The REALM of POSSIBILITY

The REALM of POSSIBILITY

DAN DALMONTE

gatekeeper press

Published by Gatekeeper Press
3971 Hoover Rd. Suite 77
Columbus, OH 43123-2839

ISBN: 9781619849655
eISBN: 9781619843608

Printed in the United States of America

CONTENTS

Part I

Part II

Part III

Part IV

PART I
CHAPTER 1

A FEW YEARS ago, Ruth, the daughter of Jim Morris, had started to play ball with the Morris family dog, Rascal. Jim's regrets began at this moment. Why hadn't he warned his daughter about the dangers of running out into the street before she left the house? Rascal was a small, blonde-haired puppy at the time. Ruth was eleven, a lanky girl who always wore a headband over her brown hair. She would toss the tennis ball with a soft grunt, pushing it with a thrust of her upper body, and Rascal would run to the spot where it ended up landing, often batting it away with his muzzle instead of catching it.

"Go fetch, Rascal," Ruth cried in her high, sweet girl's voice.

Running parallel to the Morris's yard was a fairly busy street. Blackmun, Missouri was a quiet town, but a lot of traffic to Minneapolis came through it at certain times of the day. The street in front of the Morris's home was windy as well as busy. Drivers coming toward the part of the road that passed besides the Morris's home could not see this stretch until they had fully rounded the bend right before it. On warm nights, when it was nice to let some fresh air into his bedroom, the sounds of the frequent traffic disturbed Jim's rest. As he kept getting up to shut the window and then to open it again as the room became stuffy, his wife Sarah would complain.

"Would you make a decision!"

One day Jim was watching Ruth play with the dog through the kitchen window above the sink. He was washing some dishes and humming to himself. Soft, slow jazz crooned from a radio in the kitchen. Outside, Ruth alternated between tossing the ball high into the air and hurling it straight before her. Rascal eagerly watched the ball, bolting after it once it was thrown with his tongue lolling.

Having finished cleaning the dishes, Jim switched off the jazz and retired to the family room, where he flicked on the television after collapsing into his recliner. Here was another moment that he regretted. Had he stayed in the kitchen, he might have seen Ruth as she charged into the street after the tennis ball. Instead, Jim had listened to a broadcaster talking about the local baseball team with his eyes half-shut.

"Esposito has a pinched nerve in his neck and cannot pitch tonight, but Bailey will fill in…"

Jim had wrapped a blanket around his body, since the evening had grown chilly. When he first heard the sirens, he continued to lie in his recliner, too tired to move. He was sure later that it wasn't laziness that had kept him in the chair. Instead, he had ruled out the possibility that the sirens could be associated with him. The sirens were allows howling for other people. Through his eyelids, though, Jim Morris continued to see the revolving lights of emergency vehicles; these, and the ongoing sound of the sirens, forced him to wrench himself back to his feet.

He peered out the family room window, grumpy about having to move. He glanced down and saw that Rascal was not curled in his bed, even though it was now almost totally dark outside, except for the red pulse of the siren lights.

The screen door creaked open as Jim let himself outdoors. An ambulance and two police cars had pulled onto the shoulder of the road that ran before his home. Jim could hear the crackling walkie-talkies of the two policemen who were surveying the scene as they exchanged comments. One of them noticed Jim.

"Hello, sir, are you the owner of this property?" The policeman was a tall, solidly built man. Jim nodded.

"Well, sir, I think it must have been your daughter who was the victim of the accident. She's in the back of the ambulance right now. The paramedics are doing what they can, but the situation is dire, sir."

Jim stared at the policeman blankly.

"Where's my daughter?" he asked, taking his glasses off in order to wipe the pale film of dust that had gathered there.

Ruth ended up dying in the hospital. A car had come around the bend just as Ruth came running into the road to get the ball she had thrown unusually far. The driver had not seen the girl in time to swerve out of the way.

As Jim sat in the hospital waiting room after the doctor had broken the news to him, scenes from Ruth's life kept unfolding themselves in his mind. He remembered her tiny, soft body as he cradled her in his arms for the first time. He had held her as carefully as if she were a precious work of art. Then, a scene from later in Ruth's brief life surfaced. She was wielding a bat as she waited for a pitch at a softball game. The coach looped the ball towards the plate, but missed his target, and Ruth did not have the reflexes to prevent the ball from striking her helmet. The coach had tossed the ball very gently, but Ruth still dropped the bat and began to cry, shaking her hands in shock. Jim and Sarah had trotted from the stands, chuckling at their daughter's melodrama. They took her out for ice cream afterwards, and the smooth, sweet treat calmed her.

When he went home from the hospital the night of the accident, he instinctively went to Ruth's room to see if she was sleeping soundly. He recoiled when he saw an empty bed instead of the bulge of her small body under the covers. Ruth would never get dressed up for the prom, smile as she received her diploma at a college graduation ceremony, or cry on his shoulder after her boyfriend had broken up with her. She would always be just eleven, a bright-eyed girl with a headband who liked to play ball with the dog.

The most awful part of the whole situation was that Jim could not change any of it. He had had his chance while it was happening, but once the events occurred, they were part of the past and no one had the power to undo them.

CHAPTER 2

JIM MORRIS, JUST as he did every morning, punched his employee ID number in the keypad adjacent to the door of the factory warehouse. Within the warehouse workers had dragged and dumped broken machinery which Jim had to repair. Andrew fidgeted in line behind him. Andrew was talking about a girl he had brought home the previous evening. Jim cringed and tried to focus on the shrill grinding noise made by the opening rear door of a truck. Other workers milling behind Andrew laughed heartily. Little did they know that Andrew's boastfulness was empty, since his job at the factory was in jeopardy.

Jim walked through the door once he heard the locks click and entered into the familiar atmosphere created by the din of the stereo and the metallic gleam of rows and rows of machines. He stood still and sighed before moving on slowly to a busted conveyor belt.

Minutes before, he had lingered in the cool early morning air after climbing out of the door of his compact car. All he could hear here in the distant corner of the packed parking lot was the steady chirping of cicadas, nature's lullaby. Inside the warehouse, grating heavy metal from the stereos replaced the sound of cicadas. Andrew, his coworker, worked better in these conditions. Jim, on the other hand, felt a sense of dislocation when listening to this music. It was so harsh and loud that it walled him off from his very thoughts.

The factory where Jim worked produced shingles and siding for homes. He had to start working at six thirty in the morning, and he lived an hour away from the factory in Blackmun, Missouri. While winding his way through the twisting streets on his way to the factory, Jim could savor the near total stillness of his hometown.

On clear winter mornings, a plenitude of stars was visible in the sky. The weariness at these times Jim felt was pleasant, acting like a calming intoxicant. Only the local gas station bore any traces of life at the time at which Jim commuted. Its illuminated interior always displayed to the road the same solitary, often idle attendant.

Attending to the machines now, Jim Morris pulled over his hands and wrists the gloves he used to get a better grip on tools and to protect himself from sharp edges. His instincts were drawing him back to the quiet parking lot and the comfortable interior of his car, not the cacophony of the workplace. A motorized cart shot past him and its driver honked at Jim for forcing him to pull to the side to avoid a collision. Jim hitched up his pants by his belt and began to loosen a bolt with a wrench in spite of the ache in the muscles of his arm.

After a couple hours of work, his head buzzing with the sounds of electric guitars and the rat-tat-tat of drills, Jim lowered himself into one of the hard plastic benches in the break room. He had coaxed a candy bar from the often dysfunctional vending machine. He tore off a piece of it, then wiped his fingers on his pants, since some caramel was clinging to them. The caramel reminded him of the tacky glue he sometimes used to mend machines. He could not escape from his work.

Andrew thumped across the floor in his oversized boots. He had gotten a bag of heavily salted nuts from the vending machine. His fingers shoveled them up so eagerly that a few fell onto the floor. Jim nodded curtly when Andrew sat across from him.

"Another day at the factory, huh, Morris?" Andrew asked after licking some salt from his index finger.

That morning, Jim had recalibrated a drill that a new employee had dislocated; there was a blade for cutting the siding that needed sharpening; and he had had to burrow into the greasy engine of one of the motorized carts that circled the factory carrying heavy equipment. The last morning, he had performed basically the same tasks. The only novelty had been the rat's nest that he had to spray with exterminator fluid. Jim had worked at the shingle and siding company for the past seven years.

He couldn't hold back a smile, though, when Andrew interjected, "Y'know what, Morris, that man, Jeremy, he better take some medicine!"

Andrew cackled at his own jibe. Jeremy was the manager of the factory warehouse, and often an employee miscue would send him into fits of howling and fist-waving. During these episodes, Jeremy's face would turn as intensely red as the flame of some blowtorch. As Jim watched Jeremy, along with the other coworkers, branching light blue veins would pop out against the skin of his face. The other day, Jim had been the victim of one of these vivid, apoplectic tirades. He had used the wrong color of paint to fill in a warning stripe that had faded. It was only a shade too dark, though. Jim appreciated Andrew's humor this time.

"Man, I wonder what Jeremy's parents did to him to make him get so angry," Andrew continued. Other employees had overheard the banter, and they hooted and clapped.

The laughter was an anodyne for the pain in Jim's limbs and back. There was also a deeper pain gnawing at his heart, though, which hadn't left him since the death of his daughter, Ruth. Andrew noticed that Jim was chuckling along with everyone else.

"We're on the same side, aren't we Jim? We don't have the power!" Andrew slapped Jim on his shoulder, which shook with laughter. The playful swat, however, caused the pain in Jim's arm to flare up again and, along with this physical pain, more searing memories of Ruth, whom he had lost.

CHAPTER 3

JIM HAD LEARNED of the way Jeremy felt about Andrew while sitting in Jeremy's office a few weeks ago, waiting to hear how the temperamental manager had evaluated his work for the past year. When company evaluations took place, employees worked more quickly, responding to requests from those in charge with an extra bounce in their steps. Attendance would become more consistent too, so that Jim often found that the slot in the vending machine where his favorite candy bars had stood in a row was empty.

Jeremy had his own office, with a large window overlooking the bedraggled lawn at the rear of the factory. His desk was shiny with polish, and an array of trophies from his days as a high school football star gleamed on his desk. When Jim entered the office, Jeremy was on the phone with his chair swiveled towards the window at the rear of the office. Jim saw two Canadian geese marching through the rubble-strewn weeds.

Jeremy talked for a while Jim sat waiting.

"Yeah, oh yeah, Smith really roughed him up. I think he's the new star of boxing," Jeremy said to whomever he was conversing with over the phone.

Finally, Jeremy swung around to face his desk as hung up the phone with a sharp clatter.

"Hi, Jeremy, I'm here for my evaluation," Jim said, as the large, square frames of Jeremy's glasses targeted his face.

Jeremy wheeled his chair over to some filing cabinets and pulled out a thick folder. He explained how Jim had done well in the previous year, then went on for a lot longer about how he still needed to improve. When he wheeled back to the filing cabinet to return the folder, Jim rose to leave. But, Jeremy, after clearing his throat with a couple dry coughs, called out, "No, no, Mr. Morris, there's one more thing I wanted to ask."

Jim lowered himself into his chair again. He leaned forward a little. He was interested, since Jeremy rarely said more than was necessary.

"Jim, what's your take on Andrew?" Jeremy scratched his goatee. With his other hand, he tapped the eraser of his pencil against the glossy desk.

Jim paused, wondering why Andrew was a source of interest for Jeremy. He stammered out his response.

"W-well…Andrew…well, w-what about him?"

"His work. And his attitude. We're supposed to have positive attitudes here at Sisco Roofing."

Jim shifted in his seat and nodded.

"Okay, okay. Well, Andrew is late now and then, but generally he's pretty punctual. Sometimes he jokes around, but I'd say he gets the job done most of the time. Yeah, Andy's a pretty good worker."

Jeremy nodded; he scratched some notes on a legal pad. He was silent for a while, with his head lowered. Jim unfolded his body and turned towards the door.

Management, then, was giving Andrew's case some extra scrutiny. Jim looked at Andrew mournfully when he spoke with him, since it was clear that he might not be around for much longer, even if Jim had defended him. Andrew was in a situation similar to Jim's—facing the consequences of decisions he regretted but which he could no longer change.

CHAPTER 4

A FEW DAYS after Andrew sent ripples of giggling throughout the break-room, Jeremy advanced into the factory warehouse with determined strides. Jim looked up from the torn conveyor belt he was replacing. Jeremy clumsily wove his way through all the broken machinery in the warehouse to finally stand before Andrew, who lifted his baseball cap to run his hand through his hair after Jeremy tapped him on the shoulder.

Soon, both men were walking over the cement floor of the warehouse, one with a red tie and a white, button down shirt, the other in sweat pants and a Hulk Hogan t-shirt. Andrew's face had lost some color. Later, Jim would compare the moment of seeing Andrew walk away with Jeremy to the sight of his daughter leaving the home to play with Rascal on the last day of her life. Jim was starting to see life as a gradual process of loss, in which everything you have—people, possessions—is steadily taken away from you.

Andrew was, in fact, late to work almost every day. Sometimes, Jim could even smell alcohol on his breath, and at these times, Jim tried to distract Andrew from working on the more dangerous machinery. Now and then, Andrew's squabbles with other employees had escalated to blows. The forms of Jeremy and Andrew grew smaller and smaller as they moved through the vast interior of the warehouse. Jim shouted over to a coworker named Joey.

"Hey, Joey, did you notice the wet spot on Jeremy's pants? I hope that was water!"

A small smile flickered across Joey's face, but he quickly returned to painting a rusted machine. The lyrics to a heavy metal song screeched among the rafters and the huge bulbs hanging from the ceiling of the warehouse: "THE BEAST IS ALIVE, YEAH, THE BEAST IS ALIVE!"

The hours of Jim's shift dragged on through the middle of the day. Andrew did not return to the warehouse. Jeremy walked through to see how everyone was doing, with the wet spot still darkening his pants. All the employees were strangely withdrawn that day, even while in the break room. Jim sat there chewing a candy bar, listening to the whirring of the refrigerator built into the soda machine, a sound he had never noticed. There was a similar silence in his home in the weeks after Ruth had died.

Andrew did not come into work again for five more days. The eerie silence that had prevailed after Jeremy had led him away continued in the warehouse in the form of a general feeling of uneasiness. Whenever Jeremy moved through the warehouse, with his hands in his pockets and his eyes roving back and forth around football-field sized building, employees peeked over their shoulders. It was as if Jeremy were the Angel of Death, waiting for the right time to tap the shoulder of his next victim.

After a long day of work on the fifth day after Andrew had slunk away, Jim was standing in the parking lot, taking some deep breaths to recuperate. He paced over an elevated, grassy area that divided some spaces with a cigarette hanging from his lips. Out of the corner of his eye, he saw a figure approaching. It was Andrew, carrying a red folder in his right hand. Andrew kept his eyes fixed on the cracked concrete of the lot. He chewed so energetically on a piece of gum that muscles in both his jaws and temples bulged.

"Hey Andrew, where've you been?" Jim called out, standing still now.

Andrew kept walking for a few seconds, but eventually stopped, turned around, and stared back at Jim as if Jim were some sort of fantastic creature, like a talking animal or an alien from outer space. Finally, Andrew responded, "Oh, hey Morris. Yeah, just getting the paperwork done with Jeremy."

"What kind of paperwork, if you don't mind my asking?"

Andrew blushed, then said, "Well, I'm not going to be coming back here anymore. I got fired."

Andrew walked quickly away after this confession. Jim tracked Andrew's form as he disappeared into the tastelessly assembled concrete block where he had worked for the past five years or so.

Twenty minutes later, Jim was still in the lot, sitting on the curb with his arms looped around his knees. Sweat had formed on his forehead, even though the sun was level with some tall trees far away in a field adjacent to the factory. Andrew came walking again past some glimmering fragments of a broken beer bottle.

"So long, buddy," Jim said. He had walked up to Andrew, and had given him a pat on his shoulder. Andrew, wearing a torn grey shirt, rejoined, "Yeah, so long. Don't let it get to you, man."

Andrew shuffled off on a slightly indirect route to his truck, almost as if he were intoxicated. The old engine of the pickup rattled to life. Soon, it was puffing exhaust fumes as Andrew waited for an opening in the traffic at the road that led into the factory. The truck's tires screamed as they gripped the pavement, and Andrew was gone.

CHAPTER 5

ING JEREMY, AS his subordinates derisively called him, summarily replaced Andrew with a new employee named Mike. Mike was much younger than Andrew, having just graduated high school. It was great surprise to Jim later that such a young man would have such significance for his life. He had curly brown hair and often fits of stammering hampered his attempts to communicate. His pale, slender hands shook sometimes when Jim told him he was doing something wrong.

"No, no, that screwdriver won't work there, Mike…"

A couple days after Andrew lost his job, a circle of employees, not including Mike, formed in the break room halfway through the morning shift. Jim overheard their hushed voices as he came out of the din of the warehouse.

Jim was headed for the candy machine, but the sight of the circle of employees interested him and he drifted towards it. The group of mainly men all had serious faces.

"I wonder who's next?" one man with a large belly and a blonde mustache asked.

"Yeah, and I've got two kids to take care of," a woman wearing safety goggles lamented.

The tension in the room was as palpable as the heat radiated by a machine gone haywire. Jim started to inch back towards a lonely corner of the break room, where he chewed on his candy bar for ten minutes or so while most of his coworkers continued to huddle in an angry mass.

Jeremy walked through the warehouse with an extra strut in his step for the remainder of that day. He yelled at Jim fiercely when he caught Jim taking some extra time at the water cooler.

"Hey, Jim, we're not paying you to stand around!"

The newest employee, Mike, walked up to Jim while this rebuke still stung. Mike's face was boyish, lacking even the beginnings of facial hair.

"Is that what I'm going to have to put up with? Geez, I thought high school was bad."

Jim chuckled, then reignited the blowtorch he had been using to remove some paint. As it hissed to life, Mike ambled away with one hand in his pocket and his shoulders swaying from side to side. He wore heavy boots that clunked against the floor each time he took a step. Jim saw that he was looking behind his shoulder and grinning. Mike had adapted to the warehouse quickly. The workers liked him, and he was comfortable enough to make small talk with an older man like Jim.

By the end of his shift, Jim's fingers were stained with grease, and he needed to pass a paper towel over his forehead a few of times to wipe off the sweat. After stepping into the cab of his car, he turned on the air-conditioning so that it caressed his baked skin.

When he spun the steering wheel and turned into his driveway back in Blackmun, he surveyed the stretch of road where the car had struck Ruth. He and his wife Sarah had stuck a white cross, with some flowers wreathed around its arms, in the ground besides the road. The cross was stained, and the garland of flowers had wilted long ago. Jim could see Sarah faintly through the kitchen window. The pane of glass oddly twisted her features.

She looked very similar to Ruth. They both shared bright blue eyes and straight, light brown hair. Before she died, Ruth had picked up Sarah's habit of humming while working in the kitchen. Jim paused to try to identify the tune that was playing in Sarah's mind as she scrubbed off bits of food from the dishes.

"Oh boy, what a day," Jim said with a groan after kissing his wife and landing heavily in one of the kitchen chairs.

"Is King Jeremy at it again?" Sarah inquired.

Their conversation, and the heavy meal, lulled Jim to the point where he was ready to drag himself to bed. Once upstairs, he saw the beams from the headlights of cars passing by swinging across the walls of his daughter's old bedroom. Jim and Sarah had kept Ruth's bedroom intact after she had died. They had encased the ball she had thrown into the road in glass and placed it on the nightstand where her favorite books still rested in a casual pile.

CHAPTER 6

DURING LUNCH BREAK the next day, the employees clustered into separate groups and talked lightly. The revolutionary fervor of the previous day had cooled, at least for the moment. Jim found an open bench across from Mike, who held a bottle of soda in his slender hand.

"How do you like it at Sisco, Mike?" Jim asked, sending some crumbs flying as he tore at the stubborn wrapper of another candy bar.

Mike's Adam's apple bobbed in his hairless neck as he swallowed down some soda.

"It's fine," Mike said. Mike lowered his eyes to the table surface and kept nervously running his hand along the back of his neck. Like any teen, he could get uncomfortable around adults.

"I've been working here for seven years, man. Do yourself a favor—quit after one!" Jim's face lit up as he guffawed. Mike gave only a small grin in return.

"Hey, though…it's a lot better than school," Mike responded after a couple moments. He shifted his body in the bench so that he sat up a little straighter. He drank eagerly from the soda bottle.

"Oh yeah," Jim rejoined, "y'know what my favorite subject was?" Mike was already chuckling. "What, man?"

"Recess!" Jim laughed so hard that he bent over until his head was lower than the tabletop.

A uninhibited smile now spread across Mike's face. After their laughter subsided, he said, "You're pretty cool for an old dude, Jim." Jim was forty two years old.

Mike leaned against the back of the bench and interlaced his hands behind his head. Jim looked at his bony arms. Mike would have a hard time moving around heavy pieces of machinery.

Jim had started to talk about Jeremy. He had set aside his half-eaten candy bar and spoke with unusual animation.

"Well, one day Larry—yeah, that guy in blue over there—found King Jeremy leafing through a magazine in his office. When Larry walked in, Jeremy slid open a drawer of his desk, stuffed the magazine in there, and slammed it with a bang. Jerry thinks that Jeremy was looking at some dirty pictures."

Mike's eyebrows lifted and his mouth hung slightly open as he attended to the twists and turns of the story. Jim observed that his blue eyes were as bright and hard as Ruth's. He also noticed that they were close to popping out of his skull.

"Are you alright, man?" Jim asked, leaning forward a little. Mike leaned back in the bench and composed himself. His features relaxed as he grinned cynically.

"Oh boy, what a loser!" Mike covered his mouth with his hand as he scoffed. "No, I'm alright. Man, I wish I could have seen King Jeremy's face when Larry walked in."

Jim watched Mike closely. For a couple of seconds, the young man's features had betrayed complete shock. It seemed disproportionate. Jim had thought the story about Jeremy was rather funny, not disturbing.

Mike slid lower in his seat, stretching out his legs and slipping one frail-looking hand into his pocket. He raised his soda bottle high in the air, tilted it, and took an ample swallow until all the soda was gone. Afterwards, he belched.

"I'm going to get another candy bar. Want one?" Jim asked his young coworker. Mike, who was wiping drops of soda from his mouth, shook his head.

Once again, the bar Jim wanted got stuck in the coil that guarded the end of the slot where it was resting. Jim rocked the machine with his weary arms. Finally, the bar clattered down to the well at the base of the machine.

When Jim returned to the table where he and Mike had been chatting, he stopped as he noticed that the place where Mike was sitting was now vacant. Mike had left behind his empty Sprite can. Jim inspected the break room, but Mike had not joined any of the other groups there. Jim walked back and forth, keeping an eye on the bathroom door to see if Mike would emerge. But Mike's boyish face was nowhere to be seen.

Jim's disappointment overtook him as he opened the second candy bar on a bench closer to the entrance of the break room. He wanted the conversation with Mike to continue. Ruth, of course, had never become a teenager and therefore Jim had little experience with the sometimes erratic behavior of people this age.

CHAPTER 7

J IM WALKED THROUGH a late afternoon drizzle to collect his mail. He lowered his head to keep the rain out of his eyes and tucked the mail underneath his sweater. Upon entering his home, he stomped his feet on the doormat.

"Hey, Sarah, I'm home!" The house was silent, but Jim had seen a light on in the second story laundry room when he pulled into the driveway. He sorted through the mail on the kitchen table. Some rainwater had softened the paper of a toy store advertisement.

In the middle of the pile, Jim found a gleaming white envelope with his name and address written on it in elegant cursive. In the right-hand corner, there was a stamp depicting a reindeer and a snowflake, even though it was September. In the left-hand corner, Jim saw his former coworker's full name: Andrew Bretton. Jim recalled the lewd jokes Andrew used to tell, as well as his diatribes about Jeremy.

He laughed to himself, expecting the envelope to contain some hilarious prank. Jim tore the envelope open and pulled out a card with pale mauve and blue stripes limned on its cover. Golden letters forming the message "Thinking of You" flowed across the top of the card. Jim's eyebrows lifted in amusement. This sentiment was so unlike Andrew.

A folded piece of loose leaf floated out of the card. It crackled as Jim opened it. Neat handwriting covered one of its sides. Jim pushed his chair closer to the chandelier suspended above the kitchen table.

Dear Jim,

It is quite regrettable that we will not be seeing each other any longer. I was too outspoken and uncouth in my criticism of Jeremy Salia, and now I am struggling to find another job. It seems impossible that anyone would ever hire someone like me after what happened at Sisco Roofing, but I, nor any of us, must give up hope amidst life's struggles.

Jim stopped reading for a moment. He started to giggle so hard that he began to stomp his foot.

"I'm doing laundry, Jim. Make your own dinner!" Sarah hollered from upstairs. Jim took some deep breaths, and once again positioned the letter in the pool of light coming from the chandelier. He wiped a tear from the corner of his eye with a tissue.

Jim, I want you to know that you should not imitate me. Don't ever repeat my dirty jokes, especially around children. And please be more kind to Jeremy Salia. As manager, he is entitled to lead the repairmen in the warehouse, and this role often generates animosity among those who are subordinate to him. Just think: would your attitude to Jeremy be different if he were your coworker, and not your boss?

I also want you to know, Jim, that I know how much pain you must be in because of the loss of Ruth, but you must not let your grief prevent you from attending to your duties with diligence and enthusiasm. When I worked with you, I noticed that you were getting more and more shiftless, and I think this may be due to your brooding about a loss that is now in the past. But, I'm talking too much.

Miss you!
Andrew Bretton

Along with the letter, there was a photograph tucked into the card. Jim had elbowed it to the edge of the kitchen table, but he now lifted it up to the light. It depicted Andrew sitting on a couch, wearing sweat pants with holes in the knees. His hair was disheveled, and the photograph had been taken while he waved away the person using the camera with an annoyed look. Jim flipped the photo over, and found that Andrew had penned a message there as well: *Who's going to hire me?*

Jim set aside the card after enclosing both the photo and the letter within it. He shook his head, chuckling some more. When the surges of laughter subsided, he released a long sigh. Andrew had never been sympathetic to Jeremy. Jim thought back to an earlier incident as he heard his wife's feet pounding through the upstairs rooms. One day, Andrew had arrived early at the warehouse. There were only a couple of janitors still around, so he was able to sneak into the managers' offices and pour some water over the tile floor in there, just enough to make it slick. When the managers started to file in, Andrew peered through the window looking into their offices as they slipped and even fell as if someone were shooting at them from a perch in the factory.

The oddly courteous and formal letter seemed to be another example of Andrew's buffoonery. Jim placed it on a stand next to the kitchen table. Sarah was still upstairs, so Jim went ahead and put together a sandwich for himself. He scanned the paper as he ate. Jim thrust it aside, though, when he read the headline, GIRL STRUCK BY CAR, UNTIMELY END, leaping from it in oversized letters.

He glanced up through the kitchen window to the stretch of road where the car had collided with Ruth. The driver had finally mustered the courage to visit the Morrises a few months after Ruth had died. He was a short and portly man, and his hands were shaking when Jim found him standing on the front porch after swinging open the door. He held a bouquet of flowers, which he offered to Jim after stammering, "I'm...s-so sorry ab-bout your d-daughter." The man had not been at fault—he had not been speeding or drunk. Jim had had a curt, tense conversation with him and had not seen or heard from the man since.

After watching a couple sitcoms after dinner, Jim shuffled over to the staircase and climbed up, his body slumping with fatigue. The upstairs rooms were silent and dark; Sarah had called it a night. In spite of his weariness, though, Jim pushed open the door to Ruth's old room, where he turned on the ceiling light and lowered himself into a worn-down recliner.

Jim would often sit in his daughter's old room, where almost every item brought back bittersweet memories. Her favorite teddy bear still sat on her bed. She had hugged it so tightly that the cloth binding the leg to its body had frayed and eventually broken. On the nightstand, there was a photograph of Ruth playing softball. In the picture, Ruth's arm was a twirling blur as she wound up before a pitch. Jim studied this picture lovingly for a few moments. He had been sitting on some bleachers when taking this picture. He remembered how the other parents around him fanned themselves with folded pieces of paper or wore broad-brimmed hats as the summer sun glowered upon them. They would shout out encouragement to their daughters when the ball came to them in the field or they crouched in the batter's box.

Jim lowered the picture into his lap and then stared blankly at the wall. After a few minutes, though, he stopped mulling and rose. He needed to sleep, he had to work tomorrow. Andrew's words flashed through his mind: *you must not let your grief prevent you from attending to your duties with diligence and enthusiasm.*

As he groped the wall of the dark hallway with his hand, Jim wondered again at the strange language his roguish coworker had used in the letter. A priest could have written it.

CHAPTER 8

A T WORK THE next day, Jim pulled the cardboard cover from a grim-looking, shiny new buzzsaw. As Jim held the jagged blade in his palms, its weight surprised him, and one of its teeth sliced into his finger when it escaped his grip.

"Damn," Jim cursed. He squeezed his bleeding finger. Another employee saw the stripe of blood on Jim's forearm, and trotted over to the first-aid box located on a shelf that ran along one of the warehouse's walls. Soon, the employee was wrapping a bandage round and round Jim's wound. His blood had left a garish stain on the new buzz saw.

"Just keep pressure on it," the other employee told Jim. Jim lowered himself onto a bench, grimacing. The sound of the machinery in the warehouse thundered around him.

That evening, though, before returning home and rebandaging the cut, Jim decided to visit Ruth's grave. It was a mild fall evening, and bright russet leaves littered the vast cemetery grounds. Jim, with his wounded finger still smarting, ambled up to the flat stone which bore the name of his daughter. Pine needles fallen most likely from a nearby grove of coniferous trees hid the inscription. Jim bent down and swept the block clean.

He stared glassily at the years etched on the stone: 2006-2017. It was now 2022. Jim had often visited the cemetery during the past five years. He recalled the lavish ceremony, with the elevated language of the priest and the crowd of mourners clad in black suits and dresses. After that climax, he had gone to the cemetery with a lawn chair, sometimes accompanied by his wife, to simply sit and reflect. The cemetery was on the outskirts of Blackmun, and thick walls bordered it, so it was quiet. After brushing the flat stone, Jim pulled out the lawn chair from the back of his SUV, and unfolded it in his customary spot. A flock of geese flew up and their flapping wings stirred the air.

Jim smoothed out a crease in his pants. After a minute or so, the rumble of an engine droned into his range of hearing. Jim looked in the sound's direction, and saw a cloud of dust trailing behind the wheels of a pickup truck. Lawnmowers , rakes, and hoes protruded from the bed behind it.

Jim had turned to face the ground again, but the sound of the engine kept churning right behind him, popped and screeched, then fell silent. Jim then heard the grass softly rustle. Soon, the round form of the groundskeeper loomed next to him.

"You come here a lot, don't you buddy?" The folds of fat on the groundskeeper's face wobbled at each syllable he articulated. His face was lined and weather-beaten.

Jim shielded his face from the sun as he looked up at the groundskeeper's towering form. He wore a green uniform, with the words "St. Michael's Cemetery" sewn into one of the shirt pockets.

"Yeah, I do. It's nice here. You people do a good job." After responding, Jim turned back to his daughter's grave. But the groundskeeper kept standing beside him.

The large man swallowed moistly before answering and his right hand fluttered a little. "Y'know sir, there's no point getting so upset. Being upset doesn't get you anywhere."

Jim scratched his face with the fingers of his bandaged hand. He was annoyed that this stranger insisted on talking to him. "What's that? What do you mean?"

The groundskeeper pointed a meaty finger at the gravestone. "It's all over. All of us die." The groundskeeper moved closer to the gravestone and bent over it. "Let's see—Ruth. Ruth is gone now. Stop crying about it. It doesn't change anything."

Jim stared off at the setting sun; he swatted at a fly that was pestering him.

"I should know, sir," the rotund man continued. "I work here all day, and I talk to all sorts of people. Car accidents, disease, even murder. I wonder how I'll go."

The groundskeeper's thick, deep voice pounded in Jim's mind like the thrumming of one of the motors he had to repair. He glanced at the man's sunburned face, then rose up from his chair and began to hastily fold it.

"So long, sir. I'd like to end this conversation right now," Jim said, slicing the air with his hand firmly and then marching back to his vehicle. The groundskeeper rotated his body and stared at Jim's departing figure.

"It's true, though, sir. Everyone you know is going to end up here." The groundskeeper's voice faded behind him as the grass crunched beneath Jim's retreating feet. Jim caught sight of the sharp points of a rake and the gleaming blades of an overturned lawnmower in the pickup truck the groundskeeper had been driving. The array of lawn care tools made Jim think of instruments of torture.

CHAPTER 9

THE GROUNDSKEEPER'S WORDS hovered over the next day like a stubborn fog. Jim worked deliberately at the factory warehouse. Jeremy sauntered up to him around one o'clock.

"Hey, Jim," he interjected in his nasal voice, "you've been working on the same machine since an hour before lunch break."

An image of the sagging, freckled skin of Jeremy's face lingered in Jim's mind after his supervisor had left to speak with someone else. Jim imagined a cancerous sore breaking out on Jeremy's face. In his mind, the inflamed area stood out from the rest of Jeremy's face like a badge of condemnation. Jim had become acutely conscious of the prospect of death.

About an hour later, Mike passed Jim on his way to the water fountain.

"Are you alright, man?" Mike asked as he touched Jim's shoulder with his fingertips. Jim looked back at Mike dully. He nodded, but watched Mike as he headed to get a drink. Even someone as young as Mike was not immune. Getting behind the wheel after a raucous party could be the final step before the plunging over the proverbial precipice.

Jim moved slowly out into the evening air when his shift had ended, as if the force of gravity had grown stronger since the previous day. There was a vortex at the heart of the universe that wrapped everything up into itself, suffocating it. Jim ramped up the volume of the radio in his car while he drove home. When he arrived at the doorstep, beads of perspiration had formed on his forehead.

"Are you alright?" Sarah asked, with a puzzled expression. Jim's face was pale.

"I'm just a little under the weather. I'm going to lie down." Jim moved past Sarah towards the couch in the family room, in front of the TV. He extended his body upon the rough fabric of its cushions and then pried off his shoes with his feet.

Sarah switched off the lamp on the table besides the couch. Jim, grateful for the sudden dimness, closed his eyes, and laid the back of his hand against his forehead. The rising pressure of a headache throbbed there, like the remnants of the heavy metal that still created tumult on a daily basis in the warehouse, even with Andrew's departure. Jim's chest rose and fell rapidly; images of the demise of Jeremy and Mike had wrecked his peace of mind.

All Jim could hear was the ticking of the grandfather clock that towered above the television set. Sarah had retired to the downstairs study to read a book. Jim rolled over onto his side. As he rested, he thought about how his wife had dealt with Ruth's death. Sarah's eyes had been moist during the funeral, but a few weeks after it, she was bustling around the house again, chatting about the latest episode of her favorite sitcom or complaining about the fact that her office at the Michaelson Insurance, a company located just a few miles outside of Blackmun, had no window. She often counseled Jim over dinner.

"What could you have done? The chances of Ruth's accident were so small...there was no reason to take precautions," Sarah had said one day, looking earnestly into Jim's eyes as she shook salt over a slice of chicken.

Jim wrapped himself in a blanket folded up near one of the arms of the couch. The sweat that had formed on his forehead kept flowing and began to roll over his eyebrows into his eyes. Jim turned again, so that he lay on his left shoulder. He opened his eyes, and found his own image, in a picture from his wedding day, looking back at him.

Both he and Sarah were young and good-looking in the picture; behind them, a tablecloth on which various bowls and platters rested fluttered in the breeze. Caterers had brought watermelon slices, crackers and cheese, about seven different types of soda and bottles of wine packed in ice for the outdoor reception after the wedding. Jim's best man had been a member of his fraternity in college. In the picture, he stood beside the table in the background, sipping from a plastic cup filled with orange soda.

The grandfather clock began to chime as six o'clock arrived. Jim could hear the gears within it click and whir. He listened for Sarah, but all that he could hear once the grandfather clock had stopped tolling the hour was a fly buzzing against a windowpane in the kitchen. Images of dying rushed back into his mind like agitated bees.

Death had been invisibly leering at the revelers at his wedding reception. His college buddy had had so much to drink at the party that, by the end of it, he was walking around tipsily, high-fiving strangers and tripping over his polished black shoes. A few years later, Jim learned that this young medical student, whose future had looked so promising, was out of a job because he couldn't stop showing up to work drunk.

Ruth had not been around during the reception, but now Jim knew that death had been looking hungrily at him and his new wife, even in their hour of glory. Jim imagined death as an old man with a triumphant, lustful glow in his eyes. The old man rubbed his hands eagerly and chuckled with a toothless grin, as if he were anticipating some salacious image.

Jim sat up a little on the couch. He listened carefully for any sign of Sarah. A neighbor at the end of the street started up a lawnmower.

Jim sat fully erect in the couch. "Sarah? Sarah? Are you alright?" The sound of his voice ricocheted all the way from the closet besides the front door. Sarah, though, made no reply.

Jim nearly tumbled to the floor as he rose to his feet. In his haste, he knocked the remote and sent it sliding into a cobwebbed corner of the room. Jim looked at it briefly, but, instead of retrieving it, started to move through the kitchen. He began to swing open the doors of each downstairs room; he clattered down the basement stairs and surveyed this drab storage area. There was no sign of Sarah.

"Sarah?" Jim yelled, this time with still greater urgency. He clambered up the stairs to the bedrooms, tugging on the railing as he leaped over steps. He shouldered his way through the door of the bedroom he and his wife shared.

His wife was sleeping on the bed. Her legs were drawn up against her body and her stomach gently expanded with each breath. Jim touched her shoulder.

His panic subsided as he wiped some more sweat from his forehead with his shirtsleeve. He noted with some embarrassment that he was breathing heavily. When Sarah stirred and began to stretch her arms, Jim staggered back on the bedroom carpet and collapsed on his back. When Sarah woke up, she called 911 to get help for her unconscious husband.

CHAPTER 10

JIM GROGGILY OPENED his eyes upon his bedroom, which a shaft
of morning sunlight illuminated. He saw his wife still asleep on
their bed. He pressed his hands down on the fuzzy surface of
the light brown carpet underneath him.

Jim wondered why he had been sleeping on the floor. After
sitting up for a minute, though, he reclined again on the carpet.
The sight of his sleeping wife, and the ray of sunlight that formed a
luminous block on her hair, had begun to spin dizzyingly.

Jim closed his eyes as he waited for his mind to clear. He inhaled
deeply. Finally, he thrust himself to his feet with his hands. Groggy
or not, Jim had to be at work.

Headed toward the bedroom door, Jim came to a halt at the
sight of a man's body sprawled on the same carpet from which he
had recently arisen. The man lay on his stomach; the formal clothing
he wore appeared to be some sort of uniform. Jim inspected the
intruder's body.

"What the hell?" Jim asked out loud as he looked at the man
with disgust. Jim stumbled on the way towards his cellphone, which
he kept on a nightstand while he slept; he would have fallen were it
not for the support of the doorframe, upon which he braced himself.

Jim discovered another unexpected guest in the hallway,
though. Andrew, his former coworker, was just entering the hallway
after climbing the stairs. Jim frowned with bewilderment.

"Andrew? What's going on?"

Jim's ribald former coworker displayed a kindly smile. He
extended his hand towards Jim, and placed his other hand atop Jim's
shoulder.

"Relax, brother. It's just your old buddy Andrew, here for a visit."

A shade passed across Andrew's face, perhaps because his dismissal from the roofing company came back to mind at the sight of Jim. But the kind smile soon returned. Andrew looked so happy it was as though he had not only found another job, but that his new job was the job he had always dreamed of having. It was as if Andrew had just signed a multimillion dollar contract to play for the Yankees.

"Why are you so damn happy?" Jim asked with open hostility.

Andrew held out his palms in a calming gesture. In spite of Jim's agitation, Andrew seemed to remain placid.

"We don't have time right now, Jimmy, to answer all your questions. See, look at the time, it's time to get to work." Andrew pointed with one of his leathery hands towards a clock hanging from the hallway wall. It was 8:02, Jim was already late. Andrew's calm smile, and his beckoning hand, had a hypnotic effect on Jim.

"Okay," Jim grunted. Andrew clapped his hands.

"Oh, good!" He began to skip down the stairs while snapping his fingers. But before leaving his home, Jim peered in at his wife, who still slept. On the floor besides her, the unconscious man still trespassed. Jim shrugged his shoulders as the bedroom clock kept ticking.

He was so confused by the whirl of strange events that he decided to just follow Andrew. Outside, a car horn was honking.

"C'mon Jim!" Andrew's voice became faint after it passed through the pane of the closed window. Jim headed down the wooden staircase; the screen door swung open with a screech of rusty hinges. Andrew already sat in the driver's seat of Jim's pickup.

Jim lifted himself into the truck as the engine roared to life. A cool breeze and a clear sky promised a pleasant day. Jim turned to Andrew as he maneuvered them out of the driveway.

"Have you been drinking, man? Why are you so happy all of a sudden?" When Andrew had been on the payroll at Cisco Roofing, his attitude towards work had been reliably dour. Jim would often join Andrew as he smoked a cigarette just before his shift began. There, Andrew would beguile him with vicious complaints about the other people who worked at the factory.

"That Larry is a moron! What's confusing about the idea of a board one foot long? He was supposed to make each of the longer boards on the rack in there one foot long—instead, he makes'em six inches long! Tell me—when did I say that? Huh?"

Jim would scoff at Andrew's cynicism. Now, though, Andrew sat behind the wheel with the same radiant smile with which he had greeted Jim, praising the scenery the on the way.

"Look at that beautiful patch of flowers by the mailbox, Jim!" Andrew slowed the car to gawk at the circle of tulips. The Andrew from the past would have seen this patch of flowers as a place in which he could hide his cigarette butts from his wife. Now, Jim saw him bring the truck to a complete halt to lovingly contemplate the radiant plants.

Finally, though, Andrew pulled into the roofing factory parking lot. The large number of employees arriving for work created a traffic jam around the entrance. Andrew inched his way into the factory parking lot, then swung into a tight space between a minivan and a compact car whose owner had not bothered to park within the lines. Jim could barely squeeze his way out of the pickup's door without scratching the surface of the compact car.

"People here just never learn," Jim complained to Andrew. Jim had to smile after he said this. The morning had been strange, and it was good, oddly enough, to see a familiar sight like an improperly parked car.

"It's selfish, just human selfishness," Andrew said, his face hardened like a preacher's as he tapped the tire of the compact car with his shoe. Jim just watched Andrew dumbly as memories of the pranks Andrew had played in the past ran through his mind. When had he become such a zealot for unselfish behavior?

Both he and Andrew tried not to slip on the loose gravel scattered in certain areas of the parking lot. Cisco had not bothered to pave the lot for years.

Jim punched in his employee number, just as he would on a normal day. Amidst the tangled cacophony of percussion and electric guitars that pervaded the interior of the warehouse, he was able to make out some lyrics: THE RAGE IN MY MIND... AS THE FLAMES CONSUME. He saw a lathe in need of repair. The numbers on its micrometer dial had grown indistinct as time passed. Jim assessed the dial through his safety goggles.

The familiar task of repairing the lathe helped Jim sort through the weirdness of that morning. He thought back to the painful feelings of the previous night. He and Sarah had looked so joyous in their wedding photo. Tragedy had not yet disrupted their lives. But, Ruth's death had stolen their innocence. Now, Jim brooded over the prospect of death, and considered the possibility that he was going mad. Who had been lying on his bedroom floor? Jeremy's presence broke through Jim's thinking, though.

"Yeah, that machine's real old. Our workers can't read the numbers on that dial anymore. They've created some botched products because of it."

Jim nodded, his eyes flickering towards Jeremy's pudgy face and then right back again to the lathe. He wasn't in the mood for a conversation with his boss. Jeremy loomed behind Jim for a few minutes, though, watching him sand the micrometer dial over his shoulder. Finally, Jeremy moved on to oversee another employee.

Jim wiped his forehead with a paper towel he kept in his pocket and sighed once Jeremy had left him. His hands had begun to shake a little as Jeremy studied his work. But, Jeremy evaluated his employees every day.

Little flashes of pain burned inside Jim's heart. Life took so much out of a man. He was befuddled by the perplexing events of that morning—Andrew walking right into his home, and the comatose trespasser. The warehouse was as loud as some zoo full of upset animals. He suddenly recalled how, years ago, a cold sweat had broken out as he picked up the phone again and again, contacting relatives and friends to share with them the news of his daughter's death.

The pain and hollowness within worsened, and he stepped back from the lathe, his hands in his pockets and his eyes directed towards the floor. A moment later, he felt a soft hand on his shoulder. Out of the corner of his eye, he could see the hand's hairless surface.

"You alright, Jim?" The boyish voice was unmistakable. Jim turned around to face Mike. He had a couple new zits on his fresh face.

Jim stood upright and began to adjust his hair. "Oh, y-yeah, I'm alright Mike. Just thinking about some stuff."

Mike nodded and then reached into the back pocket of his baggy jeans. From there he pulled out a crisp white envelope.

"Here, Jim, I want you to have this." Jim saw the long blue veins standing out clearly against the underside of Mike's forearm as he extended the envelope towards him.

"Oh, thanks, Mike. But- what's the occasion?" There was a bemused expression on Jim's face. Yet, it seemed to him that only by experiencing more strange events could he unlock the secret of the events that had occurred earlier in the day. Rather than stay to answer his question, Mike abruptly shuffled off down the aisle. Jim laughed.

"Yeah, thanks for the letter, man!" He shrugged his shoulders as he watched Mike's retreating form. After glancing at the envelope, upon which someone had written his first name with a black sharpie, Jim stuck it into his pocket.

Jim put off opening the latest envelope and fired up the sander once again. But he could not focus on his work. He had laughed when he first read Andrew's letter, but the way it was written still puzzled him. His confusion nagged at him until he decided to take a look at Mike's letter.

Jim glanced around to see if Jeremy was nearby, then shut off the sander. The other employees around him did not stop working when the whine of the sander stopped. Jim went to the break room, which was nearly empty since it was a couple hours after lunch. The only other person there was a man with a walrus mustache which was sprinkled with white powder from the donut he was eating.

Jim sat at a table at far away from the donut-eater. After looking towards the entrance of the break room and seeing that no one was coming in, he began to tear open the envelope. He noted how shiny and crisp it was. One of its sharp edges even made a thin incision in Jim's palm as he opened it. The paper inside was equally fine.

"The same black sharpie…" Jim said as he saw the writing on the paper that he pulled out of the envelope. The heavy ink seemed to be same that Andrew had used for his letter. Jim read, in large print, the words:

Dear Jim,

You ought to go to the part of the road in front of your house where the car struck Ruth

five years ago. Go there tonight, right after nightfall.

Your friend,

Mike

Jim stared at the sheet of paper in his hand for a few minutes. The man with the walrus-mustache coughed a couple of times at the other end of the room. Outside the door of the break room, Jim could hear the hum of a conveyor belt as someone started up its engine. The paper in Jim's hand crackled as he folded it up, put it back in the envelope, and then slid the envelope into the back pocket of his jeans.

Jim rested his chin in his palms. His glum stare took in the crumbs and scuff marks on the break room floor. What was Mike's intention?

Jim let out a sigh and lifted himself from the table. As he walked by the trash can at the entrance to the break room, he dropped in Mike's pristine envelope. He didn't appreciate it that people were making a joke of his late daughter.

For the rest of the day he worked quietly. The paper cut on his palm still smarted. He popped a stick of gum into his mouth and slowly chewed it to distract himself from the pain. He was working it methodically around his mouth even as he walked through the parking lot to his truck. The gum had long ago lost is minty flavor, but it helped him to relax.

Driving to the slow melodies of jazz, he took some deep breaths. He imagined the steaming food Sarah would have ready on the dinner table: casserole, or perhaps shepherd's pie. Afterwards, he would lower himself into his recliner and sit before the television set for a couple hours, as if he were content about everything in his life.

But, after dinner, when he had let his shoes slide off and began to peel his sweaty socks from his feet, the sight of a river of silver moonlight on his front lawn roused him. He got up, and by the light from some houses across the street, he was able to see the stretch of road that was the scene of the accident through the window.

Jim couldn't tolerate how desperate he had become, but, even so, he was putting on his socks and shoes again. Then, he got a drink of water and pushed open the screen door, which swung shut behind him with a metallic bang. The letter had directed him to go to the scene of the accident right after nightfall. He pulled out a lawn chair from the shed where he kept a lot of his tools and, after unfolding it shakily, he took a seat. Darkness kept accumulating like a slowly spreading oil spill.

Jim in his self-disgust almost walked right back inside, but he saw that the pooling darkness had completely blotted out the final traces of the sun. His jeans whooshed through the long grass that bordered the road. He climbed onto the root of a tree, and looked down at the buckled pavement.

Jim stared at the road with his hands in his pockets. A car stormed around the corner and then past him. Jim's eyes grew heavy. He started to shift towards the house, waving his hand at the road, as if to say goodbye to the false hope that had led him there.

But, out of the corner of his eye, he saw the headlights of the car, which grew in brightness as they neared. They caught Jim's attention; he paused and turned towards the road again.

Behind him, he heard the cry of a young girl.

"Go, fetch, Rascal!"

There was a rapid patter of feet moving through the grass behind him. As the whine of the car engine came nearer, a shaggy dog came into sight, as well as the glowing green flash of a tennis ball streaking through the air. He could see the scene in spite of the fact that it had grown dark. The dog and the ball were luminous; a fuzzy brightness encircled them.

The tennis ball was rocketing high up into the air. It was clear that it was headed for the opposite side of the street. It was hidden by the upper branches of the trees that bordered the road. Rascal lost sight of it, and veered to his right, having found a scent. He ran his nose along the ground greedily.

Jim turned around completely when he heard shallow breathing coming from behind him. His eyes riveted upon the figure of his late daughter. Her long, thin limbs bent awkwardly to the side as she ran towards the ball. She, too, was aglow, so that Jim could see her as clearly as if there were daylight.

"Ruth!" Jim shouted. Surges of shock and joy shook him as he saw the girl he had lost. But Ruth did not notice him. She brushed some of her long hair away from her mouth and kept jogging in the direction of the tennis ball.

As Ruth passed him, Jim spun around to face the road. The car that had been nearing now began to thrust its nose around the corner. It had a heavy grille attached to its front. Its tires squealed as its driver brought it around the bend too quickly. It, too, was visible in spite of the dense cloak of the night.

Ruth's shoes were clapping against the hard dirt near the road as the car began to accelerate down the straightaway that ran past Jim's house. Ruth was carrying a walkman. Jim panicked: its headphones must have been filling her ears with rhythms and melodies. The thick-trunked trees that ran along the road screened the sight of the oncoming car. Ruth was set up for disaster.

Jim started to sprint towards Ruth's gawkily running body. He neared quickly and lunged to tackle his daughter before she ran right before the prison bars of the grille of the car coming down the road. But, as his arms were about to encompass Ruth's waist, the vision of his daughter disappeared. Jim lunged at air, and fell heavily on the ground. The car had similarly vanished, leaving behind only the stillness of the night.

When he stood, Jim found that grass stains covered his sweater. It was proof that he had dove. He looked around him. He saw nothing but the same dark, vacant scene that had been there before Rascal, the car, and stunningly, Ruth, had emerged.

Jim tried to sort through his racing thoughts. When Ruth had died, he had not had the chance to rescue her. He had been resting inside. If only he had been out watering the lawn or even on his knees pulling up weeds. Then, perhaps, everything would have been different. He could have tackled Ruth and pinned her to the ground while the car rumbled past, sending waves of harmless hot air over their bodies. He would let her up only when the car's engine could no longer be heard. Then, he would hug her, and say, "That was a close call, honey. Please look both ways next time!"

But that was not what had happened. Instead, he had to watch her stare blankly at the hospital ceiling with the tube of an IV and the wires of machinery snaking around her body like a spider web.

Jim rested against the trunk of a roadside tree and stared out into the night. The night remained undisturbed, though, and Jim's fatigue led him back inside.

Jim peeled off his stained sweater and slid into bed. The flurry of mysterious events that day caused him to fall quickly into a deep sleep.

CHAPTER 11

THE SHRILL YOWLING of the alarm clock brought Jim awake. He saw through his drooping eyelids that Sarah was already putting on makeup in front of the bedroom mirror.

"I made scrambled eggs. Please eat something!" she said as she added more lipstick.

Jim glanced at the floor. The comatose man he had seen the day before was no longer there.

"Good, I guess you had him taken away?" Jim asked Sarah. Sarah frowned at his reflection in the mirror.

"What are you talking about?" She tapped her mascara bottle against the surface of the dressing table.

"The man who was lying here. Some sort of intruder." Jim ran his hand through his disheveled hair.

"Honey, that was you! You passed out. You were out for a while, and the doctor said that you need to eat more."

Sarah had gotten up with only her lower lip coated with lipstick. She pressed her hand against Jim's shoulder.

"C'mon, you've got to take better care of yourself."

Jim got up, threw on a bathrobe and slid into some slippers. Sarah clattered down the hallway in her high heels. Yawning a few moments later, Jim arrived downstairs to see the steaming bowl of scrambled eggs Sarah had mentioned, as well as a carton of orange juice.

"So was that all a dream?" Jim asked as he rubbed the stubble on his face. First, he had seen the body of the unconscious man stretched out on his bedroom floor. Then, another intruder had entered his home: Andrew, with a new, strangely sunny personality.

It had all ended with the lambent figure of Ruth glowing in the night, rushing towards disaster. The events in the dream had been so vivid.

Jim stopped spooning scrambled eggs into his mouth. Sarah was moving around the kitchen. The heavy scent of her perfume trailed the clapping of her high heels against the wooden floor when she passed Jim.

"So, the unconscious man was me?" Jim asked, looking quizzically at Sarah.

"Yeah, you were unconscious for a while. I was getting worried. But—did you see yourself while you were passed out? That doesn't make sense." Sarah's thin, false eyebrows furrowed. She slid a chair away from the table and sat down in it.

"Yeah, I guess I had a dream and I saw myself while I was lying there in the bedroom. I guess it was an out-of-body experience."

Jim noticed Sarah's long, painted fingernails as she gripped a coffee mug with both hands. Thin strands of steam rose up before her face.

The tense conversation faltered and petered out, and, before long, Jim was on his way out of Blackmun to work again. He veered into a parking spot in the rapidly filling factory lot. A couple of hours into Jim's shift, Jeremy summoned all the repairmen for a meeting in his office. The entire group, in jeans and T-shirts with streaks of grease on their hands, crowded in the small room while Jeremy rocked on his chair.

"Well, folks, there's been a problem." Jeremy held up two yellow pieces of paper with a long, single-spaced message typed onto both sides of each of them. "Cisco is going to have to recall the four truckloads of siding that got shipped to Wisconsin. They're all the wrong size. I've talked to management, and we think that the reason this happened is because you people didn't fix the roll forming machine we entrusted to you. We're going to send it back to you. We've got to do a better job, people. I also want to talk to Jim in particular. Jim, please stay and chat with me a little after everyone else has left, alright?"

A couple of guys around Jim turned to leer at him, as if he had some gross deformity. Jim's face already glistened with sweat. There was a hot light above Jim's ahead. Jim had done a lot of work on the roll forming machine. Soon, after a few employees had asked questions about financial penalties and if management was going to fire anyone, he stood alone before Jeremy, who pointed to chair in front of his desk.

"Look, Jim, let me explain something to you." Jeremy plucked a sharpie from a cup on his polished mahogany desk and began to sketch a diagram on a yellow legal pad. On one side of the paper he drew a triangle. From the triangle, he drew several long lines.

"Alright, now the triangle is Cisco Roofing. Cisco Roofing sends trucks full of roofing materials to places all over the country. Two weeks ago, we sent four trucks along these lines," Jeremy traced the four lines extending from the triangle like sunbeams, "to different towns in Wisconsin: Madison, Abrams, Calamus, and Prentice. Then, the trucks had to go back to the company who sent them to us. We were supposed to pay for the return trip as well as the trip to Wisconsin. So, Cisco pays for the material for the siding, the salaries of employees like you who help make it, and the fare for the trucking company responsible for delivering the siding."

Jim shifted in his chair. Jeremy looked into his eyes unflinchingly through the thick, square lenses of his bifocals.

"Now, none of this would be a problem if we were able to sell the siding that we shipped to Wisconsin. But, as I said, it's defective. Not only is it the wrong size, it's slightly asymmetrical. And," Jeremy's stubby index finger extended towards Jim's chest, "you did most of the work on the broken roll forming machine. Why did you think it was fixed?" Jeremy's voice rose in volume as he built his case.

Jim swallowed through his tightened throat. His grip on the arms of his chair was firm. "Well, I guess it was just an oversight. I'll try not to do it again."

Jeremy leaned back in his chair, removed his glasses, and studied Jim's sullen face. "Well, Jim, trying is not good enough here at Cisco. Anybody can try. We need people to be *successful.*"

Jim sat up straighter. There were other companies. Many other companies used machines. He had a good mind for machinery.

Jeremy's pause was prolonged. The stuffy air of the office enveloped Jim like a heavy wool coat that was too small for him. "Jim," Jeremy finally asked, "is something bothering you?"

Jim did not want to talk about Ruth with Jeremy. He cleared his throat and placed his ankle atop his knee. "No, not really. Maybe the bad weather we've been having."

Jeremy frowned, and shook his head. "No, Jim, I'm not convinced. I'm curious. You're not still upset about your daughter, are you, Jim?"

Jim had opened up to Jeremy about Ruth when he requested a week off after her death. Jim sat silently before his heavyset, prying manager.

"Well, naturally, I am…" Jim said softly. The muscles on his hands bulged. They were strong from the years of handling wrenches and hammers.

Jeremy breathed so deeply that the intake of air was clearly audible to Jim. "Jim, can I give you some constructive criticism?"

Jim nodded. His heart began to beat faster and blood began to flood his face.

"Jim, everyone experiences the death of a loved one now and then. A couple of years ago I lost my uncle." Jeremy flipped around a silver-framed picture propped up on his desk. Jim saw the bespectacled face of a man with high cheekbones just like Jeremy's. "You might be thinking that he was just my uncle, but he and I were really, really close. But, Jim, we've got to move on. I've moved on. In the two years since I lost my uncle, I've gotten two raises. Jim, you're letting your grief interfere with your work, and that's unacceptable."

Jeremy crossed his hairy arms atop his desk. He removed his bifocals in order to clean them with a small rag he pulled from his pocket. Hot blood flowed in Jim's arms, hands and face. He eyed Jeremy's flabby neck.

"Alright, Jeremy. May I be excused?" Jim had already risen. Jeremy waved his hand towards his office door, and then buried himself in more paperwork lying on his desk.

Jim walked slowly back to the broken machines. He looked at the floor as he walked: a couple of centipedes scurried along the dusty concrete. He clutched a hammer, and began to pound a nail into a board with great fierceness. Other employees turned to watch him, since they could hear the sharp crack of his hammer even above the raucous sound of the music playing in the warehouse.

Memories of Ruth rose up in his mind once again. He had coached her as she made her first stumbling attempts at walking. With his large, masculine hand he gripped her's. Eventually he would let her go, watching to see how long she could manage on her own. At first, she would collapse to the carpet right away, where

Jim cushioned her fall with his cupped palms. Slowly, though, she was able to take a few clumsy steps on her own.

Jim stood up straight and stared at the gray blank area where the wall met the ceiling at the other side of the warehouse. The memory was bittersweet, of course, since his daughter had left him soon after she had arrived.

He kept hammering, but a new scene floating up before his consciousness distracted him from his work. It was from the vivid dream he had recently: he was standing by the road while Ruth headed past him looking for the ball she had hurled across the street. Out of the corner of his eye he could see the headlights of the approaching car slicing through the darkness. His foot jerked forward as he saw Ruth and the car converging. He shook his head, though, and broke free from the reverie. He did not want to witness its gory ending again.

As he began to work with a drill, which whined as it spun, yet another scene played itself in his mind's eye. People kept coming into Wisconsin stores hauling siding on carts. They all told the store employees that their siding was the wrong size. He saw people in fancy suits signing papers, on the letterheads of which were written the words "Recall Approved". Then, he pictured large panels of siding being loaded into the backs of trucks, with neon posters hanging from their sides. The posters read "Defective". The two situations he imagined—his reflexive movement towards Ruth and the recall of the asymmetrical siding—were similar. Both involved attempts to undo a mistake, to edit life the way one would edit a manuscript.

Jim felt the sweat collecting on his forehead. He stopped drilling as saw that his hand was trembling. The scene around Jim— other workers, the machines and the light reflecting off the office windows—began to spin. His body thudded to the floor, and other workers clustered around him rapidly.

CHAPTER 12

JIM CLOSED HIS eyes just as a few workers had gathered around him, leaning with their hands on their knees and staring. Their voices faded to an incoherent babble. Soon, complete darkness blocked out Jim's consciousness.

After an indefinite period of time, a thin shaft of light broke the total darkness. Gradually, it expanded, until it had consumed the blackness. The incandescence was so fierce that Jim covered his eyes.

"Hey, stop it, stop it!" Jim cried. The pain in his eyes forced out tears. As if someone had heard him, the intensity of the light waned. Jim noticed that the brightness of the light had concealed some objects. He could now make out the faint outlines of a chair and a desk. He looked to the side and saw that he was lying on his back on a couch with cushions that were dark blue, almost black.

"It'll be alright, Jim," someone with a soft, boyish voice said. Jim jerked his head in the direction of the voice. Since the light had continued to grow dimmer, he was able to discern the silhouette of a person sitting in the chair he had already seen. The figure, which appeared to be male, twirled a pen with his fingers. He propped a clipboard on his lap.

"Where the hell am I?" Jim barked. He tried to roll off the couch, but his body was unresponsive.

There was some whispering behind him. Soon, someone stood above him and handed him a cup of water with one hand and a pill with the other.

"Go ahead and take this, Jim," the tall figure said. Jim could still not see clearly because of the extraordinary brightness of the light that had broken through the darkness of his unconscious state.

Even though the figure standing above him was a blur, Jim snatched away the cup and poured half of its contents down his throat to wash down the pill. Within seconds, his agitation left him. It was as though he were relaxing in his living room after a trying day.

Jim's eyes steadily recovered from the shock they had received. He could see, as he rested on the couch, that he was in a small room with framed diplomas hanging on the wall. The hum of an air-conditioner lulled him. Tropical fish in a large, square fish tank across from him darted back and forth through weeds and in and out the door of a miniature castle. After he had watched the brightly colored fish circle around the tank for a few minutes, he felt a gentle tap on his shoulder.

"Hello, Jim." Jim looked up at Mike's young face. Mike was not wearing his usual tattered jeans and T-shirt, though. Instead, the cherub-faced youth wore a black blazer with a white button-down shirt underneath. A red tie hung from his neck. Jim looked curiously at Mike.

"What happened to you, kid?" Mike looked like a kid on Halloween who had decided to dress up as a businessman or a professor. Mike cocked an ear and listened intently to Jim's question. Then, he made some notes on his clipboard. He pointed up at the diplomas on the walls. Through the glistening glass, Jim was able to notice Mike's name on each of them.

"So, what are you, some kind of doctor?" Jim giggled. He decided that he would refuse the pill if they offered it to him again.

"Actually, Jim, I'm an engineer. A special type of engineer. I'm here to help you. We have a lot of work to do." Mike pulled a chair up towards Jim's bedside. He sat down and slid his pen behind his ear.

A tender light gleamed in Mike's eyes. He stretched one of his delicate hands towards Jim and placed it on Jim's shoulder. Jim frowned at the boy's face before him. This new dreamscape was weirder than the one with Andrew. Mike noticed Jim's befuddled expression.

"Well, okay, I know this is confusing. Let me just start out with the basics." Mike cupped his hand over his mouth and cleared his throat. Jim tried to sit up, but his body still would not cooperate.

Mike breathed deeply before beginning. "I think the best way for you to understand your situation is for you to go into the TV room." Mike raised his eyebrows when he mentioned the room.

"Why is that scary?" Jim asked. He tried to fight back a drug-induced yawn.

Mike got up and smoothed out his blazer. He placed his clipboard atop his desk while he said, "Well, Jim, you'll just have to see. Now, get up."

Jim limbs shook a little and tingled. It was as though a faint electrical current were passing through his body. Once the tremors ceased, he was able to move his arms and legs. Soon, he stood beside Mike. Mike had pulled out a ring of keys, which tinkled as he searched for the right one. Once he had found it, he swung open a closet door. He pushed apart a row of coats and blazers that blocked the wall at the rear of the closet. Jim peered into its dim interior. He saw, abruptly, the golden gleam of a door knob. Mike turned to address Jim.

"Only a couple of people know about this room, Jim. Consider this an honor." There was a grinding and a rattling noise as Mike pushed a key through the slot in the golden doorknob. Jim could see flashing, colored light knifing into the closet through the now open door.

"This, my friend," Mike said with the verve of an actor, "is the TV room."

The soft murmur of a million different voices filled the hall. Jim saw two seemingly endless rows of televisions stretching before him. He and Mike strolled down the aisle between them.

"You see," Mike said as he pointed at one of the screens, "here's the scenario where you're watching *Return of the Jedi* while Ruth plays outside with Rascal." Jim looked closely at the screen to which Mike was pointing. One side of the screen showed Jim stretched on the living room couch with the remote control in his hand. Light from the television rippled across his face. In the other part of the screen, Ruth was winding up to toss a tennis ball up in the air while Rascal waited with his tongue lolling.

"But, no, I wasn't watching a movie the evening Ruth died. I was watching a sports talk show." Jim frowned as he studied the image.

"Well, let's look at the next screen." Mike took one step ahead of Jim and stood in front of the next screen, which was exactly the same size as the first one.

Jim bent to see this new screen. His breathing had grown rapid and beads of sweat had started to form on his temples. A black bar ran down the middle of the screen. On one side, Jim saw himself working in the factory warehouse alone. At one point, he removed his safety goggles and wiped his face with his sleeve. In the other half of the screen, Jim saw Ruth again back in Blackmun, holding a tennis ball up before Rascal's rapt gaze. Jim watched the split-screen for a few minutes. The images froze just before the car coming up the lane and Ruth's long-limbed body collided.

"In this scenario, you decided to work overtime instead of come home." Mike watched Jim's face carefully. A fire burned in Jim's eyes as he looked at Mike.

"Hey, what is all this supposed to mean, kid? That night...that night, I wasn't working overtime. Or watching *Star Wars*. I was watching...I don't know, I just wasn't where I should have been." Jim moved closer to Mike. His body was well-muscled and thick, especially in comparison to Mike's scrawny frame. Mike remained still, though, with his hands hidden in his pockets.

"I know what you chose to do the night your daughter died, Mike. But, here in the TV room, we have put on display all the choices you and Ruth could have made that awful night. Neither of you had to do what you did, y'know. See, here's a screen that shows Ruth sitting in the living room watching the sports talk show with you."

Jim moved a few paces down the hallway. Indeed, the image on the screen there showed Ruth with her head resting on her father's shoulder. Jim was sipping from a bottle of beer and pressing a button on the remote.

"So...Ruth never dies...in this...other world?" Jim asked Mike. He could not stop staring at the peaceful domestic scene: Ruth had closed her eyes and Jim began to stroke her hair.

"Nope," Mike said as he adjusted a sleeve of his blazer, "she decided not to play outside in this scenario. You'd still have her if she had made that decision. Or, if you had invited her inside to watch TV with you—that would have been a good choice, as well." Mike pointed to another screen that depicted the same scene that

Jim had just been contemplating. The only difference was the letter "J" was glowing in the bottom right-hand corner of the image. "The 'J' means you invited Ruth inside in this scenario," Mike said.

Mike watched Jim's expression. Jim breathed heavily as he strode down the hall, glancing to his right and to his left at the various monitors. He nearly tripped over a wire that extended across the hallway floor. Mike began to rush to him, but stopped when he saw that Jim remained upright. But, even after Jim had avoided stumbling over the wire, his steps were unsteady and soon, he did fall. Mike moved swiftly towards him. He caught his body just before it crashed to the concrete floor. Mike pulled a walkie-talkie out of his pocket and hastily switched it on. It crackled for a few seconds before he began to speak.

"Help, I need help in the TV room. This is Mike, and I need help immediately." Mike's hair hung over his head as he looked at Jim's pale face.

CHAPTER 13

J IM'S EYES OPENED upon a gray ceiling. He rolled onto his side.
"What are the other possibilities? I want to see other
screens," Jim said in a half-stupor as he swung his feet over
the edge of the bed. He heard soft, regular breathing coming from
behind him. He peered over his shoulder: his wife Sarah was still
asleep. Through the window behind her, Jim could see sunlight
dappling the browned, fragile leaves of a tree. A breeze made the
spots of brightness dance. His alarm clock began to wail.

Jim blinked a few times and shook his head, as if he were
emerging from underwater. He was trying to make sense of
his shifting experience, his sudden entrance into the familiar
environment of his bedroom.

"Are you going to be able to go to work today, Jim?" Sarah asked
in a sleepy voice. Her blonde hair glowed in the light that had just
begun to come in from the window behind her.

"Work?" Jim rubbed his hair, pieces of which were sticking
straight up.

"Well, yeah, work. You fainted again yesterday. Don't you
remember?" Sarah masked her yawning mouth with her palm.

Jim's searched his memory. He recalled Jeremy reprimanding
him for botching the siding that was sent to Wisconsin. His jaw
tightened when he thought how Jeremy had told him to stop
mourning the loss of his daughter, his only child. He had gotten
dizzy while working with a drill.

"I fainted again?" Jim asked, with surprise in his voice.

"Yeah, honey, I'm starting to worry about you." Sarah placed her
hand on Jim's shoulder. Jim responded by placing his own atop hers.

Slowly, though, Jim pulled himself away; then, he began to dress himself briskly.

"It's nothing, honey. It's probably just a passing bug. People keep calling in sick at the warehouse." Jim jumped into a pair of jeans as he spoke. After this, he wrapped a glossy leather belt around his waist. The belt had the outline of a charging horse inscribed into its buckle.

"Yeah, just make sure you wash your hands. I don't want to get that thing." Sarah was bustling to the bathroom. She emerged with a cup full of water and a pill. Jim gulped it down, then glanced at the digital clock on the nightstand.

"Hey Sarah?" Jim said, with a timid look on his face.

"Yes?" Sarah answered as a smile began to stretch the corners of her mouth.

Jim cleared his throat before saying, "There's still time for you to make me my favorite breakfast."

Sarah held her forehead in her right hand as if irritated, but a broad smile illuminated her face. Jim looked at her with pleading eyes.

"Oh, alright. But, you have to do the laundry on Saturday if I do."

Jim agreed. Soon, he was pounding down the staircase to wait in the kitchen while Sarah changed.

After Jim had eaten, it was clear he would be about ten minutes late for work, even with the recent change in his shift. But, even Jeremy would be lenient to someone who had fainted while working the day before. Jeremy did not want Cisco Roofing to lose money in court because he had mistreated a sickly employee.

Jim therefore strolled through the front yard to his car. Three Canadian geese were waddling across his lawn, bending their long, hooked necks to pluck at the grass now and then. Jim had a granola bar in his pocket and he broke off some fragments and strewed them in the vicinity of the geese. They all walked stiffly but rapidly to the crumbs. Jim chuckled, then began to whistle as he kept walking.

With his engine thrumming, Jim waited for traffic to clear on the road in front of his house. The drive on the way to work was very familiar, and the dream—or vision or trip to an alternate world, whatever it was—he had after fainting the day before began to preoccupy him. If he had been outside with Ruth the evening she had died, like some of the monitors in the hallway behind the closet had shown, he would have been able to block her progress with his body and rescue her. Instead, he had been paying attention only intermittently to people talking about professional baseball. Someone was bragging about his thirtieth homerun of the season while a three-ton vehicle plowed into his daughter's body.

His brooding continued as he drove past the pizza parlor where he and Sarah had taken Ruth for her ninth birthday. Perhaps he should not have fed the geese. Perhaps some kids in the neighborhood saw him feed the geese that morning. Later, they would decide that they should imitate him. Soon, hundreds of geese would come flocking to his lawn and the lawns of his neighbors. Their droppings would cover the lawns. People would get sick. Some would even die, all because of his whim that morning to toss some pieces of his granola bar onto his front lawn. It started to dawn on him as he drove that every choice he made, no matter how trivial, had far-reaching ramifications. How many deaths had he caused, in addition to the death of his own daughter?

Jim noticed the gleam of his belt buckle when he glanced to the side to switch on the turn signal.

He had the obscure fear that he should not have chosen this particular belt as he traced the image of the horse on its buckle with his finger. He began to hold the steering wheel tightly while scrutinizing the buildings and trees around him. There was no way he could avoid another catastrophe.

His face had grown pale by the time he pulled into the factory parking lot. He crossed paths with a crowd of workers from the early shift, who were looking glum as they complained about another day of work. Management had shifted Jim to a later shift because they feared for his health.

"Man, it just never ends. I keep telling my wife that we've got to save up so I can retire."

Another employee responded: "Yeah, but y'know what happens to my wife when she goes to the mall? I'll be working until I drop dead."

Jim ran his clammy hand along his cheek as he moved along with the pack. His fingers played with his belt as he looked around the lot. On one side, there were some homes and on another there was a small museum with artifacts from the abandoned coal mines in the area. Jim had been in there one day and looked at the pictures of the men involved in the subterranean treks through the mines. Their smeared, listless faces had stared back at Jim. The memory evoked an upwelling of hopelessness within Jim.

Jeremy walked back and forth across the warehouse once Jim's shift had begun, surveying the work of each employee with his sleeves rolled up just above his elbows. He crossed his beefy forearms before his chest when addressing one employee. At one point, Jim heard Jeremy say to an employee beside him, "Hey Tim, can we speak for a few moments?"

Jim peeked towards Jeremy as he addressed Tim in the shadow of a tall shelf piled randomly with tools. Tim's face had a beaten-down look as he nodded at Jeremy. Jeremy eyed Tim seriously. He gesticulated with his hands. He was clearly reprimanding Jim's coworker, and this exacerbated Jim's malaise.

Soon, it was time to take a break for lunch. Jim shuffled off into the swelling line of sweaty, quiet men toward the break room. A janitor who had been washing the break room floor began to erect "Caution: Slippery" signs before the men entered. Jim watched as the shoes and boots of the men added new stains to the shiny floor. Jim brought his candy bar to a table where Larry, a black coworker, and two other employees whom Jim did not know, sat. Larry was holding one of his hands about a foot above the floor.

"He was about this big. Not a very big dog, you see. I didn't check my mirrors, anyway, so even if he had been the size of a St. Bernard, I wouldn't have seen him. I guess there was an interesting scent behind the rear bumper of my truck. Stupid dog turned into a pancake."

The other two employees shook their heads. Larry smiled ruefully.

"When my daughter heard the news, she started bawling. She loved that dog, but I told her we could get a new one. She didn't want to hear that, though."

Larry took a gulp from the soda can in front of him. Jim watched his face intently. When no one spoke for a few moments, Jim interjected, "Y'know, you better be careful about what you drink. That soda—it could end up being your downfall!" Jim pointed at the soda can as he looked at Larry with wide eyes. Larry frowned at Jim, whose face was still without color.

"Oh, you mean soda's not healthy. Hey, man, but it sure tastes good!" Larry tilted the soda can back and poured it down his throat so that his Adam's apple bobbed up and down with each deep swallow he took. The other two coworkers' noses crinkled as they laughed.

Jim stared at Larry with his eyebrows raised in shock. He rested his chin on his fists. After a few moments of silence, he shook his head vehemently.

"No, no, that's not what I mean. Think of it this way: what did you have to drink this morning for breakfast?"

Larry looked down at the surface of the table with a puzzled frown, then made eye contact again when he answered, "Orange juice. I have orange juice every day."

Jim rose up in his seat. "Y'see, if you had had coffee, then maybe you wouldn't have hit your dog. Because you would have been more alert." Jim shrank back when he saw that some spit had flown by accident from his mouth into Larry's dark face. Larry wiped it off with a handkerchief he kept in his shirt pocket.

Jim kept going as his hands shook. "Sorry. I mean, everything we do matters. Do you realize that? That soda—take this can of soda, for instance."

Jim held up the can before the eyes of the three men. They exchanged nervous looks with one another.

"Let's see. This can could be recycled, and used to make a gun, say, that is used to shoot someone! There! It could happen, right! There's aluminum in some guns, right?" Jim looked at the faces of the three men. Larry grimaced.

"Hey, man, you better calm down. People just don't think about all that stuff. Nobody worries about all these—possibilities." The vein running up Larry's neck was beginning to swell. It throbbed visibly with each beat of his heart. His bald head glistened.

"Yeah, well, I guess..." Jim's voice faltered. He began to quietly chew his candy bar. The three men across from him began to converse amongst themselves. Soon, Jeremy was going through the break room, clapping his hands and barking, "Alright, everybody, time's up, back to your stations!" Jeremy's lunch break was twice as long as that of the people he supervised. After summoning them back to work, he would return to his office, where he kept a small portable television.

Jim began to walk back to the warehouse with slumped shoulders. Larry and his friends watched him with narrowed eyes. They covered their mouths with their hands as they exchanged gossip.

Jim had a hard time working once he got back from lunch. He was clutching a large, thin slab of aluminum with both hands. Suddenly, he paused. A couple of seconds later, he continued to walk haltingly across the warehouse floor with the piece of aluminum. Then, he stopped so abruptly that the aluminum slid out of his hands and rang as it tumbled to the floor. The choice to turn on the television and watch the sports talk show had led to his daughter's death. Why couldn't another tragic event follow from his next decision?

Other employees looked at Jim and the fallen piece of aluminum.

"What the hell happened, man?" a man said. Creases of confusion formed on his forehead.

"Well," Jim explained in a weak voice, "I was just worried that this aluminum would end up falling on someone. Someone—a worker—might, y'know, drop it on someone. Later on, when they're attaching it to a house. I didn't want to be to blame for that, too." Jim looked around at the crowd of which he had become the center. People looked at Jim with concerned expressions.

"But that wouldn't be your fault," a man with a large potbelly and shoulder-length blonde hair said. "The guy carrying it has a job to do. Dropping it's on him." The blonde-haired man pointed in the air before him, as if the clumsy worker were standing before him.

Jim became animated. "Oh, that's what people might think. But, listen to this. If I don't get this piece of aluminum ready for shipment, then the accident would never occur, right? So, I'm responsible. Me!" Jim laid his palms against his chest.

Another coworker had stepped forward to join the debate, but Jeremy had cut through to the center of the crowd.

"Hey, what's going on here? We're here to work, not chat. Are you guys going to start a union or something?" Jeremy's voice echoed brassily from the metal pipes that formed a tangle near the ceiling of the warehouse.

The employees began to fidget. Jim turned his head aside as he blew his nose into a tissue.

"Tell you what," Jeremy said when no one responded, "I don't want to know what you guys were talking about. Is there some hot new porn star you guys like or something? Get back to work, you bums." Jeremy glowered at the retreating figures of the workers. He chewed his gum slowly. Jim bent down to pick up the slice of aluminum that had slipped out of his hands.

After another hour of work, Jim moved over to the corner of the warehouse where the safety goggles were kept. He needed a pair, since he was about to slice up some shingles with a buzz saw. Holding a pair of goggles up to the light coming from above him, Jim saw two thin scratches marring the surface of one of the lenses.

Jim thrust the goggles back onto the dusty rack so forcefully that they rattled off of it and onto the floor. He searched the warehouse for Mike. Jim finally spotted him heading towards the bathroom. Jim walked so quickly towards his young coworker that the employees who saw him tittered. Jim heard one of them say behind him, "Got the runs, Jimmy?"

Jim was panting by the time he swung open the bathroom door. Mike was flattening out a cowlick with his hand when Jim entered. Jim investigated the interior of the bathroom. No one else stood amidst the urinals and he could see no feet under the door of the one stall. Jim grabbed one of Mike's shoulders.

"Mike, how can I make one of the other scenarios on those screens happen? C'mon, tell me, I'm desperate."

Mike backed away from Jim's hot breath and forceful grip.

"What are you talking about?" Mike eyed the door behind Jim's taller frame. His shoulders came up against the hardness of the hand dryer.

"Y'know, the screens, with me doing different things." Jim moved even closer to Mike. He rested one of his hands atop the apex of a curved faucet.

Mike frowned. "What?" After looking into Jim's eager eyes for a couple seconds, he squirmed around him and then flew out the door.

"Hey, Mike, I just wanted..." Jim stared at the door, which swayed from side to side from the force of Mike's exit. He held out his hands in dismay.

Turning to the mirror, the sight of his face pulled him up short. He ran his hands along his cheeks. They had grown thin. His newly lean face looked hard and almost cruel. The patch of gray near his bangs had broadened. Sarah had recommended recently that he take more vitamins.

"You're starting to look old, honey. I don't want to fall out of love with you," she had said as she mixed in some frozen orange juice with the water in a pitcher.

Jim studied the reflection of his own eyes. He placed his hands in his pockets and a cocky smile twisted the corners of his lips.

"Just relax, buddy, everything will be fine." He had coached his own reflection on other occasions of his life. He had done it before Jeremy had interviewed him for the position he now held at Cisco and also when Sarah had gone into labor in the hospital in St. Louis. He inhaled deeply. Then, he walked slowly back into the warehouse.

"Hey, Steve," Jim said as he passed a coworker. Jim forced himself to smile. He stretched out the ribbon of a tape measure and began to check if some pieces of siding were the right size. The rest of the day was uneventful. At one point, though, Jim did observe Mike talking to Jeremy. Mike started to gesture towards him. Jeremy eyed Jim, then looked back at Mike, who pointed to the bathroom door. Jim's lips tightened.

Jim recognized the ominousness of the sight. His negligence had already forced the company to recall the shipment of siding to Wisconsin.

Jim met with every employee still in the warehouse before leaving. He patted some guys on the back, and congratulated the receptionist on her son's college graduation. In the car, he adjusted the radio knob to the local soft rock station.

"Here comes the sun, here comes the sun…" Ruth was gone, but there was still sunlight, good food, friends and baseball when the weather was warm.

More disturbance, however, followed the placidity of the evening. A vivid dream troubled Jim's sleep. It began with him standing atop a skyscraper above the vibrant glow of a city still active at night. He wore a shirt with a superman logo covering the cloth that stretched across his chest. A long cape fell almost to his feet. When he leapt off the roof of the skyscraper, he found himself hovering in the air instead of falling.

Like a hawk, he was able to see the streets below in explicit detail. Drunks hobbled down sidewalks, singing. Crowds of people emerged from a stadium, decked out in their team's apparel. Vendors still sat in illuminated booths stocked with magazines, bubble gum and hot dogs. Jim's eyes sifted through all this activity. He was looking for a particular villain.

After a few minutes of scanning the city while hovering amidst the needles of towers, Jim spotted the villain he wanted through the window of a basement. It was next to a sewer grate. The villain had painted himself so that he resembled a clown. Solid, black armor encased the villain's long, slender body. He towered above Ruth, whom he had tied up in a chair.

Jim descended to the roof of an apartment complex that rose a block away from the small basement window. He looked soberly at his daughter's torturer. The Joker-Darth Vader combination smiled with gratification as Ruth watched his every move, terrified.

"I'm coming, Ruth," Jim bellowed hoarsely, even though his daughter could not have heard him. He sprung from the roof of the apartment building and dove into the air. Yet, his flying power had deserted him for some reason. He flailed as he kept plummeting to the road. He could hear the exuberant laughter of the villain who was holding Ruth captive, or perhaps imagined it. Jim saw that he was destined to fall in front of a speeding SUV. Just before crashing to the ground, though, his eyes opened upon his dark bedroom.

"What…why can't…"Jim struggled with the blankets. His movement woke Sarah.

"What's wrong with you now?" Sarah hissed. Jim's breathing was rapid. With his eyes staring at the ceiling, he recounted the dream to Sarah.

"It was a nightmare. All of a sudden, I couldn't fly. I couldn't save Ruth."

Sarah turned the switch of the bedside lamp. With her unkempt hair, she looked wild.

"Look, Jim, you've been acting awful funny lately. The fainting spells, now this dream. You're making mistakes at work. Y'know what? I think you should seek counseling."

Sarah tapped his shoulder with her finger. Jim felt a drop of sweat running down his cheek.

"Maybe that's what I need, Sarah, maybe you're right. Didn't your father go to a psychologist when he was going through that age-discrimination lawsuit?" Sarah nodded and tapped Jim again to emphasize her point.

"Absolutely. It really helped him. Honestly, Jim, you're turning into more and more of a…well, basket case, every day." Jim's eyes returned to the ceiling. He saw the cracks in its dull white surface.

"Well, give me some time. I want to beat this on my own."

Jim had been able to fly in the dream before jumping from the top of the apartment complex. He wondered why he had all of sudden lost this power.

CHAPTER 14

JIM PREPARED HIMSELF for work after twisting sleeplessly in bed for a few hours. Sarah waved goodbye as he walked out of the house toting his paper bag lunch.

"Remember what I said, Jim. It could really help!" She watched him through the wire mesh of the screen door. Exhaust fumes soon began to billow from Jim's pickup truck.

Jim thought about Sarah's advice on the way to work. While he worked, Jim kept glancing in Mike's direction. He had said that he was some sort of engineer, but it seemed to Jim that he could have some knowledge that might be helpful. He had had an official role in the place with all the television monitors. When Mike had moved to a deserted corner of the warehouse to get some equipment, Jim broke away from the shingles he was trimming and walked towards him. Jim looked around the entire warehouse. Jeremy was in his office, and Jim felt free to bring up his questions.

He approached Mike with a smile. His hands, however, shook noticeably in his pockets.

"Hey, Mike, how've you been? How's the family?" Jim gave Mike a pat on his bony shoulder. Mike returned Jim's gesture with a broad, brilliant grin. A warm light glowed in his eyes.

"I'm great, man. How's your family?" Mike placed his hand on one of Jim's shoulders and looked at Jim expectantly. "What's up?"

Jim breathed deeply and let his shoulders relax. Even after the incident in the bathroom, Mike was open to talking to Jim. Jim grinned as his cheeks flushed.

"Well, sorry about the…the…uh, y'know, incident in the bathroom." Jim coughed in a clenched hand. Mike patted Jim's shoulder again. Mike's friendliness emboldened Jim, and he decided to raise another difficult issue. "Y'know, Mike, was that dream, or whatever it was, real? I mean, it was so vivid! I've just got to know—do you have access to this TV room?"

Mike removed his hand from Jim's shoulder and nodded. Light from a window behind him lit up the outline of his head with shiny fringes. Mike glanced towards the center of the warehouse. None of the other workers seemed distracted by them.

"What you saw after you fainted—the office, the televisions—is real." Mike spoke slowly and dramatically. Jim's eyes widened as he bent closer towards Mike.

"Really?" Jim stepped backwards a little. He fumbled with the top button of his shirt and, after a couple unsuccessful attempts, eventually unloosened it.

"Yes, it's real. That place, it's called," Mike lowered his voice to a whisper and raised an extended hand to shield his lips from prying eyes, "the realm of possibility." Jim's face reddened in his excitement. After a few seconds of thought, though, a tense frown appeared on his face.

'What the hell's that—this realm?" Jim's hands lurched towards Mike's shoulders as he waited for an answer, but he held them still just after they had risen above his waist.

Mike raised an open palm towards Jim to caution him. Jim rested back on his heels and breathed deeply. Once Mike had brushed some hair from his eyes, he began his explanation.

"You've been given access to the realm of possibility. In the world you've lived in up to this point, possibility exists only in the future. But, as people make choices, the originally endless array of possibilities gets narrowed down to just one scenario, which becomes actuality. This actuality, whether it's good or bad, is what we all have to live with." Tears began to pool in the redness in the corners of Jim's eyes as he listened to Mike. All the new information was overwhelming. "Yes, I know this is a lot, Jim. But, in the realm of possibility, the possibilities that attend every situation are still available. In this realm, for instance, if you bought a candy bar at the grocery store, instead of being stuck with that choice forever, you can go back and buy something different, or nothing at all."

Jim swallowed down some saliva that had been pooling at the back of his throat. Mike continued.

"I can imagine that you want to find out how you can get to this realm." A beseeching expression made Jim look like a criminal begging a judge for leniency. "Yes, well, here." Mike reached into his back pocket and pulled out a rusty key. He held it up in the air before Jim. The parts of it that were unmarred by rust glinted in the warehouse light. Jim snatched at it with his grease-stained hand. He clutched it there so tightly it was as if Mike were trying to steal it from him.

"Where's the door?" Jim's voice was unnecessarily loud. Mike looked around the warehouse. A female employee was staring at them.

"Jim, you've got to keep it down. The door is in your basement. It's really small, but it's possible to squeeze through it. It's behind the stack of paint cans. Watch out for the spiders down there. You hardly ever use those cans."

Jim nodded rapidly, and had begun to walk away briskly, when he spun and reversed direction, and came close to Mike again. "Why are you so, um, helpful, all of sudden?" Jim recalled how Mike had charged out of the bathroom when Jim had tried to ask him then about the TV room as if Jim were a deranged person.

Mike smiled. "I wanted to see how much you cared. Only really desperate people are allowed into the realm of possibility. The technology is still in its experimental stages, and we use it only if there is a need."

Jim pulled a rolled-up piece of tissue from his pocket. A trail of tears had begun to run from the corners of his eyes. "Oh, man, I'm so grateful." Jim held Mike in a tight embrace as he swayed back and forth. Mike struggled to extricate himself from the hyperemotional man.

"Jim, c'mon, that's enough," Mike said as he wrenched himself free. Flustered, he hissed, "Get back to work. People are going to start wondering what's going on." Indeed, the female employee who had been staring at the pair had begun to walk towards them.

"Are you two alright?" she asked as her boots clunked against the floor. Mike turned towards her as he motioned to Jim with his hand to move back to the shingles he had been trimming.

"Oh, we're fine, Brittany, no need to stop your work." Jim pounded away from Mike. He reached into his pocket to feel the cold, rough metal of the key again. He pushed it down among the dust and crumbs in his pocket as deeply as he could.

CHAPTER 15

JIM MANAGED TO mask his excitement around Sarah as he ate dinner with her and then watched television. He kept reaching, though, into his pocket to touch the key Mike had given to him. Sarah peered down at his hand once when he reached for the key again while they were both watching television.

"What've you got in that pocket?" Sarah slapped Jim's shoulder playfully. Jim's face colored, but he chuckled to deflect Sarah's curiosity.

"I'm just fidgety, there's nothing in there but a couple coins I keep playing with," Jim said. He turned back abruptly to the television set. Different colors radiating from the set flickered across his face. Sarah ran her hand along Jim's shoulders. Jim sank deeper into the couch.

Late that night, though, after Sarah's breathing had become deep and regular as she slept, Jim slithered out of bed. He slid into some sweat pants and then lifted the key out of the drawer in which he had hid it. The whites of his eyes flashed in the moonlight when he looked back at his sleeping wife. She shifted in the bed and moaned softly, but did not wake.

Having made certain that he had not wakened his wife, Jim padded on the soft carpet of the bedroom towards the hallway. A loud creak issued from staircase when it received the weight of his body. Jim stood still, scarcely breathing. He listened intently for any sounds coming from his bedroom. But there was only the sighing of the wind.

Soon, he had made it to the basement door. The Morris's hardly ever used their basement. It had never been finished and was primarily a storage space. Ruth had kept a lot of sports equipment and old toys down there. Boxes of old clothes that Sarah used to wear gathered dust amidst the cement and pipes. The stuffy air of the basement wafted into Jim's face after he had slowly and quietly opened the door.

Jim saw that pools of water had collected on the basement floor, most likely the result of a recent violent thunderstorm that had bombarded the area. Jim turned on the basement light, which dispelled the darkness only partially. His eyes veered to the corner of the basement where the paint cans were stacked.

Jim rubbed his hands together in anticipation of the task of setting aside the paint cans to get to the door. One by one, he began to remove them. The stack was three rows deep. Jim had once worked for a painting company, and one of the company perks was free cans of paint. He had more than he needed.

Jim's arms had begun to ache by the time he could see the gray surface of the wall. Behind one of the cans, near the basement floor, Jim uncovered the intertwined threads of a cobweb. A fat-bodied spider crouched in the center of it. Jim jumped back, pulling a paint can down with him. The can knocked others in the stack, which began to teeter over from the impact and soon came crashing to the floor.

Jim lay on his back while the cacophony subsided. The metallic sounds of the falling paint cans echoed throughout the basement. Jim's face tightened. He waited for the sound of footsteps and Sarah's questions.

But, even after five minutes, there was no sign of Sarah. She slept two floors above the basement. Jim wiped his forehead and let out a long sigh—it seemed his wife had slept through the noise. He clawed his way back to his feet and got back to work.

Soon, he had exposed a large swath of the wall. Jim could not see a door, though. He thought back to Mike's face when he had handed him the key. Had there been a mocking light in his eyes? Was this a kid's cruel prank? But, Jim began to brush away at the wall and bent down to get a closer look. He slowly discovered that the dust and flecks of paint that drifted to the floor hid the outline of a door about four feet high and four feet wide.

Jim stood up and studied the small door he never knew existed until now. He was breathing heavily from the strain of moving the paint cans. He pulled out the key. A golden arc of light flashed through the air as light shone on the surface of the key. Jim aimed the key at the black keyhole protruding from the door. He forced it in after a brief struggle, then turned it.

Jim stepped back as the door opened. It had coughed out a thick cloud of dust. Its interior was utterly dark. Jim clicked his tongue.

He treaded softly up to the kitchen, where he slid open the drawer where he and Sarah kept the flashlight. He froze, though, as the headlights from a passing car shone through the kitchen window onto his face. The light revolved past him. After it had passed, he exhaled, and snuck down the basement stairs again.

He stood a few feet from the opened door as he pinched the small flashlight in his fingers. Jim's body was tense, and there was a haunted look in his eyes. Nothing, though, emerged from the small passageway: no villain in a Darth Vader suit, or Ruth's ghost. The thin beam of light from the flashlight showed nothing but a gray-walled crawlspace. Jim craned his neck to glance towards the basement door at the top of the stairwell. He could only see the shadow of a swaying plant Sarah kept in the kitchen. The house was silent.

Jim crouched down on the ground and peered into the crawlspace. He inched towards it and soon had squeezed in his upper body. He tested the air within the narrow tunnel. It was warm and had an unidentifiable sweet smell, but Jim began to crawl through anyway. He was like a soldier crawling along the ground to avoid a stream of bullets flying overhead.

The flashlight revealed nothing but more crawlspace followed by a dark abyss. Jim dragged himself forward for a couple more yards. Something tickled the top of his hand.

Jim shone the flashlight on the back of his hand. At the edge of the circle of light emanating from the flashlight, Jim saw the long, orange body of a centipede. He recoiled, slamming his head against the low ceiling of the crawlspace.

"Holy hell," Jim hissed as his flashlight uncovered a centipede nest a couple feet away from him. The insects crawled around in an intricate, frantic tangle. Jim began to pound the nest with his flashlight. He flattened a couple centipedes, but the rest became agitated and went on the attack. One crawled up under Jim's jeans and along his calf. Jim rolled on his side, hoping to crush the invading centipede. But a flash of pain paralyzed him and he screamed. Tears began to roll down his cheeks as he tried to push himself out of the crawlspace with his hands. He glanced down at the crevice from which the centipedes were coming. He could see a massive swarm of the ugly insects down there, busy laying eggs, multiplying, and growing.

The pain in Jim's leg grew. His vision became more and more dim. He reached with his foot behind him, trying to hook it around the entrance of the crawlspace, but he could not feel the cement ledge. Dizziness and nausea forced him to stop moving. Soon, all was dark as he became unconscious again.

A chaotic scene replaced the darkness. Jim realized after several moments of stunned confusion that he was in the midst of a battle. Booms of cannons muffled the sound of the general's voice. The man, who towered above Jim, wore a three-cornered hat and directed the troops with a saber. Jim could see the blue uniforms of the enemy soldiers on a hill opposite the one on which the army among which he had suddenly found himself was stationed. The enemy soldiers all fought to remain upright in the mud as they charged with their swords and rifles ready. The general pointed his saber at Jim. Jim focused on the man's face. Jim's anxiety was making it hard for him to understand the man. The general's forceful shouts swelled his jugular vein.

"Light the cannon! Do it—now!" The general's horse reared up into the air as the imposing man looked at Jim with a sneer. Jim noticed that the man wielded a long sabre in his hand, which shook as he surveyed the hordes of enemy soldiers. Jim reasoned that the cannonball would tear apart the flesh of a number of these men. But the general kept waving his saber at Jim. Jim got up to shield a match from the drizzle and tried to steady his trembling hands. Out of the corner of his eye, Jim saw that another soldier was glaring at him. This man growled, "Do it, before they fire their own, you bloody coward." Jim looked once again at the dark forms of horses and bayonets scurrying through the mud on the opposite hill. His chest rose and fell rapidly, but the scene shifted before he could light the match.

The din subsided almost completely once the battlefield had dissipated piece by piece. Jim's only sensation was a hand patting his shoulder. He looked to his right. A woman with heavy makeup on and white gloves was trying to get his attention. Her lips wrinkled as she said, "Say something, please, don't you remember what we talked about?" Jim looked around to take in his new surroundings. At the end of rows of pews full of finely dressed people, a tall man beamed as he held the hands of his bride before the altar. The young lady before him stared into his eyes adoringly. A clergyman faced the congregation while holding a book open with his right hand. Jim gathered that the priest had just asked if anyone in the pews had an objection to the marriage that was taking place. The woman's efforts to get his attention became more aggressive.

"Say it, Jim, tell everyone why they shouldn't get married!" Jim looked back at the couple before the altar. The groom towered above the bride by more than a foot and it seemed to Jim that his smile had spread a couple of inches while he attended to the woman. But, just as the clergyman lowered his eyes to the book in his hand to continue the ceremony, the scene whirled away once again.

Jim stood on a shiny rooftop on a dark, wet night. A man with a heavy beard, dressed in a white T-shirt with holes in it, was eying him with his chin held challengingly in the air. He stomped his foot and said, "Alright, Jim, I'm fed up. Y'know what I'm going to do! I'll show you, man!" Tears filled the man's eyes. Jim looked at him with a puzzled frown.

"Oh, you know what's wrong, man. Don't play your funny games on me. I'm gone, dude, gone!" The bearded man swung around towards the skyline, where rows of towers cut into the light pollution of the city. He began to walk quickly towards the edge of the rooftop. His shoes clapped against the concrete rooftop. The bearded man then spun around and held out his raised middle finger towards Jim. He leapt backwards over the edge of the building, and just after his body had fully disappeared, Jim crashed onto the leather surface of a couch in an air-conditioned office.

"Hey, what are you doing, stop that!" Jim shouted before he recognized the diplomas and family pictures hanging on the wall. Once he did, he relaxed in the couch and breathed heavily as the air-conditioner lavished his sweaty face with cool air.

Jim heard footsteps behind him and a shadow blocked the light in the office. Out of the corner of his eye, Jim saw someone pulling a chair alongside the couch. Jim rolled onto his side, and saw Mike, who once again was dressed crisply in a blazer and tie.

"Hello, Jim. I see you had a rough passage out of Blackmun." Mike offered Jim a box of tissues. He snatched a couple and began to wipe his face and nose. Outside a window across from Jim, a bumblebee moved among long-stemmed flowers.

"Yeah, there was a war, a freakin' wedding with this big tall guy and this woman kept trying to get my attention…" Jim began to cough spasmodically. His head spun and he was disoriented. Mike got up and took a couple steps to a water cooler. He came away with a paper cone full of the cold liquid, which Jim gulped down greedily.

"Just relax, Jim, I know your passage here was crazy." Mike pointed to the cushion at one end of the couch. Jim sighed and let his head fall against it. He was too tired to protest. Mike sat up straight in his chair and, in spite of Jim's fatigue, began to talk.

"Now, Jim, I want to explain to you again where we are. This is the realm of possibility. In your world, once a choice is made, all the other possible choices that could have been made are no longer available. So, if you buy two percent milk at the grocery store, it's impossible for you to reverse that specific decision and buy skim milk instead. There's an inflexibility in your world that, at times, can have unpleasant results." Mike glanced at the clock hanging above his desk. He was about to continue his explanation, but Jim abruptly interjected, "How do I get my daughter back?" He had lifted his upper body from the couch, and looked at Mike with the whites of his eyes bulging from their sockets. Mike recoiled at the violence of Jim's motion.

"That's what I'm getting to. Just lie down, we'll get there." Mike pointed with a skinny arm towards the cushion of the couch again. Jim pushed himself back into a prostrate position, and Mike sighed softly as he moved some chewing gum around in his mouth.

"Alright, as I was saying, in your world, there's no way you can change what you did on the evening that Ruth died. You chose to stay inside watching television, and, in your world—or, rather, I should say the part of your world to which you have had access so far—this is the decision you'll have to live with for the rest of your life."

Jim's eyes began to glisten as moisture filled them. Mike's discussion of Ruth was probing at a huge burden of pent-up emotions. Even so, Mike wheeled his chair over to his desk and brought back a picture. He held it before Jim.

Inside the frame Mike held in his hand was a photograph of Ruth. She had a plastic shovel and a bucket in her hands. Sarah bent down above her with her hands on Ruth's shoulders while a white-crested wave reared up in the background. Jim wrested the picture away from Mike and inspected it.

"How do I get her back?" Jim asked again after staring at the picture for a couple of minutes. Mike loosened his tie a little and got up to turn down the temperature on the thermostat. Jim's distress was shaking Mike's composure, but he had a new idea.

"Okay, I'm going to let someone else do the talking. You obviously want to get your daughter back, and you can do that in the realm of possibility. Jim, do you remember Andrew?" Mike stood up and went to the door of the office.

"Come with me, Jim," he said as he stepped out into the hallway. The wooden floor beneath him creaked at each step he took. Jim followed Mike's slim figure. Jim was about a foot taller than the young man. It was strange to Jim that Mike seemed to occupy a position of authority in this so-called 'realm'.

They both wound their way through the hallways until they came out into at a small garden in front of the building which housed Mike's office. Amidst the bushes and vivid colors of the flowers, Jim saw a man bent over and digging. When the man turned his smudged face towards Mike and Jim, Jim recognized Andrew. Andrew shook some dirt from his forearms before striding towards Jim.

"Nice to see you again, partner." Andrew's gray eyes looked grave. Jim tapped one of his toes and glanced around randomly. He was flustered by how surreal his life had become. It was as if he had dived into a Dali painting.

"You remember Andrew, right, Jim?"" Mike asked, since Jim appeared distracted. Mike tapped Jim on the shoulder and pointed to the warehouse prankster. Andrew lifted one of his hands and smiled. Jim finally gave a barely discernible nod.

"Well, Andrew's going to take you to a place that I think will be of great interest to you, Jim. Andrew has been elected for the realm of possibility, too. That's why his personality changed so drastically after he was fired. He became aware of the consequences of everything that he did. Right, Andrew?"

Jim looked into Andrew's eyes. He was looking for a signal from his former comrade, since he was not comfortable trusting Mike, whom he didn't know as well. Andrew nodded with his eyes lowered and his hands clasped behind his back.

"Alright, Andy, you know the way, right?" Mike checked his watch, as if he had to meet someone else soon. Andrew gave him a thumbs-up and beckoned Jim towards a compact car parked alongside the curb in front of the office building.

Jim toyed with his collar after he had slid into the car. He kept adjusting the seat, though he ended up in the same position in which he had started. When the car started moving, he pressed his hand against the glove compartment in front of him. Andrew had driven so fast when Jim had known him, but in the realm of possibility, Andrew drove a few miles slower than the speed limit. Jim still had not fully grasped where the trip through the three weird situations—the wedding, the battle, the suicidal man—had led him.

"Okay," Andrew said after he had fished out a scrap of paper from his pocket, "we're looking for 127 Pleasant Drive." They were moving down a two-lane highway. Kids were playing basketball on a concrete court adjacent to a school. Andrew kept glancing at the street signs.

"Ridge, Concord, Oak…"

Jim rolled down the window of the car. His face was hot, but the air outside was also warm. It rushed at his body in fetid, exhaust-tainted billows. His eyes kept darting along the roadside, but he found nothing about the realm of possibility that was different from a suburban town in the world with which he was familiar.

"Where are we going?" Jim asked. The tension in his face caused him to mumble.

"We're going to a place that is very important for you, Jim, but which you know nothing about. It's the home of Eddie Drake and his nephew, Steve." Andrew tapped his hand on the steering wheel in rhythm with the music that tinkled softly through the interior of the car.

"What the hell does Eddie Drake have to do with Ruth? Who the hell is Eddie?" Jim's fidgeting and shouting made him seem drunk. He began to cough violently. When he was done, he spit onto the road that rushed beneath them.

"You'll just have to trust me on this, Jim. What Eddie Drake did two nights before Ruth died is crucial—Ruth would not have died if Eddie hadn't done it. We're pretty sure about that." Andrew's eyebrows rose after reading a street sign. They were getting close to Pleasant Drive.

Jim stared out the window after hearing Andrew's explanation. As the buildings, stores, and schools flickered by along the road, Jim realized that many of them were recognizable. There was the drugstore where he would pick up headache medication when he needed it. A block later, he spotted the high school where he had starred on the baseball team years earlier. A tractor with a rake dragging from its rear sent up clouds of dust as it went over the surface of the infield of the high school's baseball diamond.

"Are we going to, like, fix what this guy did?" Jim asked. He rolled up his sleeve and blew into his cupped hands as if it were cold outside.

"We're going to try, Jim," Andrew replied. The muscles on his forearms twitched as he gripped the steering wheel a little tighter. Suddenly, he slammed the brakes. The tires of the small car screeched, and loose gravel from the road rattled against the undercarriage.

"Shoot, I missed it. Sorry, man," Andrew said as he shook his head in self-reproach. Jim peered frantically behind him.

"Pleasant Street...Pleasant Street! There it is!" Jim pulled at Andrew's shirtsleeve.

"I know, I know, stop pulling me!" Andrew swatted at Jim's hand. After seeing that the road behind them was clear, Andrew put the car in reverse and then pulled down Pleasant Drive.

"We're going to approach just before he does it," Andrew whispered to Jim, but Jim didn't understand exactly what Andrew meant. Jim stared ahead, transfixed by the shadow-dappled street. The prospect of rescuing his daughter intoxicated him. House after house ran past them. Finally, Andrew pulled gently to a stop before a one-story home coated in brown stucco. He patted Jim's shoulder.

"We'll wait 'til it's dark. Here, let's listen to some music." In spite of Andrew's change in personality, he put on the same heavy metal that often assaulted the interior of the warehouse while work was taking place. It was already evening, and Jim and Andrew had to lower the visors attached above the windshield to block out the reddish, horizontal light of the setting sun.

As darkness fell, the large window of the home Andrew had pulled up next to became more and more transparent. Jim began to make out a tattered couch illuminated by the vivid glow of a television set. The large form of an overweight man emerged into the room and then faded from it. Soon, though, the man returned and seated himself on the couch.

"That's Eddie Drake," Andrew said while pointing at the man on the couch. "His son Steve is about to take the car out to the local library." Jim looked at the driveway that ran alongside the Drake home. A red station wagon was parked there. The passage of a tall, slender man through the Drake family room caught Jim's attention. The man was lifting a jacket over his shoulders and talking to the old man on the couch. The old man chuckled at something his son had said. After the exchange, Steve came out into the darkness. Jim shrank in his seat, fearing that he would somehow thwart Andrew's plan by allowing Steve to see him.

"The moment Steve leaves…" The unfolding scene in the Drake home transfixed Andrew, though it was apparently mundane. He spoke in a whisper. The engine of Steve's station wagon began to purr. Its headlights swung as Steve backed out, and then zipped down the rutted one-way street where he lived. Andrew hit Jim's shoulder so hard it stung.

"Now, watch Eddie. This is the key moment!" Jim obeyed. Eddie was peering out the family room window. Once Steve's car was no longer audible, Eddie disappeared into a dark part of the house behind the family room. He came out with a wireless phone and sat down on the couch again. He pushed up his glasses with his finger before punching in the numbers on the phone.

"He's calling his friend Jerry." Andrew still spied with constant attention.

"How do you know, though? Has this situation occurred before?" Jim gestured towards the illuminated interior of the Drake home.

"No, no, of course not, it's a replay. Anyway, be quiet, just watch." Jim looked through the car window once again. Eddie patted the sloping folds of his stomach after he had dropped the phone into a crevice between cushions. While he watched television for the next ten minutes or so, he kept glancing towards the window facing the street.

Jim heard the rumble of a large engine coming from behind Andrew's parked car. Soon, the headlights of this vehicle streaked the back of Andrew's head. Andrew sat up straight and twisted his body to look at the oncoming car.

"That's Jerry, it's Jerry!" Andrew said quietly while tapping Jim's shoulder. Jim snarled at his old coworker.

"Would you stop touching me and tell me what the hell all this is about?"

But Andrew just silently watched the pickup truck as it parallel parked in an empty spot a few houses beyond where Eddie Drake lived. Jim saw Jerry come out from the truck. He was an old man who wore a hat that had a logo of the Marines stitched above its brim. Jerry walked up the steps to the porch of the Drake house with his hands in his jacket pockets. Eddie Drake had disappeared; he reappeared when the front door opened. Eddie shook Jerry's hand and walked down the steps behind him. Both men walked to the pickup truck. Jim could overhear their banter as they walked past Andrew's car.

After Eddie and Jerry had climbed into the pickup truck, it rolled past them down the street. Jim could see the silhouettes of both men through the rear window. Andrew's breathing slowed as he reclined.

"Alright, they'll be back in a few minutes. This is the fatal series of events, we're sure of it." Jim was almost motionless for half a minute. Then, he tried to turn on the car radio. When no sound came and Jim tried again, Andrew batted away Jim's hand away and said, "Let me put the battery on, hold up." Lights came on all over the dashboard as Andrew twisted the key in the ignition. Jim rotated the knob of the radio to find a soft rock station. He flapped his hand along the handle of his door in time with the beat of the music once he had found the station. Andrew, though, pounded the radio knob to shut it off once the rattle of the pickup's engine broke through the slow, soft love songs that were playing.

"Now, watch what Eddie is carrying when he comes out of the truck. Jerry has taken him to the nearest grocery store." Eddie stepped down from the truck alone. He waved to Jerry, who sped off into the night. He held a small box against his waist.

Andrew's eyes widened. "There it is! See the little box? It's a carton of ice cream." Jim looked out the window at Eddie's rotund figure and the ice cream carton that became visible whenever he walked through the transparent puddles of light cast by streetlights. Stinging tingles ran up his spine. He turned to Andrew and began to scream hoarsely.

"What kind of sick joke are you trying to play, you worthless scumbag? Who—what—I don't have the faintest idea who Eddie Drake is and I—I've come all this way for this! Ice cream!" Spit flew from Jim's lips as the tantrum escalated. Andrew thrust Jim back against his seat and held him there.

"Jim—Jim! Quiet down, man, relax. You've got to trust me. We're trying to help you get your daughter back. Trust me, all this is about your daughter." Sweat traced faint, vertical lines on Jim's cheeks. He breathed heavily, with an open mouth. Andrew nudged the side of Jim's head and pointed in the direction of the Drake home.

"Now, watch big Eddie eat. He's not supposed to be eating ice cream, since he just had a heart attack. But, he waited for his son to leave and his buddy Jerry doesn't mind helping his own friend hasten his death." Eddie had sat down on the ragged family couch once again. His face had a contented look. He grabbed a spoon which rested atop the container of ice cream and, after prying open the ice-crusted lid of the container, he dug into the contents inside with the spoon. Soon, he was bringing spoonful after spoonful of ice cream up to his mouth. Streaks of fudge began to run down his chin. Eddie cleaned it up with his tongue. Jim gawked at this orgy of eating.

Andrew watched with a grimace. The expression on his face twisted more and more with each spoonful that Eddie lifted to his lips. Finally, Andrew lowered his head and began to weep. Jim peered at Andrew as he sobbed into his lap.

"What's the big deal, dude? The dude's old, he's going to die soon anyway." But Andrew shook his head as more tears and snot dribbled from his face. He was trying to say something, but his grief made it unintelligible. Finally, though, he was able to hold his tears in check long enough to speak.

"This is how Ruth died! It's all connected, this is the source!" Andrew pointed towards the overweight old man, who kept digging into the carton of ice cream and bringing out clumps of gooey sweetness. Andrew spoke as if the man he was pointing at were in the process of murdering someone, or beating his wife. Jim scrutinized the old man with narrowed eyes. He couldn't sympathize with Andrew's response.

"I'll have to get Mike to explain all this to you. It's good that you saw this, though." Andrew had composed himself somewhat. He started up the car and began to maneuver it away from the curb. Eddie kept chipping away at the block of ice cream he cradled in his lap. The colors from the television ran across his body like flowing, multicolored water.

Chapter 17

ANDREW DROVE JIM through the dark streets back to the office building where Mike worked. Jim stared sleepily out the car window, but he grew tense again when he saw light penetrating the night and people coming out of their homes. Jim checked the digital clock on the dashboard: it had been dark for only a couple of hours, so it was confusing that the sun seemed to be rising. He sat up straight and stared through the windshield with a frown. Soon, it was as bright as it had been in the afternoon and people were out walking and running errands in their cars.

Andrew took notice of Jim's edginess. Andrew began to explain to Jim the sudden appearance of daylight.

"Remember, Jim, we're in the realm of possibility. It's not like our world, where we could never change what had already happened. We need to go back to the time before Eddie ate the ice cream—otherwise, how are we going to stop him from doing it? That's why it's daylight again—we're going back in time."

Jim just kept staring through the windshield with a scowl. His doubts about his sanity, and that of Andrew, kept getting more difficult to dismiss. Andrew glanced at him again.

"Don't worry, man! Mike can explain all this much better than I can." Jim started to drum his fingers nervously on the door handle. Wind coming in through the open window had ruffled his hair so much it was as if he had just rolled out of bed. Andrew stopped at a traffic light, turned and wound his way back through the increasingly crowded streets to Mike's office building.

Mike was standing in front of the office talking on his cellphone when Jim and Andrew arrived. He slid the phone into one of his pockets when he noticed who was in the car and, with his pants flapping in a breeze, he walked towards Jim and Andrew.

"You guys saw him—Eddie, I mean?" Andrew had rolled down the window and Mike had thrust in his thin-boned face.

"Yeah, Mike," Andrew replied after coughing, "we saw Eddie eat the ice cream." A shadow passed over Mike's face. Jim couldn't comprehend why everyone was so tormented by Eddie's eating habits, and he was getting frustrated.

"Yep, that's the key event. A linchpin event, to use the technical term." Mike motioned with his hand for the men to follow him as he strode to the glass door of the building. Soon, Jim and Andrew were seated on two comfortable chairs with wheels while Mike crossed his forearms on top of his desk. Both Jim and Andrew were sipping from cones of water from a large water cooler in the hallway of the office building.

"Alright, where should I begin?" Mike muttered as he rubbed his chin. He began to draw on a yellow legal pad with a pencil. When he had completed the diagram, he held it up before the two men. There were two large X's and many small o's. Mike used the pencil as a pointer once he began to lecture.

"Okay, Jim, this X represents Ruth's death. That's the event we're interested in. There are people all over the realm of possibility interested in different tragic occurrences that they are trying to reverse. I just spoke to a man yesterday who's trying to change Hitler's development— to prevent him from becoming the murderous dictator he was."

Jim held the cone of water still in his right hand. His eyes were fixed on Mike's diagram. Jim desperately wanted to trust Mike. Mike moved the tip of the pencil to the other X, which marked the opposite side of the paper.

"This X represents Eddie's night of gluttony, which you just witnessed. Now, these small o's represent all the noise with which we are not interested. In the realm of possibility, noise means events that don't have a causal relationship with the events that followed them. If they didn't happen, Ruth would still have died. So, for instance, your purchase of your dog Rascal did not guarantee that Ruth would end up dead. Another dog your family purchased could have run across the street and Ruth could have chased him or her as well. You see the distinction I'm trying to make, Jim?"

Jim's hand shook as he brought the cone of water up to his lips. A little of it spilled on his lap as he nodded.

"Now," Mike went on, "the fact that Eddie disobeyed doctor's orders and ate ice cream was relevant, we have found, to your daughter's death. In fact, these two events are so intimately connected that the only way that we can undo Ruth's death is to prevent Eddie from eating the ice cream. That may sound far-fetched, Jim, but my team and I have studied the consequences of Eddie's action and we've found that it *must* lead to Ruth's death. If Eddie doesn't eat the ice cream that night, Steve doesn't find the ice cream smeared on the couch when he's on it the following evening. If Steve doesn't find this smear, then he doesn't take Eddie to the doctor to be lectured. The series goes on, up until Ruth's death."

Andrew brought one foot up to his knee and wrapped his fingers around his calf. "What we're going to try to do, Jim, is, quite simply, prevent Eddie from eating the ice cream." Jim sat with his head lowered. A tiny bird had perched on the windowsill and was staring at the three men.

"That's right," Mike said, clearly uncomfortable because of the silence. "Now, what would happen if we prevented Eddie from eating the ice cream is a recalibration between the realm of possibility and the realm of actuality. So, if we prevent Eddie from eating the ice cream in the realm of possibility, then he won't eat the ice cream in the realm of actuality, in Blackmun. What once was an actuality— Eddie eating the ice cream—would then become a possibility. If, for whatever reason, we change our minds and decide that Eddie *should* eat the ice cream, then, in this realm, we can make that change, and we'll swap a possibility for an actuality and vice versa. The realm of possibility allows for endless revisions. It's the perfect environment for flawed human beings like us. We never have to suffer for a long time from our mistakes—we can just go back and change what caused them."

For a few seconds, the only sound was the soft grinding of the office air-conditioner. Mike rose from his desk.

"So, Andrew and Jim, I want you to get some rest tonight. Then, tomorrow, you guys will have to figure out a way to prevent Eddie from eating the ice cream. Remember, you just have to trust me that Eddie's action is essentially related to Ruth's death—the reasoning process behind this conclusion is very, very complex." Mike began to page through a black appointment booklet. Jim and Andrew continued to sit in their chairs quietly. Just before Mike left the office, he turned towards them again.

"Well, are you guys with me?" The men looked up and began to lift themselves from their chairs.

"Sure, absolutely," Jim said. A healthy glow had returned to his face. When he stood up, his posture was erect. He looked about the office alertly. He harbored doubts about his sanity, but Mike's confidence was enough to override them.

"There are a couple of cots in the room at the end of the hallway," Mike said while pointing down the long, carpeted hallway. Jim and Andrew began to file down it. Mike patted Jim on the back after he had passed and looked deeply into his eyes.

"We're going to do this, Jim. We're going to make it."

Chapter 18

Jim hardly slept the night after Mike's explanation. He was awake as the sun rose. At that point, since he was eager to get the day started, he began to shake Andrew's shoulder. Andrew had been snoring with an open mouth. He rolled onto his back and moaned after Jim had shaken him.

"I'm still tired," Andrew groggily complained. He swallowed a thick pool of saliva that had collected in his mouth. But, Jim kept shaking him and Andrew eventually came out of his stupor.

"Oh, I'm sorry man, I'm just not used to waking up this early." Andrew rose from his cot and looked out of the window. No clouds obscured the red light of the rising sun, just like the day before.

"Let's get to work," Jim said while slipping into his pants. Andrew gave him a nod and he also began to dress. Soon, the two men were in the car and driving among people commuting to work. Andrew pulled into the parking lot of a McDonald's.

"We need to strategize. This is not going to be that easy," Andrew said as he and Jim walked through the parking lot. They both ordered egg sandwiches and hash browns and then exchanged ideas at the table.

Andrew swallowed a piece of his hot hash brown before saying, "I mean, neither of us know Eddie. We need to establish some sort of foundation before we can talk him out of his unhealthy eating habits. I mean, we can't just walk right up to him and start talking to him about ice cream—it'd be weird."

Jim had taken just one bite out of his egg sandwich and the hash brown was still lying untouched on the plastic tray. "Steve wasn't able to convince Eddie to change his ways. Neither, presumably, was his doctor. Maybe we can use force."

Andrew eyebrows lifted a little. "Only as a last resort. Hey, people are pretty reasonable. If we do this the right way, we can get Eddie to change. You know all those ads about the dangers of cigarette smoking? Maybe we could use some similar scare tactics on Eddie."

Jim stroked the gray and black stubble on his chin. "Yeah, maybe we could get him to come with us to a hospital and show him all the people there suffering from heart disease, heart attacks, and strokes. We'll show him some people who have to deal with paralysis because of a stroke. That'll set him straight."

Jim stared intensely at the trash can next to a soda fountain. A woman dressed up for work glanced up at Jim as she slid the boxes and wrappers from her meal into the can. When she saw his fierce eyes, she moved away quickly.

Andrew put his hands in his pockets and leaned back on the hard plastic bench. "Well, Jim, we don't want to traumatize the old man. Here, let's try this. I want you to pretend that your Eddie's new neighbor. Around eleven every day, Eddie comes out to get the mail. When he does this, you can introduce yourself as Eddie's new neighbor..."

Before Andrew could continue, Jim intervened in a voice so loud that a whole family nearby turned to stare. "You want me to tell a lie? Andrew, I'm an honest guy!"

Andrew chuckled at Jim, who a moment ago had advocated the use of force. "But, Jim, it's for a good cause. You tell a little lie to build a rapport with Eddie, and then you can steer the conversation to the topic of eating and healthy diets and all that, and then, when evening comes, Eddie calls Jerry and guiltily tells him not to run that errand."

Jim lifted his hash brown to his mouth and nibbled at it. "Whatever it takes," he said after absently wiping some crumbs off the table onto the floor, "I'll do whatever it takes to get Ruth back."

Andrew pointed to Jim's egg sandwich. "C'mon, Jim, eat that, you're going to need it." Jim's mouth soon became full as he took rapid bites of the sandwich. "Yeah, just tell a little lie," Andrew continued, "and, hey, y'know what? You really are Eddie's new neighbor. I mean, you're new to the realm of possibility, aren't you?"

Jim chuckled. "Yeah, I guess, technically, I am a new neighbor. But, whatever—I'm game for it. You guys have an admirable agenda here—helping me get Ruth back and letting people fix problems in their lives. You just have to prove to me that you can actually accomplish these things."

Andrew stretched his closed fist over the table and he and Jim bumped knuckles. "Trust us, Jim, trust the people here." Andrew waited until Jim had finished his breakfast before beginning to drive again.

Andrew parked a block away from Eddie's house. Jim had to appear as if he were walking from a house in a different part of the neighborhood from Eddie's. If he claimed to have moved in near him, Eddie would have recalled that he had seen no moving trucks near his home recently and therefore suspect Jim of deceit. Andrew rested one of his hands on Jim's shoulder and leaned near him.

"Alright, here's the plan. You're new to the neighborhood and you're taking a walk. Eddie's going to come out of his house to get the mail right when you walk by. Approach him and introduce yourself as new to the area. Start talking to him and find an opportunity in the conversation to bring up the topic of weight loss and dieting. See if you can get Eddie to change his mind about eating ice cream behind his son's back."

Jim nodded after each sentence. His eyes were wide and his breathing was audible. He stumbled on the curb on his way out the car, nearly falling. He walked down the shadow-dappled sidewalk towards Eddie's house. He stopped, though, when he heard Andrew shouting.

"No, no, it's the other way!" Andrew was pointing down the street. Jim raised a hand in the air and spun around to head in the opposite direction. He passed some kids playing basketball in their driveway. A car backing out stopped courteously before he passed. Finally, Jim saw the broad front window of the Drake home. Just as he approached, Eddie hauled his corpulent frame through the door and then down the concrete front steps. Jim walked across Eddie's lawn to accost him.

"Howdy neighbor!" Jim said, extending his hand towards Eddie. Eddie glared at Jim. A couple of days ago, a member of the Jehovah's Witnesses had come to his door with a handful of pamphlets. After a brief exchange, Eddie had slammed the door shut with a crash.

Jim, still with a broad grin, glanced up at the two trees that towered over the Drake's front lawn.

"It's—it's a nice day!" Jim said as he stared up at the sky. Eddie's feet were rooted to the lowest step of the front porch. He kept staring at Jim with annoyance and confusion. Jim's face reddened when his eyes met Eddie's again.

"Oh—well, I'm sorry, yeah, I'm Jim, your new neighbor!" Jim reached his hand out once again towards Eddie, who remained motionless.

"Y'know, I just moved in." Eddie finally gave a small nod. A stiff smile pushed aside the fat of his cheeks, but quickly vanished.

"Well, nice to meet you," Eddie said in his hoarse smoker's voice. His hand was fleshy and sweaty. After the greeting, Eddie waved to Jim and began to walk down his driveway towards his mailbox.

"Wait, no, Mr. Drake—I mean, sir—could we talk a little more?" Jim remembered in mid-sentence that he wasn't supposed to know Eddie's last name. Eddie had paused suddenly when he heard Jim use it. Jim grimaced.

"How do you know my name?" Eddie asked with his bald head gleaming in the sun. His lips were curled away from his teeth. Jim lowered his eyes to the unmowed grass.

"Well, y'know, word gets around. Anyway—well, how's your d-diet?" Eddie's scowl intensified. Jim clapped his hands together in front of him in an effort to make light of his gaffe. After Eddie had remained a half a minute in sullen silence, though, Jim put his hands in his pockets.

"Oh, I know, I know I'm no movie star. I don't want to be, either," Eddie said with his voice raised slightly. Out of the corner of his eye, Jim could see a woman peeking out of the bedroom window of the house next door at the two men. "But, quite frankly, it's none of your business what I eat, sir. It takes time to become someone's friend, and I've known you for what—ten seconds?" Eddie, having made his point, continued to pad down the driveway. But Jim trotted closer to him.

"Eddie, I know—this is all kind of weird—but you just can't eat that ice cream tonight. Please." Jim was bent at the waist and he had clasped his hands. Eddie's face grew bright red.

"Get off my property, you damn spy! Get away before I call the cops!" Eddie had thrust one of his beefy arms out to point down the street. He shouted like an inexperienced schoolteacher before an unruly class. "Leave, you weirdo!" As Jim ran off, tears of disappointment filled his eyes. When he got to Andrew's car, he supported his body by resting his hands against the car doorframe. His breathing was audible.

"I blew it, I really blew it, Andy." Andrew's body was hidden in the shadows that covered the interior of the car. "I just got flustered," Jim continued, "and I didn't build up to talking about ice cream and stuff, I went right after him, and now we're never going to get Ruth back!" The outline of a vein running under Jim's neck was clear as it pressed against the skin. Andrew waited for Jim to finish venting.

"That's alright, though, Jim. Remember, we're in the realm of possibility. A different course of action is always available to us here. You can reverse what you just did. We just have to start the day over again." Andrew motioned to Jim to open the car door. Jim slid into the car and brushed some hair off of his forehead.

"That's right. It's hard getting used to this place," Jim said as his breathing slowed. "This is embarrassing. I can't be this nervous. A little suavity, and I would have succeeded." Andrew pointed to Jim's open window. Jim rolled it up and Andrew turned on the air conditioning.

As he pulled away from the curb, Andrew kept trying to soothe Jim. "We'll tell Mike what happened and he'll just start the day over." Jim nodded. He was looking in the side view mirror to neaten his hair. Soon, Andrew was maneuvering through the crowded parking lot in front of Mike's office.

"He must have a lot of clients today," Andrew noted. Both men walked through the entranceway of the building and down the quiet, cool main hallway. Mike was alone in his office when they entered, writing.

"Well, did you guys get Eddie to start going down the straight and narrow?" Mike asked with a smile.

Andrew spoke for Jim. "No, it was Jim's first time, and he, y'know..."

Mike nodded. "It's to be expected. No problem, though. Let me show you something, Jim."

Mike stuck his pen into his pocket after putting a cap on it. He led Jim and Andrew out into the hallway and then down a corridor where a goldfish bowl with no goldfish rested on a table.

Jim could hear murmuring in the doors he passed. Finally, Mike stopped before one of these wooden doors and whispered to Jim and Andrew when they caught up with him.

"This is where we keep the clock!" Jim frowned as he cut in front of Andrew to step into a dimly lit, windowless room that was empty save for one bare desk. Andrew and Jim moved to one side of the desk, while Mike stood on the opposite side. A digital clock was set into the wooden surface of the desk.

"This, Jim, is the clock. The way it works is quite simple. Right now it says eleven thirty-three AM. If I change the time on the clock, we'll literally be set back—or forward, depending upon what our goal is—to the time I punch in. So, if you make a mistake, we can just go back to the time before you made the mistake and you can try again. Pretty sweet, huh?" Mike rubbed his palms together and grinned at Jim. Jim watched him intently.

"So, now I'm going to punch in eight AM. We'll go back to the morning, before your encounter with Eddie. You can prepare again and learn from the problems you had your first time. What a luxury, huh?" Mike looked into Jim's eyes with his eyebrows raised. After a few seconds, Jim stirred.

"Uh, yes, I'm ready." Jim's hands were in his pockets. Mike bent down over the desk and clicked one button a couple of times, then another button thirty or forty times. As Jim watched Mike leaning over the clock, he noticed that Mike's body was getting more and more transparent. At first, Mike's skin seemed to be growing paler. Later, though, Jim noticed that he was starting to be able to see the wall behind Mike's body. The outline of Mike's body steadily lost solidity and it soon looked like a swirl of tiny particles. At first, the particles maintained a tight rotation so that together they still formed the shape of a body. But, slowly, the particles began to branch out in various directions. One veered into a corner of the room by the floor. Another broke off from where Mike's head had been and zipped up to the ceiling. Jim's heart started to pound.

Suddenly, though, the trend reversed and the particles began to condense. Soon Mike's body was reconstituted before Jim's eyes. Mike had an easygoing smile when he had fully formed.

"Alright, mission accomplished. It is now eight o'clock in the morning. Let's talk about the improvements we need to make in our strategy for Eddie."

Jim, though, lifted a hand from one of his pockets and pointed at Mike. "Wait, that was weird—you started to disappear, it was disturbing."

"Yes, that's what happens when we need to change times. What you saw, Jim, is just how insubstantial we really are in the realm of possibility. We are the product of events that occurred in the past. Our psychology is in part the product of choices we've made. Our bodies were built up by the food our mothers ate when they carried us in the womb. In the realm of possibility, none of these constitutive events had to happen. When we change the time in this realm, the reversibility of all these events is exposed. That's what you were seeing—there was a momentary instability in which it was possible that all the events that created me could have been undone."

Jim's eyes widened. "Did I look like you did, too, when I was coming here?" He had been fixated on Mike while the change in time was underway.

"Yes, you did. But, you shouldn't be alarmed. We have a good amount of control over the reversal engineering process. We can change pretty much exactly what we want to change—everything else remains in place."

The three men stood silently for a few seconds as they took in what had just occurred. Andrew turned towards Jim. "Do you have any more questions, Jim?" Jim lowered his eyes to the carpet. He was mulling over a new idea and he began to speak with fervor.

"Yeah," he said after clearing his throat, "I've got one. Can just anyone access this clock? I mean, what if there were some guy who was a total sadist—let's say he enjoyed killing people. In the ordinary world, he would murder someone, and the people who knew that person would see that he or she was missing, and detectives would analyze the body after people found it, and let's say officials identify the sadist and catch him. So, problem solved. But, here, a sadist could murder someone, run to this clock room, and go back to the time before he committed the murder, when there was no dead body to deal with and no fingerprints. I mean, he could have the pleasure of killing someone without the unpleasant consequence of getting caught. As many times as he wanted to! I know this is all kinda morbid…"

Mike leaned over the desk towards Jim. "Oh no, Jim, your point is well taken, well taken indeed. We're very aware of that potential problem here in the realm of possibility. But the chances of it happening are…well, let me put it this way: a scenario like the one you described could never occur, Jim. First of all, to become an engineer like myself, you have to endure what we call a biorenewal. This means that all the problems in your life are removed. If your father was abusive or you did some recreational drugs as a teen, the biorenewal will change it so that your entire past is free of the slightest glitch. At the end of the biorenewal, you're as psychologically healthy and well-adjusted as a person can possibly be." Mike gave Jim a broad smile and rested his hands upon his hips. The pose suggested confidence and happiness. "Furthermore, this room is the best-kept secret in the whole realm. If anyone whom I find suspicious finds out about it, I just go back a few minutes with reversal engineering before they do and make sure this discovery doesn't ever happen. Yeah, so consider yourselves fortunate. The inner sanctum of the realm of possibility!"

Mike gave a hearty, biorenewed laugh. Jim peered out the window and saw that the sun was lower in the sky than it had been. It was, indeed, morning once again.

"Well, I guess we better head back out," Andrew said as he patted Jim on the back. Jim was drained from all the new information. "Do'ya need a break, my friend, or should we just get this over with?" Jim stared glumly at the gray carpet. Then, he sat erect and broke the silence.

"No, no, I'm ready, let's tackle this." Jim adjusted the collar of his shirt and pulled the band of his wristwatch tighter, since it was ready to slide from his arm. Andrew, seeing the determination in Jim's eyes, nodded and marched out of the office. Jim trailed behind and Mike gave the two men a broad wave.

"Good luck, guys! And Jim, just relax this time! You don't have to do it right." Andrew and Jim walked down the hallway again, past the doors behind which they again heard hushed conversations. Behind one door in the particular, they heard the whine of a machine. Outside, a squirrel hopped around the lawn in the soft morning light and then chewed on a nut it held in its tiny paws.

"Now, let's rehearse the plan," Andrew said as he steered the car to Eddie's neighborhood once again. "Just introduce yourself as a new neighbor, and then make a natural transition to the topic of weight loss and health. Y'know, develop the conversation in a way that's not awkward and that will give you away. And, hey, if you mess up, we can always try again." Jim nodded after each of Andrew's sentences. A smile came to his face as the wind ruffled his hair. After parking, Jim and Andrew waited for the time just before Eddie would be coming out of his house to get the mail. When it came, Andrew gave Jim a light shove as he exited the vehicle.

"Break a leg, man!" Andrew said. Jim glanced around the neighborhood. It was deserted save for an old woman rocking on her porch. She was not looking in Jim's direction.

Jim strolled down the sidewalk, which was broken in different places by the roots of trees. When Jim was about twenty feet away from the Drake house, Eddie Drake once again shuffled out of his front door onto the porch. Jim looked towards the opposite side of the street at first, so that it seemed as though he were passing by casually. Slowly, he turned in Eddie's direction. He paused before the Drake yard and waved.

"Howdy, neighbor!" Jim said. His voice cracked slightly, since he was still nervous. Eddie studied the newcomer with suspicious eyes.

"I don't think I've met you before, sir," Eddie responded coldly. Jim noticed the thick patch of white chest hair emerging from the top of Eddie's T-shirt.

"That's right, I'm new to Blackmun." Jim walked up Eddie's driveway and extended his hand when he neared Eddie. Eddie did not smile, but he reached out and shook Jim's hand once he was close enough.

"Where're ya from?"

Jim stammered a little, but replied, "Tallahassee, Florida. Yep, I got a new job out here and brought my family with me."

"Why the hell did you come up to Missouri for? You like freezing?"

Jim laughed. "Actually, it's pretty nice out today. Nice, mild, early summer day." Jim's eyes darted to the side for a second as he thought out his next move. "Perfect day for a jog." Eddie looked up and down the street.

"You jog, huh?" Eddie held a hand above his eyes as sunlight found a gap in a cluster of leaves.

"Oh yeah, every day," Jim answered. "Great way to burn off calories and stay trim." Jim's speech was a little rapid, but he still grinned at Eddie.

"Yeah, good for you." Eddie lowered his head and began to walk down the driveway again. Jim, though, sensing an opportunity, moved closer to him and blocked his path. Jim began to expand on his lifestyle.

"Yeah, I try to stay fit, but I've got a sweet tooth. Last night, I had two bowls of ice cream—I think it was fudge ripple—and my wife got on my case for it. I've gotta admit she's right." Jim laughed briefly and then watched Eddie closely to see if he had made an impression.

Eddie's face reddened. He pushed up the bridge of his glasses with his index finger. He muttered something Jim could not hear, and then circled around Jim to the mailbox.

"It was nice to meet you," Eddie said gruffly, without looking at Jim. Jim watched the back of Eddie's bald head. He stood on the driveway for a few seconds watching the old man. Finally, he called out to him.

"Nice meeting you too! Take care now!" Jim smiled and then walked off quickly, as if he were eager to explore more of Blackmun, his new town. After he had reached the end of Eddie's block, he slowed and watched the cracked concrete of the sidewalk pass beneath him.

Jim concluded, as he passed the old woman on the rocking chair, that there was a good chance this last attempt had been successful. Judging by Eddie's body language, Jim's openness about his eating habits had perturbed the old man. Jim noticed that the old woman on the rocking chair was staring directly at him. She wore large sunglasses whose deep black lenses hid her eyes. Jim approached Andrew's car, pulled open the door and bent over to sit in the passenger seat.

"So what's the scoop?" Andrew eagerly asked. Jim's face was expressionless.

"Well, I managed to play my part pretty well this time. I'm not sure Eddie will change, but I think I at least made him reconsider his plan for this evening. I guess we'll see." Andrew nodded and smiled.

"That'll do. We'll just chill out until tonight, monitor Eddie's behavior in the TV room, and see if what you said worked. If it did, great. If not, we'll just start the day over again."

Jim peered over at Andrew as they drove back to the office building. "Yeah, I've been in the TV room. We can just watch Eddie from there, huh?"

"Oh yeah, we'll know if he eats ice cream without having to drive over here again."

"Man, Mike must have a helluva lot of power." Jim had to raise his voice over the sound of the car engine. "I mean, he can watch anything that goes on out here in that TV room, and then change it if he wants to with that clock?"

"Yeah, he's got power, but remember the biorenewal. Didn't someone say that tyranny was the best form of government, so long as the tyrant was benevolent?"

Jim was looking at a group of sweaty men playing a game of basketball. "It makes sense." Jim was tired, though, so he adjusted his seat in order to recline. He rested with his eyes shut until Andrew had pulled into the parking lot.

Once there, Andrew and Jim filed into the office building where Mike worked. This time, they had a different result to report. Before they entered Mike's office, Jim turned to face Andrew.

"It's weird—the mistake I made earlier today has just been erased?"

Andrew shook his head. "Not quite erased. What you did when you messed up the first time is still real, but real only in the sense that it is still possible and can be made actual if you were to go back and try to make the same mistake again. That mistake you made, in other words, is still an option, just not, thank goodness, an actuality."

Jim rolled his eyes. "Whatever," he said with a chuckle. He was happy that the project seemed to be headed in the right direction, and didn't care for the moment about the intricacies of the new realm he had entered. The two men found Mike waiting at his office door.

"Come in, gentlemen, let's talk," Mike said genially as he beckoned with his hand.

Once again, Jim and Andrew seated themselves before Mike's desk. Mike crossed his hands above a leg that he had swung over one of his knees. Jim noticed that there was a bright gold ring on one of his index fingers.

"You want to tell him, Jim?" Andrew nudged Jim's shoulder. Jim rubbed his eye and then looked towards Mike.

"Well, I did manage to bring the conversation—in a, y'know, reasonable manner—to the matter of the ice cream. And I think I might have caused some gears to turn in Eddie's mind."

Mike smiled and patted the surface of his desk with his hand. "That's good, that's good. It seems like, depending on how stubborn Eddie is, we've got a reasonable chance of success. What exactly did you tell him, Jim?"

Jim ran his hand along the top of his knee a couple of times. "Well, I, well, I made up this story about how my wife was getting on my case for eating ice cream and how I, y'know, jogged every day. I actually probably should start doing that, now that I think of it."

Mike leaned over his desk and placed his clasped hands on top of it so that his fingers pointed at Jim. "That's good, Jim, excellent. Y'know, there's no harm in telling a lie now and then, so long as it's for a good cause. You can trust me, y'know." Mike pointed to the series of diplomas hanging on his wall. Jim looked pleased.

"Now, gentlemen," Mike said as he rose up from his soft, leather chair, "I am going to have to monitor Eddie as the day goes on. I suggest that you two wait for the results in the waiting room we have here. There's stuff to do in there—there's a bookshelf, a TV with some movies stacked on the rack underneath it. There's also a couple of couches if you two feel tired. Here, I'll walk you to it." Mike reached into his pocket as he crossed the threshold of the door. "Oh, I nearly forgot my keys."

Jim and Andrew were both sitting in the office waiting room when Mike stood beside the television set he had mentioned and waved. "I'll keep you guys posted."

He closed the door softly behind him. Jim and Andrew looked at each other. Light, mediated by filmy curtains, came through the large window in the waiting room and illuminated their faces.

"Well, looks like we've got a good chance of getting Eddie to change, Jim." Andrew was the first to break the silence. Jim looked at the ground with his brows furrowed.

"Man, I don't lie much, Andrew. I hate doing it, it always makes me feel a little queasy. I mean, this guy, Eddie, trusted me!"

Andrew responded while watching a bird outside that was perched on a tree branch. "You're starting to come under the influence of the realm of possibility. Being in this place makes you more sensitive to the consequences of your actions. But, yeah, you've got to remember that if your conversation with Eddie works out, Ruth will be alive when you go back to the realm of actuality." Jim lifted his head and looked at a picture high up on the wall, close to the ceiling. The lighting in the room was such that Jim could only make out a hodgepodge of bright colors.

"That's right," he said with wonder. "I keep forgetting that somehow or other this old man's gluttony led to my daughter's death!"

Both men were silent for a few minutes. Jim finally rose from the chair on which he had been sitting and walked to a couch. He stretched out upon it and pulled a blanket over his body. In minutes, he began to breathe heavily and rhythmically. Andrew, after chuckling paternally at Jim, went over to the bookshelf and pulled out a beat-up paperback. For a couple of hours, he read while Jim slept.

A knock on the door led Andrew to dog-ear the page he had been reading and ask, "Who is it?" The knob turned, and Mike stepped inside the waiting room. He looked excited.

"Hey, Andrew, I've got some news. Is Jim asleep? Yeah, wake him up." Andrew walked to the couch and began to shake Jim's shoulder gently. Jim rolled onto his back and lifted his fists above his head.

"My gosh, what time is it?" he asked as he squinted at the faces of the two men. As he sat up, he tried to put his hair in place with his hand. Mike rattled some coins in his pocket.

"C'mon, Jim, I've got something to show you. Follow me, we're going to the TV room again." Jim pushed himself to his feet, but nearly tripped over a toy truck on the waiting room floor. He and Andrew followed Mike as he walked rapidly down the corridor until Mike disappeared into a door on the right. Mike and Andrew followed him into a hall lined with televisions.

"It's this one, Jim, we've got it on tape." Mike pointed at one of the monitors. Jim moved quickly towards him. Mike's hand was trembling slightly. Jim looked down at the monitor to which Mike was directing his attention. He saw an image of Eddie talking on the phone. Captions ran along the bottom of the screen. Jim read: *No, Jerry, not tonight.*

"Your talk worked, Jim!" Mike almost whispered the news to Jim. He grabbed Jim's shoulder with one of his bony hands. "Here, watch Eddie. He made this phone call at one o'clock this afternoon." Jim turned away from Mike's face and watched the screen. Mike was pressing a button, and the action moved backwards for a while— Eddie put the phone down and then backpedaled to the couch, where he sat. Then, Mike released the button. The video played at a normal speed and began to progress in the opposite direction.

Jim was mesmerized as Eddie dragged his heavy body up from the couch. A blanket slid off of him. He shuffled towards a narrow table on which a phone rested. A few seconds after dialing a number, Eddie began to talk.

"Hey, Jerry, it's Eddie!" A smile compressed Eddie's red cheeks. Jim leaned over the monitor so that his face was quite close to it. "Hey, Jerry," Eddie went on, "I've decided I don't want that ice cream tonight. I better listen to doc… Yeah, you can still have the Mantle card you've been bothering me about. You've done a lot for me over the years… Oh yeah, I definitely remember Loretta, how could I forget?" Eddie cackled loudly. "Alright, Jerry, I better get going. Bye now. Huh? No, Jerry, not tonight." Eddie hung up the phone and turned around to walk back to the couch. Mike stopped the video and turned back to face Jim. His eyes were glowing.

"Y'see? The awful night of indulgence has now been erased. Your conversation led Eddie to change his mind!" Mike was so excited he looked like someone who had just won a game show. Jim frowned at him and Mike, recognizing Jim's chagrin, grew sober. Mike placed both of his hands on Jim's shoulders.

"Don't you know what these means, Jim?" Jim backed away a couple of steps and shook his head. Mike removed his hands from Jim's shoulders, but maintained eye contact. "Don't you remember what we've been talking about? Ruth's alive now!" A tear in Mike's eye began to glisten in the crazily dancing light from all the television sets. As Jim looked down at the floor, Mike whispered, "Ruth's alive, Jim!"

Suddenly, Jim's shoulders buckled as tears rushed to his eyes. He gasped deeply and sharply while clutching his forehead. Andrew rested a hand on one of Jim's shoulders. A strand of mucus ran from Jim's nose as a tumult of emotions rose up in him. Through his sobs, as he leaned on one of the monitors, Jim asked, "When can I see her?"

Part II
Chapter 1

A KEEN, RHYTHMIC SOUND broke through the darkness. Jim opened his eyes and saw a red glow illuminating the curtains that swayed beside him. Jim's lowered his eyes to the alarm clock on his nightstand. He shut off the alarm, and in the silence he could hear the soft snoring of his wife.

Scenes from the mysterious and incredible realm of possibility flooded into Jim's mind like the memory of a dream. The conversation with Eddie. Watching him on the monitor make the phone call that triggered a chain of events that prevented Ruth from running in front of that car on the night she died. The heavy sobs that shook Jim when he learned the results of Eddie's self-discipline...

Jim rolled out of bed and stood upright in one rapid, fluid motion. He almost sprinted out the door of his bedroom into the corridor. The door to Ruth's room creaked as he shoved it to the adjacent wall. In the light of the early morning, Ruth's blonde hair shone on the bedspread like a golden cloth.

Jim nearly fell after had curved around the foot of Ruth's bed and paused next to her small, soft face. Jim was so awestruck by the sight of her that it was as if Ruth had just emerged from Sarah's womb.

"Oh my goodness!" Jim whispered as the blankets covering Ruth rose and fell along with her breathing. He noted again that Ruth had Sarah's broad cheekbones. With a huge smile, Jim ran back into the corridor and back to the bedroom. He rushed up to Sarah, who still was curled up on the bed sleeping.

"Get up, honey, get up!" Jim urged loudly as he shook his wife's arm. Jim saw that Sarah's hair was unkempt as she bent upwards from the waist. Sarah squinted to guard her eyes from the light seeping in through the curtains.

"What's going on?" Sarah asked before she lifted a hand to cover a deep yawn. Jim tugged the blankets on the bed down and held Sarah's hand.

"Sarah, you've got to see this, Ruth's back, you won't believe this..." Sarah yanked her hand back and frowned at her husband, who was talking very rapidly. Jim grew quiet.

"What are you talking about? Ruth's back? From where? Don't tell me you've lost it like that crackpot Jeff Stone down the street!" Jim took a deep breath and his shoulders relaxed. He realized his wife, for some reason, did not understand his excitement.

"Well, I, uh, just wanted to say what a wonderful daughter Ruth is, I just want you to know how happy I am that we have her." The muscles on Jim's throat contracted as he swallowed. He moved closer to the foot of the bed. Ruth stared at him for a couple of seconds as if he had grown horns overnight. Then she lay back down on the bed and covered herself with the blankets.

"That's great, Jim, I'm glad you've had that stunning realization that you just had to share with me. I think I'll go back to sleep now if you don't mind." Sarah closed her eyes while Jim scratched his head. For Sarah, it seemed that Ruth had never been dead.

Jim paced around the bedroom for half a minute, then he walked back into the corridor. He peeked into Ruth's room on his way past the still open door. She had shifted positions since he had last seen her. Jim beamed as looked at his young daughter. He kept peering back into Ruth's bedroom as he moved down the corridor to the staircase.

Once he was in the kitchen, though, he began to collect bowls and spoons from the cupboards and drawers as well as eggs, milk, bread, and butter from the refrigerator. He adjusted the temperature knob on the stove to light up one of the burners. Jim tried to keep his work quiet so as not to disturb the sleep of his family, but his hands were shaky and once he dropped a pan. He stepped on it so it would stop rattling. In the silence that followed the metallic din, Jim listened for sounds from upstairs. Both Ruth and Sarah, though, had slept through the clattering of the pan.

By seven, Jim had prepared an array of dishes. Resting on the table was a bowl of scrambled eggs, a plate of moist and crispy bacon, fried potatoes, and a few slices of toast over each of which he had spread jelly and a small slab of butter. The scent filling the kitchen was heavenly.

First, Sarah walked into the kitchen. She saw the steaming array of food and crinkled her nose in confusion. "What got into you this morning?" Jim walked up to her, hugged her, and kissed her cheek.

"I just wanted to show my family how grateful I am for them." Sarah looked at Jim's radiant face.

"I think you might have taken a little too much pain medication the other night—but, hey, it looks good." Sarah grabbed a shiny plate from a stack in the cupboard and cut into the fried potatoes with a knife. In a couple minutes, Jim could hear Ruth's soft footfalls. He rose from his chair to watch the emergence of his daughter from the staircase into the kitchen. Jim took a few steps backwards towards the kitchen counter. His face grew tense as he stifled a shout.

"Morning, Ruthie," Sarah broke in when she saw Jim just stare at their daughter. "Daddy made a big breakfast." She spread her arm over all the plates that covered the table and grinned mockingly. Ruth frowned at the food, and then at her father.

"I don't like grape jelly," Ruth objected as she pointed at the pieces of toast smeared with the purple spread. Jim ran a hand through his hair.

"Oh, of course, I forgot, it's been such a long time…" Jim lifted the plate of toast from the table and dumped its contents into the trash can underneath the sink. He inspected the refrigerator and, after a thorough survey, he lifted a jar of marmalade into the air. "Here, Ruth, it's marmalade, your favorite. It's just been so long…" Jim placed the marmalade jar on the table and wrapped his arms around Ruth. His fingers were sticky from holding the marmalade jar.

"It's been so long since what?" Sarah confronted Jim after moving to stand directly before him. She pointed her finger at his chest.

Jim's face paled. He realized he was giving himself away and he sheepishly put both of his hands in his pockets. "Oh, well, since, um,

I made breakfast for the family. I hope you like it!" Jim shrugged his shoulders and coughed. He looked down at Ruth, though, with an ecstatic smile. Sarah just hooked a strand of her hair behind her ear and sat down at the table with her plate full. Ruth also began to take portions from the various dishes Jim had prepared.

Throughout the meal, Jim kept studying Ruth's face. He had decided to leave Blackmun for work later than usual to enjoy his daughter's company. The car had never struck her. She had never run into the street in pursuit of the ball she had thrown for Rascal. Rascal was moving around underneath the table, licking up the scraps of food that fell to the floor. Jim could feel the dog's warm body slide against his shins. When he looked at Ruth again, he saw that she had nearly finished her scrambled eggs.

"This is good, Dad!" She lifted an open palm into the air and Jim gave her a high-five and then pointed to the bowl containing the scrambled eggs that remained. Ruth nodded and got up to get seconds. Jim watched every movement of her body as she walked to the other end of the table.

A few minutes before eight, Sarah said sharply, "Ruth, you've got to finish now, it's time to go to school." She clapped her hands. Jim took Ruth's plate for her and scraped off the bread crumbs and pieces of egg with a knife. Ruth slipped her slim arms underneath the straps of her pink backpack. She said bye to each of her parents. Sarah gave her a kiss. Ruth's dirty blonde ponytail swung as she walked.

Jim watched his daughter as she bounced down the path that cut across the front lawn to the curb. Suddenly, he dropped the plate he was rinsing into the sink and crashed through the screen door.

"Ruth, Ruth!" Jim sprinted to catch up with Ruth. "Wait, honey!" When Jim stood alongside Ruth, he was out of breath. He held Ruth's shoulder firmly. "There's a lot of traffic on this road, doll. You've got to be careful." Ruth squirmed away from him. Some of her friends were coming out from other houses in the neighborhood. Jim let her go, but every time a car passed, he put his body between her and the street. Finally, the bus was idling in front of the sidewalk. When Ruth was sitting in the bus and looking out the window, Jim blew her a kiss and waved. Ruth looked towards the kid who shared her seat.

The temperature was mild and it was sunny. Jim walked along with a glowing smile. He chuckled to himself and the skipped the last couple of yards before he came to the door of his home. Sarah had added some makeup to her face while he was outside waiting with Ruth. She gave Jim a warm smile and they exchanged a kiss before she left. The sweet scent of her perfume lingered in the air around the front door.

Jim wiped off the crumbs that littered the tabletop. He glanced up at the clock: 8:30. He would have to come up with an excuse to stay out of trouble with Jeremy. He went to the bathroom to look at himself in the mirror. He immediately noticed that much of his gray hair was gone. In this new world, where Ruth was alive, grief had yet to take a toll on Jim's body.

Jim skipped out of the bathroom while singing the lyrics of "Here Comes the Sun" by the Beatles. He went to the refrigerator and began to pack himself a lunch. There was a yellow notepad on a countertop in the kitchen. Jim tore a sheet from it and wrote a note to himself:

Make sure you thank Mike.

Still smiling, Jim folded the piece of paper into a small rectangle and dropped it into his lunch bag. When he stepped outside, the warm sun and temperate air caressed his body. Jim thought that it was fitting for the weather to be beautiful this day.

CHAPTER 2

JEREMY NEARLY JUMPED when he heard Jim's loud greeting.
"Jeremy!" Jim raised a hand in the air. Jeremy stared at Jim's
radiant face. Finally, he smiled and then buried himself again
in paperwork. Jim gave similarly gregarious greetings to other
employees at Cisco Roofing. When he tapped an employee named
Tim on the shoulder and extended his hand with a grin still arching
across his face, Tim spun around and glared.

"Can't you see I'm working with a freakin' buzzsaw? What
are you, stupid?" Flecks of spit shot from Tim's mouth onto Jim's
face and neck, but Jim kept smiling and just moved on to the next
employee down the aisle. Finally, Jim stationed himself in front of
a motorized cart used to haul shingles around the warehouse. Its
engine had not been starting lately. Jim rolled up his sleeves and
considered the damaged equipment with a serious stare while
wearing a headlamp. He began to whistle. Ruth's presence in his life
made his work enjoyable. Jim remained focused on the damaged
engine until Mike walked down the aisle in front of him.

"Hey, Mike!" Jim's cry drew the attention of the other workers,
whose heads snapped in his direction. Mike, though, kept walking
as if the racket from the warehouse stereos had been enough to
drown out even Jim's strong shout. Jim kept fiddling with the cart's
engine.

At lunch, though, the yellow sheet he had slipped into his paper
bag that morning came out along with the sandwich he had made.
Jim unfolded it and glanced around the break room after reading
it. He did not see Mike's slender form. He went to the door of the
break room and surveyed the huge, echoing warehouse. He saw

Mike alone in a corner, holding a blowtorch that spewed a bright red flame. Jim looked back at the workers gathered in the break room. They were all busily eating and talking. Jim strode quickly across the warehouse floor.

"Mike, hey Mike," Jim called when he had gotten close to the young man. The flame of the blowtorch died out and Mike removed his safety goggles and placed them on a nearby machine.

"What's going on?" Mike asked as a drop of sweat trailed down his face. It made a faint stain. The lingering heat from the blowtorch caused Jim to move a couple steps back, but as Jim spoke, he came close to Mike again.

"Hey, Mike, I just wanted to say that I just cannot thank you enough…" Jim was having difficulty speaking. His lower lip began to tremble. Mike peered behind Jim's shoulder. A couple of burly men had just exited the break room.

"It all worked out, and there's just no way for me to repay you." As the tears started to come, Jim's voice rose in volume. Mike shoved Jim's shoulder lightly.

"Keep it down, man." Jim frowned and glanced behind him. He saw the two men that had just left the break room. They were chatting with animation. "Oh, I'm sorry, yeah…" Jim looked at the wall behind Mike and put his hands in his pockets.

"Look, Jim, I appreciate this, but I need you to keep everything that happened between us totally secret."

Jim eyebrows rose. "Oh, secret? Absolutely. I kinda wanted to tell my wife about it, but I guess I won't now." Jim rocked back and forth a couple of times and then rested a hand on the wall to his right.

"Don't tell your wife," Mike urged. His face was pale and he had brought himself inches away from Jim's body. "You don't fully understand your situation and what happened to you. Promise me: no one finds out about the realm of possibility." Mike was standing so near to Jim that some of his warm breath rose up towards Jim's nostrils. Mike pinched some of the cloth of Jim's shirt between his fingers.

Jim pulled himself from the grip of Mike's delicate hand. "Alright, alright, I'll be quiet. Sorry for thanking you." Jim smiled though, and gave Mike a strong and prolonged handshake. As Jim walked away, Mike watched him intently with one hand on a hip and his shoulder resting against the wall. Finally, he placed the goggles over the bridge of his nose again and the flame of the blowtorch surged. When Jim got back to the break room, he made an offer to every worker. "Hey everybody, who here wants a free soda?" Hearty cheers burst forth from the workers.

CHAPTER 3

THE FOLLOWING WEEKEND, Jim drove Ruth out to a local park. Jim kept taking his eyes off the road to look at his resurrected daughter. Once, he even had to slam on the brakes to avoid striking a pedestrian who had wandered in front of his vehicle. He managed to get Ruth to the park, though, without incident. Rascal, who they had coaxed into climbing into the back of the car, leapt out and begun to run around the wide, grassy area.

It was a spring afternoon, sunny and mild. Jim tossed a tennis ball high into the air. It arced up towards the treetops, then descended towards Rascal's upturned nose. Ruth followed after the dog and tried to snatch the ball from his mouth once he had corralled it. The park was a good distance from any road. Jim kept an eye on a stranger smoking a cigarette by the swingsets. There were ragged holes in the knees of his jeans and a mermaid tattoo emerged from his shirtsleeve. He just stared off into the patch of forest near the park, though. Jim sprinted towards Ruth and the dog and wrapped his daughter in a tight embrace.

"Dad, that hurts!" Jim released Ruth and she straightened out her clothing. She was tired from running around and looked absently towards a woman and her young daughter moving away from the softball field towards the swings. Jim frowned as he looked back towards the smoking stranger, who was now pacing with one hand in his pocket.

Meanwhile, in the realm of possibility, Mike was watching Ruth and Jim on a television monitor. He sipped from a cup of coffee and smiled. Behind him, on another screen, Jim was weeping at his daughter's funeral. A door at the end of the hallway clicked open and let in a shaft of light. Mike turned his head as the sound of feet approaching grew sharper.

"We've got some paperwork done, sir. Here." The man, who was also dressed in a blazer and tie, handed Mike a manila envelope with twenty or thirty sheets of paper. Mike looked through a couple of pages on the top of the stack.

"It seems like things are going pretty well," Mike said. He glanced at some monitors to his right and left. The other engineer pointed to a graph on the paper Mike was holding.

"Yeah, take a look at this value. Nothing. *Nada*. First time we've ever done things this smoothly." Mike tilted his head back and laughed.

"My friend," he said as he gave his colleague's hand a tight squeeze, "I think we're both going to be rewarded quite handsomely!"

CHAPTER 4

SIX YEARS LATER, Ruth had grown to be nearly as tall as Sarah, who was 5'9". Jim could see this as she walked to the kitchen table, where he sat paging through the newspaper. Ruth had a couple of papers in her hand, both which were marked with bright red ink. She slapped both papers down onto the table in front of her father.

"Check this out, Dad!" Her voice had grown fuller and richer as the years had passed. Jim glanced up from the paper and saw again that Ruth looked a lot like Sarah when he first met her. The same high cheekbones and piercing, intense eyes. The papers Ruth had set down were tests she had taken in school. Jim saw that she had gotten A's on both.

"This is outstanding, Ruth," Jim said as he looked through the equations and verbose essay questions on the exams. He lifted his lined face to hers. His smile was contagious.

"So does this mean I don't have to pay for tuition when you go to Harvard?" Sarah, who was washing dishes, laughed. Ruth pointed to the large red A on one of the exams.

"I got the only A in my calculus class. All the other kids are angry at me. It's possible, y'know, to do well on a Jiminez exam." Jim could see Ruth clothed in a graduation cap and gown. Then, later on, she would be wearing a stethoscope, perhaps. Sarah crossed into his field of vision.

"These other kids aren't mistreating you, are they Ruth? Sometimes the bad students will resent the good ones." Sarah placed both of her slim hands atop Ruth's shoulders.

"No, Mom, stop babying me. They're just joking." Ruth's face reddened. Sarah saw this, and returned to the sink, from which steam was rising.

"You just tell me, Ruthie, and I'll get the principal to stop that nonsense," Sarah continued. Ruth rolled her eyes and turned back to her father. Jim looked at her disgruntled face, and then said to Sarah, "She's fine, honey. She's grown-up." He reached up to pat Ruth's shoulder. Sarah remained at the sink and silently scrubbed bits of food from the plates. In a few moments, Ruth had turned on the kitchen television. A weatherman was giving the week's forecast.

"Well, folks, we are in for some unusual weather in the upcoming week. Tuesday and Wednesday are going to be rather nice fall days—fifty-five degrees and sunny. But on Friday, folks, you're going to need to turn on the AC, especially if pets or old people live in your home. It's going to go up all the way to eighty-five! This is not a joke! Susan, back to you."

Jim rose from his chair to watch the man as he pointed to images of masses of clouds rolling across the country and cartoonish images of the sun.

"I learned from Mrs. Jeltz that global warming is a scientific fact. Sea levels are rising and glaciers are melting," Ruth said. Jim was still watching the weatherman as he gesticulated before an oversized image of a personified sun wearing sunglasses. Sarah had begun to put away some dishes that were now clean. The rattle of the dishes upon the cupboard shelves drowned out the words of the weatherman and Jim headed towards the door that led to the garage.

"Alright, I'm going to get the tools I need." The Morris's lawnmower had broken down the other day while Ruth was mowing. Jim had heard a loud explosion and bolted outside to see if Ruth was alright. He had not forgotten the tragic version of reality in which he had been inside watching television while Ruth suffered a fatal accident. After the lawnmower explosion, though, Jim watched some football, then napped. The first three days of that week were, for the most part, ordinary days. Jim and Sarah went to work, and Ruth went to school. They all gathered for dinner around six. Jim had to help Ruth with her math homework on Tuesday and on Wednesday Sarah's allergies got so bad that she had to go to bed early. On Thursday, though, Jim woke up with sweat on his face. He was wearing a long-sleeved shirt and flannel pajama pants. After seeing that some of Sarah's hair was clinging to her pillow, he rose up and pulled the string of the fan above the bed.

"Wow, I didn't really believe it." It was in November, and it felt like a summer morning. The air was thick and Jim made sure that Rascal's water bowl was full. Rascal had slowed down considerably as the years passed. The once energetic dog now rarely rose from his bed on the living room floor and his corpulent frame swayed with each step. When Jim stood at the end of his driveway after walking with Rascal to pick up the newspaper he breathed in the heavy, unseasonable air. When he got inside, he twisted the air conditioning knob on and closed all the windows. Close to noon, Jim could hear the tinny and uncanny music of an ice cream truck coming up the street.

A couple weeks later, powerful gusts of wind tore at the Morris home. Jim could hear the walls creak under the strain. An antennae on a neighbor's roof teetered and then crashed down onto a shed. Ruth rushed to a window to see the damage. The antennae had gathered such momentum during its descent that it had punctured the roof of the shed like a spear. When Jim stepped outside, clouds of dust assailed his eyes and he nearly tumbled onto his back a couple of times. Ruth comfortably observed the effects of the wind through her bedroom window. She marveled at the angle at which the trees were bending and the frequency and duration of the gusts. When Sarah saw her daughter looking through the window, she chided her.

"Get away from there, Ruth. Something could be caught by the wind and crash through."

But the wind eventually died down, and the weather grew very cold, and snow began to accumulate on the ground. The Christmas that year was white. Jim spent a lot of money on Ruth's presents. He had worked especially hard that year, and he had earned a raise. The main present for Ruth that Christmas was a brand new Honda Accord. When Ruth saw it parked along the curb outside the home, Jim tossed her the keys and whispered, "It's yours, honey. Go check it out." When she got in, Jim pointed to the seat belt. "Make sure you wear this all the time. And never, never drink and drive." Ruth nodded as she clutched the steering wheel with excitement. Her nails were painted red and the teenage girl was starting to look quite lovely.

In the spring, when the baseball season was starting again and Ruth kept talking about a particular male student, Jim was relaxing on the couch after a day of hard work. He took small sips from a bottle of beer. He worked the cold liquid around his mouth before swallowing it. On the screen, a broad-shouldered hitter was crouching at the plate waiting for the pitcher to go into his windup. But the umpire began to wave his arms and the pitcher stopped just as he was rocking behind the rubber. The batter listened to what the umpire had to say and then trotted off the field. The catcher unhooked the straps around his calves as well as those around his chest. He also trotted towards the foul line and into the dugout. Jim turned up the volume after putting his beer on a small table next to the couch.

"We apologize, folks, but it seems someone has threatened to bomb the stadium. Someone here has received word of a bomb threat. The game will be cancelled and we will be switching to another program. Again, we apologize and hope to present to you more baseball in the future." Jim watched the fans in the stadium crowd the exits. People were yelling, and wrestling with others to be the first to leave. Then, the screen became totally blue. Jim switched off the television.

"Hey Sarah, you won't believe this."

"What," Sarah responded from the kitchen, "Josephson got a hit?"

"No, no," Jim said in a serious tone. "Someone threatened to bomb the ballpark."

After a sharp gasp, Sarah said, "Wow. As if the world needed another damn nutbag." But, Jim opened up the door to the freezer and pulled out a carton of ice cream. He massaged Sarah's shoulder as he spooned the sweet treat into his mouth.

A couple of days later, Mike came into the bathroom at the factory while Jim was washing his hands. Jim could see Mike approaching him in the mirror.

"Hey, Jim," Mike's reflection whispered. The image glanced back towards the bathroom entrance.

"What's up?" Jim was working the soap on his hands into a lather.

"Hey, Jim, we've got to talk. There've been some problems." Jim had risen and turned towards Mike, whose face still bore a coating of peach fuzz. Jim frowned.

"What problems? No, man, things couldn't be better. Ruth's back, she's doing great. You're being too hard on yourself." Jim gave Mike's shoulder a light punch. He walked past him towards the bathroom door, but stopped when Mike addressed him again.

"No, Jim, don't leave yet. I need to talk with you. Can we meet after work today? I'll wait for you by your car?" Jim's face reddened and he grimaced a little.

"Yeah, whatever, if you insist." Jim pushed through the bathroom door. The din of the warehouse momentarily rushed inside the bathroom. After work, Jim found Mike pacing beside his vehicle, just as he had said.

"So, what's up?" Jim fingered the keys in his pocket. He was impatient to get home. Mike looked pale.

"Haven't you noticed?" Mike spoke softly. A group of workers came pounding through the parking lot in their heavy boots. They were bantering loudly.

"I am going to get *so* wasted tonight!" one of the men said. Mike waited for the raucous men to pass.

"Haven't you noticed," he continued, "the changes that are taking place? The bomb threat from the fan? The crazy weather we've been having? The birds migrating in the wrong direction? Computer systems mysteriously shutting down?"

Jim rested an elbow on the hood of his truck. "Yeah, so what's new? Are you following the news for the first time in your life? Stuff like that happens all the time. You just tune it out and live your life."

Mike remained silent for a couple moments and stared towards the empty field adjacent to the company building. Jim moved towards the driver's side door.

"Wait, Jim, hold on." Mike followed Jim around the front of the truck. "All this stuff is not normal. I think, unfortunately, that when we brought Ruth back to life, we created some unforeseen consequences. Like, stuff that wouldn't have happened if Ruth had remained dead. Bad stuff."

Jim's mouth hung open in shock and he clenched his hands. "So, what are you saying? That we would be better off if Ruth were still dead? Go to hell, you little punk!" Jim kicked a tire of his truck and climbed into the cab. Quickly, the engine began to roar and Mike scurried out of the way.

Over the throb of the engine, Mike yelled, "It's true, Jim. We need to reevaluate. You'll see." Jim slammed the gas pedal and the tires of his pickup truck screeched as he left the parking lot.

CHAPTER 5

RUTH HAD DONE so well in her studies one marking period that she earned an award from the principal. There was a ceremony right before the winter break. On the illuminated stage, other students who had won awards were lined up; some of them wore ribbons pinned to their chests. The principal stood before a podium. He spoke in a booming baritone.

"The award for most distinguished academic performance this marking period goes to a very special young lady. She is never late for class, takes on and succeeds at the most difficult assignments, and is polite and humble among her fellow students. None of it gets to her head! This special young lady is Ruth Morris. Ruth, come up to the stage!" A small band located in the corner of the stage began to play. Ruth walked quickly down one of the aisles among the seats with her eyes upon the floor and her cheeks reddening. She received the framed certificate and shook the beaming principal's hand. A member of the group that distributed the school newspaper took Ruth's photograph. A girl who had been sitting a couple of rows behind Ruth half-rose from her seat and frowned at the sight of Ruth and the principal on the stage.

After the ceremony, the frowning girl approached the crowd of people that encircled Ruth. Everyone was happily chatting. The girl was overweight and had rough, bright pink acne. She waited for the crowd around Ruth to disperse before coming up to her.

"Hey Angela," Ruth said as she exposed her clean, straight teeth. She gave a small wave. Angela brushed a strand of hair away from her forehead.

"Hi, Ruth, I'm so happy you got that award." Ruth still held the certificate against her side. "I mean, I thought I had a chance to get it and all, but you totally deserve it." Angela lifted her green eyes from the dusty tile of the school hallway. She tapped a pencil against her dress.

"Yeah, thanks, Angela. Y'know, you did so well this marking period, too! Well, I guess I better get going!" Ruth moved to Angela's side and began to file past the heavyset girl. But Angela turned her head to follow Ruth as her ponytail bobbed behind her while she walked. Angela's voice grew hoarse as she said, "I know you kept asking Tommy Samson for help, that's why you did so well in chemistry." Ruth stopped walking and slowly turned to face Angela.

"Tommy's real smart, but he just guided me now and then, he didn't do it *all* for me. But, hey, have a nice day." Ruth walked briskly towards the glass doors at the end of the hallway. When she had gotten outside, she turned back to look into the hallway. She could see the dark, plump outline of Angela's body, twisted and bent by the glass.

On the first day of school after winter break, during chemistry class, Ruth changed her seat. She moved to a corner in the front of the class, far from the door. Angela sat in the back of the class, closer to the door. Ruth quickly drew out her textbook and notepad from her backpack and sat silently waiting for the teacher to begin his lecture.

"Alright, now, right before we left for vacation, we were talking about Boyle's law…" Ruth took rapid notes. Angela scribbled some notes too, but she kept looking in Ruth's direction. The teacher challenged the class with a question. No one raised their hand for half a minute. Finally, Ruth raised her slender arm.

"Very good, Ruth, you haven't gotten rusty over the winter break, I see. Maybe you can win another award this marking period." The skin on Angela's pudgy face tightened. She began to doodle pictures of Ruth in her notepad with grotesquely enlarged features. Beside the images, she scrawled abusive remarks, like "You're stupid," and "I hate your guts."

Ruth answered four or five of Mr. Jensen's questions that day. When the bell rang, she closed up her textbook and notepad and, even with her bookbag weighing her down, she was the first one to leave the classroom. Angela went to her locker to get the lunch her mother had bagged for her.

Angela walked into the disarray of the cafeteria. There was a foodfight going on at the long table past which Angela was walking. All the chatter created a tumultuous din. Angela brought her bag to the group of friends with whom she usually sat. She leaned in closer to the conversation.

"I got a boyfriend today!" Lauren exclaimed. She had long black hair and tan skin. Her family was Italian.

"Oh my God! Who is it?" Susanne bent over the table as she held half of a sandwich in the air. Lauren paused while she adjusted her skirt. She wore heavy lipstick and eyeshadow. She nibbled at a granola bar in between sentences.

"Tell us, you bitch!" Susanne cried after Lauren had withheld the news for another half a minute. Finally, Lauren looked at the faces of each of her friends and said, "Tim Devine." All the girls except for Angela screamed. A few nights ago, Angela had attached Tim Devine's yearbook photo to her bedroom mirror and drawn a heart around his face.

Ruth's locker was only a few away from Angela's. When school ended, they were both twisting the knobs of their lockers to pull out the textbooks and supplies they needed to take home. Angela peered past a couple other students between her and Ruth. Before Ruth could walk away, Angela caught up with her.

"Great job in chemistry today, Ruth," Angela said with a tense smile. Ruth looked away from the dense freckles on Angela's face and her yellow teeth. "You must be hanging out with Tommy Samson a lot."

Ruth ground her teeth. Her pace slowed and she turned towards Angela.

"Look, Angela, you did really well last marking period. You should be happy with your scores. Maybe if you work really hard, you could get a prize at the end of *this* marking period." Angela scarcely blinked as she looked defiantly back at Ruth.

"Did Tommy Samson do your chemistry homework for you? Did he let you look at his test while we were taking it?" Angela grinned and raised her eyebrows. Ruth was getting angry and she raised her voice.

"Angela, c'mon, get over it! Tommy helped me once or twice. Look, I'm good at school, leave me alone!" Ruth began to walk again through the swarms in the hallway, but Angela managed to keep up with her. Angela stammered before she spoke clearly again.

"W-what d-do you do to get Tommy to help you?" Ruth stopped and faced Angela with wide, shocked eyes. Angela looked at the floor for a second, but then she lifted her eyes and spoke again with the same taunting tone.

"I said, why does Tommy help you? Do you do favors for him?" Lines creased Angela's forehead as she glowered. Ruth's shoulders went slack as she stared blankly at the lockers beyond Angela. But, she pulled her backpack up and refocused her eyes in a few seconds.

"What do you mean, Angela?" A tremor went down Ruth's spine. She gripped a strap of her backpack so tightly that her hand became white. Angela drew closer to Ruth and leaned over, so that the two girls' faces nearly touched.

"You know what I mean, you, you slut!" Angela stomped one of her feet. The crowds in the hallway had thinned and the roar of the engines of the school buses from the road was clearly audible. Ruth's lips trembled as she glared at Angela.

"You take that back, right now, Angela. I deserved the award. You don't work hard enough. Take it back!" Ruth had grabbed Angela's forearm. Angela kept her face close to Ruth's. Drops of spit flew from her mouth as she yelled, "You're a slut, slut, slut, slut!"

Ruth let go of Angela's forearm. She pulled her hand back to gather force. Her hand fell on Angela's cheek with a crack. Angela placed her hand where Ruth had slapped her, then swung at Ruth's face with her fist. Ruth's neck titled back as she descended to the lockers behind her. The impact of her body against the metal made a clanging sound that echoed down the hallway. Ruth's shoes slipped on the dusty tile and she dropped to the floor. A teacher came out of his room when he heard the loud noise. He came running towards the two girls.

Ruth's left eye was black after the fight. The principal brought Angela and Ruth into his office to discuss the incident. Jim came to get Ruth after receiving a phone call. He hugged her tightly when he saw her damaged face.

"It'll be alright, honey. I hope that Angela gets what she deserves." Ruth cried on her mother's bosom as they both held each other when she got home.

The next evening, Mike called Jim's home.

"Hey Jim, this is Mike, from work." Mike spoke quickly. Jim could hear sounds of traffic in the background.

"What's up?" Jim comfortably watched a ballgame while talking.

"Um, I wanted to tell you, that, uh, I know what happened with Ruth the other day." Jim looked down towards the mahogany table where the phone rested. He snatched up a tissue angrily from a box there. After the adventure in the realm of possibility, he thought that he deserved to live without problems at least for a while.

'How did you find out?"

"Remember, the TV room? We've been keeping track of the results of our project." Jim sighed.

"Y'know, I wish you would just stop talking about that. I don't want to think about your stupid realm. Ruth's alive, and that's that." A vessel in Jim's neck began to bulge. He could hear Mike coughing while turning his mouth away from the phone.

"Well, Jim, we have to talk about the realm. We have to talk about it because there are kinks in the work we did. One of the side effects of this work, for instance, is this fight with Angela. You see, Angela needed that prize. There's so much else that's wrong with her life—she's not very attractive, she's not athletic, and Tim Devine doesn't care for her. But, Ruth is here now, and she's better at school than Angela., so Angela doesn't get the prize that's so important to her." Jim kept glancing back at the game while Mike lectured. The Twins were winning by ten runs. Jim pumped his fist when they scored again.

"Oh, is that right?" Jim said in the silence after Mike had finished. "So, um, what do you recommend I do? Murder my daughter tonight so her foul-mouthed rival can feel better about herself?"

"No, that's not what I'm saying. What I'm saying, Jim, is that we need to talk so that we can refine things. You're going to have Ruth for a very long time. But there's work to be done to eliminate unpleasant, unforeseen consequences like the fight with Angela."

Jim breathed deeply. "Alright, whatever. When do you say we should meet?"

"Great, super. Believe me, Jim, we just have to adjust some minor details. Ruth's not going anywhere."

'Okay. But when should we meet?" Jim tapped a finger on the mahogany table.

Jim had never been to Mike's apartment. Mike lived alone on the top floor of a twenty-story building in Blackmun. He owned a fish tank full of brightly colored fish that darted back and forth in concert. He offered to make Jim a sandwich, but Jim refused it.

"No, let's just get down to business." Jim pulled a chair from the small, round table in the kitchen and sat. He rested his elbows on the tabletop.

"Alright, Jim, we've fixed the major problem, right? I mean, you've got to give me some credit for helping you do that, right?" Jim looked into Mike's luminous blue eyes. The young man appeared to have lost weight. The bones in his face were more sharply outlined against his skin.

"Yeah, I guess. I mean, it's obviously nice to have Ruth back. I don't know how much longer I could have gone on in the old, um, the old world, I guess." Jim shifted his feet and drew in his elbows a little. Mike nodded slowly while maintaining eye contact.

"Thanks. That means a lot. Y'know, it's not easy be in charge of the realm of possibility. I really had to work to become an engineer." Jim nodded, then looked out at the window again at a bird perched on a nearby electricity pole. While Mike remained silent, Jim shifted in his chair again and coughed. He was uncomfortable.

"So, yeah, thanks man. Thanks a lot for all that work. But let's move on to these problems you were talking about." Jim folded up a corner of a newspaper on the table and then pressed it down again idly. Mike looked at Jim, and then rose from his seat. As he talked, he paced along the floor with his hands in his pockets.

"The problem really is quite simple, Jim. When we prevented Eddie Drake from eating the ice cream, a series of events that would have happened had he eaten it ended up not happening. This led to the eventual avoidance of Ruth's untimely death. But, the new series of events that we introduced gave rise to other events that were not nearly as positive as the fact that Ruth is still alive. For instance, this girl Angela who is harassing your daughter would not have been so upset now if Ruth had died."

Jim slammed a hand on the table. "There you go again! So we should kill Ruth so some teenage girl feeling sorry for herself can feel special? Go to hell, Mike!"

Mike had stopped pacing and taken a couple of steps towards Jim while pointing at him. "No, no, you listen. Angela's problems aren't the only bad consequences of what we did. There will be more. And, as I've already said, Ruth is going to continue to live. We don't have to kill her to avoid these bad consequences." Mike had raised his voice, and he emphasized each word. Jim relaxed in his chair and looked down at the table. A tremor shook through one of Mike's hands.

"Alright, I'm all ears. Go ahead, what's your grand plan?" Jim got up and opened the refrigerator. He poured himself a glass of orange juice without getting Mike's permission. Mike sat on an arm of a couch.

"Work in the realm of possibility is quite complicated. It's very hard to even access it, let alone make adjustments in it. He doesn't want anyone in it. It's very hard to fight Him." Jim frowned at the younger man.

"Who the hell are you talking about?" Jim asked as he gripped his glass of orange juice tightly.

"God, I'm talking about God. People aren't supposed to be able to change what's happened. We're supposed to just accept the past. It's what defines us, and it's the basis of our decisions in the present. Our work in the realm of possibility...it's all clandestine. It's a rebellion." Mike looked through the window into the smoky city air. Jim had finished his orange juice with a couple of long swallows. "So it's hard to go back into the realm. But, we have to. There's a couple events that need to happen in order to neutralize the negative consequences of your recovery of Ruth."

"Okay, what are they?" Jim's voice cracked. Wind rattled the windowpanes.

"Well, you're not going to like the first one." Jim leaned his elbows on his knees.

"Go ahead."

"Okay, Ruth does not have to be killed, like I said, but she does need to get hit by a car and hurt. She needs to at least get injured. Not necessarily by a car, but that would be ideal." Jim turned away from Mike towards the kitchen counter.

"So…are we supposed to help cause this injury? Are we supposed to actually set up a car accident?"

Mike took a couple of steps closer to Jim. "Well, yes, I know it seems weird, but it's what we have to do."

Jim looked through a window. He drummed his fingers in a puddle of orange juice he had spilled. Then, he got up and said loudly, "You're full of shit." He opened the door and marched out of the apartment. He slammed the door so hard the sound pierced the air like a gunshot.

CHAPTER 7

A FEW DAYS AFTER the fight with Angela, Ruth pulled out an envelope from her locker before the first class of the day. Angela's name was written in large cursive letters across the front. Ruth had drawn a smiling face underneath the name. There were still ten minutes before class started. When Ruth entered the classroom, Angela was not there. Ruth watched the doorway from her desk, but Angela still had not arrived even after class had begun.

Ruth kept the card in her locker, and pulled it out again the next day, hoping to give it to Angela. However, the desk which was assigned to Angela remained vacant. It stayed that way for two weeks. Ruth approached Susanne, one of Angela's friends, in the school cafeteria. She had to shout to be heard above the collective discussions of the hundreds of people around her.

"Hey, Susanne, Susanne!" Susanne was spooning pudding into her mouth. She was peering down the table and pointing. Ruth knocked on the surface of the table. Finally, Susanne looked at Ruth. She frowned.

"Oh, sorry to bother you, Susanne, but I just wanted to know how Angela is doing? Where has she been?" Susanne swallowed another spoonful of pudding and glanced down the table once again before answering.

"Oh, Angela? I don't know." A crowd of students on the benches behind Susanne started to laugh uproariously. Susanne started conversing with the girl beside her again, but Ruth rapped on table once more.

"You don't know? Don't you talk to her now and then?" Susanne set her pudding cup on the table and glared at Ruth. With her lower jaw thrust out, she said, "Haven't you heard? Angela attempted suicide. She's in the hospital." After this, Susanne turned around to chat with a boy behind her. Ruth took a couple of steps backwards until her back touched the rough surface of the cafeteria wall. She walked swiftly away from the raucous swarm in the cafeteria after standing there reflecting on what she had heard.

That evening, while Jim was reading a book, Ruth stepped into the circle of light coming from the lamp beside him. She sat on Jim's knee.

"What's up, honey?" Jim set aside his book. A shiver ran up his spine as he held his daughter's shoulder. He still kept a description of her funeral in a folder hidden under a pile of clothing and old books in his closet.

Ruth whispered. "Hey, daddy, you remember that girl Angela?" Jim's face clouded. He held Ruth's shoulders more tightly with his hands. Ruth leaned against him.

"Well, she hasn't been at school for a couple of weeks now, and I learned today that she...she attempted suicide." Jim gasped. He glanced out the window at Rascal chasing after a squirrel.

"Well, what for?" Jim's hand trembled a little as it rested on Ruth's shoulder. Ruth snuggled against her father.

"It must have had something to do with not getting that stupid prize. I don't want it anymore." Jim straightened in his recliner. He pushed Ruth's body away from him until she stood before him. Jim held her hand as he stared directly into her eyes.

"Ruth, dear, I want you to know that Angela's problems have nothing to do with you. They're *her* problems. They're her responsibility. You worked hard for that prize, and you deserve it. Y'know what, we should hang it up in your room. Where'd you put that certificate?" Jim rose to his feet and clapped his hands.

"Um, on the shelf in my closet." Ruth skipped behind her father as he neared the staircase. Jim hummed as he climbed up to the bedrooms. When Ruth had shown him the honorary certificate, which Jim had framed, he went down to the basement to get a hammer and some nails. He had stacked up the paint cans he had once knocked over to get into the crawlspace back when Ruth was still dead.

As Jim pounded in the nails to hold the certificate in place, he kept talking to Ruth.

"People make their own choices. You can't let yourself feel guilty for what Angela did. Angela's just feeling sorry for herself. Let her kill herself, who the hell cares?" Jim was pounding the hammer with great force and suddenly he pulled back his hand and shouted with pain. He began to shake his hand vigorously.

"Goddamit, sonofabitch!" His thumb was already red and swollen. Ruth had risen from her bed and was edging towards her cursing, wounded father. Jim grabbed his injured hand and held it up towards his face. He looked down at his daughter's concerned face and gave her a tense smile.

"Could you get daddy some ice, dearest?" Ruth rushed out the door and down the hallway. Jim looked at his misshapen thumb and then up at the crooked plaque hanging by just one nail.

Chapter 8

Abbout fifteen men and women sat at the long, glossy wooden table. The men wore suits and ties and the women wore stylish dresses and sweaters. The engineer Mike sat at the head of the table. He clutched his head in his hand as he pored over a document on the table beneath him.

"How did all these errors creep in? I thought we had this covered! You're supposed to be the best. You're nothing but a bunch of morons!" Mike pounded his fist. Everyone else in the room was silent. After rising and starting to pace, Mike continued his tirade.

"Angela attempts suicide! We were supposed to have anticipated this! We should have made sure she lived in a different area, so she could end up with a prize of her own." Mike reached into a pocket of his blazer and pulled out a box of cigarettes. A couple of engineers coughed as the smoke Mike puffed into the air billowed towards them. A bald man sitting towards the middle of the table stirred in his seat. Everyone looked at him when his small tenor voice broke the silence.

"Well, Mike, I hate to say this, but maybe, just maybe, the whole basis of the realm of possibility is flawed. I mean, we did the best we could."

Mike stopped pacing and he held his cigarette at his side. He glared at the short, bespectacled man. "What do you mean, Jerry?" A woman sitting across from Jerry lowered her head and cringed. Jerry continued, though.

"Well, I mean, look at what happened. We go in trying to do some good. This guy lost his daughter and we're going to get her back. We don't like the way things worked out, and we've found a way to acquire some control for a change. But the whole process is so damned complicated. I mean, to find the key circumstance that brought about Ruth's death took years and years of research. All the minutiae we had to comb through! And how the hell were we supposed to know all the possible aftereffects of restoring Ruth? There's just too much information that we need to keep track of."

Mike blew smoke out of the corner of his mouth. There was a whiteboard on the wall behind him with charts and graphs inked on it. Mike walked over to it and grabbed a marker. He began to draw a pie graph in an empty corner of the whiteboard.

"So, what you're saying Jerry, is that we just shouldn't tamper with things? A *laissez faire* attitude?" Mike faced the whiteboard as he queried his colleague. Jerry had turned his chair around and sat with his slender hands crossed atop his paunchy belly.

"Yes, absolutely, Mike. We should keep clear of this business altogether." Jerry smiled and his eyes twinkled through his spectacles. Mike had divided the pie graph into two slices. After half a minute of silence, he began to talk while pointing at the different parts of the pie graph. One of the slices was very thin.

"Okay, class, I'm going to call the small sliver in this very complicated pie graph here the H.P. slice. H.P. stands for happy people." Mike pointed at the small slice with his index finger and nodded towards the other engineers. "Is that clear?" Mike then pointed at the much larger slice on the pie graph. "I will call this other slice U.P. U.P. stands for unhappy people." Mike stepped away from the whiteboard so everyone could see his graph. He tossed his stubby cigarette into a trash can, though in his haste he nearly missed it. "In case you haven't noticed, the unhappy people vastly outnumber the happy people." Mike's face was growing redder. "So, isn't it fair to conclude that there's something very wrong with the way the world is put together?"

Jerry shifted in his seat again. He cleared his throat, and then began to speak once more. "But that's only what you think, Mike. We've been through this before. There could be a deeper logic that makes sense of all this unhappiness."

Mike took two quick steps towards Jerry and bent his body towards the bald man as he thundered, "We've been through this nonsense already, Jerry. A deeper logic? So, we should just accept all the shit that happens in life! It all will make sense in the end! After all, who are we to think that we can be critical of the divine plan? We weren't present when God made the universe." Mike rolled up his sleeves as he paced back and forth rapidly. "I'll tell you what, Jerry, you've got the mind of a child sitting on his grandmother's lap. You'll believe whatever you hear, as long as it makes you feel better. Me, though, I'm different. There's no deeper logic to war, to famine, to people dropping dead from treatable diseases, from young girls like Ruth dying! It all just sucks, plain and simple, and there is either no God or he's a monster just like you!" Mike thrust out his arm and pointed at Jerry. He kicked the trash can next to the whiteboard, sending its contents sliding across the floor. A woman sitting beside Jerry folded her arms across her blue vest and began speaking in a remarkably calm tone of voice.

"Mike, you're right, of course you're right. Please relax. The whole reason we started to try to access the realm of possibility was that we realized that the world had been set up poorly. Jerry, excuse my honesty, but you've got to either leave or change your views." Jerry squirmed in his chair. The woman adjusted her vest and continued. "So, Mike, our problem is not really that bad. We just need to persuade Jim that some minor adjustments need to be made in order to prevent the occurrence of more bad events. Let's try talking to him again. We've done all the research. Ruth just needs to put up with being injured and then all the bomb threats and depressed teenage girls will go away."

Mike's pacing had slowed. The muscles of his jaw relaxed. He leaned against the whiteboard with his hands in his pockets.

"The guy—Jim, I mean—is stubborn. I think he feels like he's already failed his daughter, and now he's fiercely committed to protecting her against anything. He got a second chance, and there's no way he's going to waste it. I don't know." Mike sighed deeply. "I guess you're right, Marianne, we just need to keep plugging away. What else can we do?" Marianne's bright white teeth shone as she smiled. Mike rose to his full height. "And, Marianne, I think you should try this time. I think you have a diplomatic gift, something that I obviously lack." Marianne's smile grew even wider after the news of her promotion.

"Oh my, I'd be honored!" The rest of the engineers in the room applauded.

CHAPTER 9

MARIANNE CONTACTED JIM by phone. Jim had been playing a board game with Ruth when the phone rang and Marianne's sonorous voice greeted him.

"Hi, there, Jim, I hope I'm not calling at a bad time?" Jim turned back towards Ruth and raised one of his index fingers.

"No, I've got a couple minutes. Are you one of Ruth's teachers?" Jim sipped from a glass of soda while Ruth watched him with her legs crossed on the family room carpet.

"No, no, I'm not, Jim. Before I tell you who I am, though, I need you to promise that you won't hang up on me. I'm a person trying to do good, just like yourself." Jim listened guardedly to Marianne's clear, ringing voice. He held still as he responded.

"Well, okay, I won't hang up. So go ahead, what's your business?"

"I'm an engineer from the realm of possibility." A pang of anger rose up within Jim and he frowned. He gripped the phone tightly.

"Okay, Marianne, let me move to another room so we can talk in private. But, be quick and to the point," Jim said in a suddenly clipped, harsh tone of voice. Jim walked over to the study and swung the door shut. Ruth looked up at the closing door and then turned to watch the colorful cartoon characters dancing around the television screen across from her.

Once he had sat down at the study desk, where stacks of paper were haphazardly piled, Jim said tersely, "You may proceed, Marianne." Marianne coughed softly before speaking.

"Thanks very much, Jim. I know that you're not pleased with the service we've provided you lately, so the fact that you're willing to listen to what I have to say means a lot." Marianne paused.

Jim interjected sharply, "Go on."

"Oh, okay, I was putting some mints back into my purse. So sorry. I first want to begin by congratulating you on the recovery of Ruth. You took some bold steps to do this. It is sometimes hard, as you can imagine, to get our clients to wrap their minds around the whole concept of the realm of possibility. I mean, not many people know that you can change the past." Jim's face glowed when Marianne mentioned Ruth's name. He looked at a picture he had just taken and had framed. It rested on the study desk, and it showed Ruth smiling with a basketball in her hands. She had just made the varsity basketball team.

"Yeah, it's just fantastic, having her back. I just couldn't have gone on without her for much longer." Tears filled Jim's eyes and he had to stop talking.

"I'm so glad we were able to do that for you, Jim." Marianne was also having trouble speaking. Jim heard her sniffle over the phone, and it occurred to him that the woman might be sincere. "What we do can be so frustrating at times and tricky, but there's nothing better than success in this profession. Nothing at all." As Marianne paused to blow her nose and dry her eyes, Jim started to drum his fingers on the desk. He looked at the gray evening through the study window. Finally, he interrupted the tearful woman.

"But, uh, what did you need? Why exactly are you calling?" Jim gazed fiercely at Ruth's image in the frame before him as he stroked one of its ridged sides with a finger.

"Oh, I'm sorry Mr. Morris, your story is just so moving. The reason for my call is…well, I just wanted to talk with you in person about your situation, I guess, to just follow up."

Jim paused. "Well, Marianne, you seem like a nice person. Yeah, we can meet. But not at my home." Jim lifted an open palm in the air and frowned.

"Okay, okay, no problem. How about, then, we meet at the Dairy Queen a couple of blocks away from your home? We'll talk over ice cream."

"Sounds fine, Marianne. We can talk for an hour, maybe half an hour. Okay, so long," Jim said abruptly. He hung up the phone, lifted himself from the chair, and shouted through the closed study door.

"Ruth, I'm coming, I hope you didn't cheat!"

At the ice cream parlor, Marianne ordered a Blizzard, but Jim got nothing from the young man behind the counter with a thin, dark-haired mustache.

"I'm not hungry. What's on your mind?" They sat near a crowd of young girls wearing cleats and green and gold uniforms. A man with a baseball cap towered over them holding a tray full of ice cream cones.

It was Saturday, and Marianne was wearing a pair of jeans and a dark blue turtleneck. She took the long red spoon from the blizzard and began to eat it.

"So good!" Marianne said after swallowing a mouthful. "You sure you don't want anything?" Jim glanced out the large plate glass window of the store at a couple ragged youths carrying skateboards. He twisted his wrist to check the time.

"No, I don't want anything. Look, I've got things to do, places to go. What's your business?" A girl on the softball team turned around to look at Jim, whose voice was harsh and growing louder with each word.

"Oh, I know Mr. Morris, your time is precious. Well, how can I introduce this best?" Marianne stirred her Blizzard and gazed into the vanilla ice cream upon with chocolate chip cookie crumbs sprinkled on top. "Well, Jim, you know about Angela, right?" Jim leaned back in his bench and clapped his hand on the smooth tabletop.

"Yeah, I know about Angela." Marianne lifted her delicate, small-boned faced towards Jim. "And—it does bother me a little, to be honest. Angela is someone else's daughter. Her father is probably going through a lot of sleepless nights himself." Jim looked up at the menu board above the cash register.

"You want something? My treat." But Jim, with pursed lips, shook his head. Marianne nodded, then continued slowly and in a soothing tone as she leant over the table.

"Jim, the world is like a web. Each event, each person, is connected to every other event and person. If you touch one thread of the web, a tremor runs through the entire web. There are ramifications for bringing Ruth back, and I think we need to deal with them."

Jim sighed and muttered to himself. He scratched the rough stubble under his chin. "Look," he said, "this makes sense to me,

I'm not stupid. Part of me wants to trust you and Mike. You guys brought back Ruth in the first place. Then again, I don't want to ever see you people again. I mean, you scare me. If you can give Ruth back, you can take her away again. And sometimes I feel... y'know, that I should never have gotten Ruth back. She died and there's something false about her still being here and I don't want to think about that. I just want to forget about you people." Marianne had slid her blizzard to a corner of the table and sat with her hands folded, listening intently to Jim. She sat up straight when Jim had finished speaking.

"And those feelings are totally understandable, Jim. Totally. We'll get out of your hair in due time. In fact, we really should be out of your hair, but unfortunately we haven't perfected this process yet."

Jim absentmindedly brushed some crumbs onto the floor. The softball team was filing past the table. One girl stuck her tongue out at another girl.

"Alright, so when are you going to get out of my hair?"

"It's really quite simple, Jim. Think of it as a surgery. The surgery in itself is bad, but it's worth going through because you feel better after it's over."

"What's this surgery?" Jim shrugged his shoulders.

"Well, didn't Mike tell you that Ruth had to get injured, that that was the only way we could correct the problems we face?" Marianne lifted a slender hand towards Jim. Her nails were long and painted red. Jim rested his chin on his thick knuckles, and then placed his hands in between his thighs.

"Alright, what kind of injury does Ruth have to get? A fractured spine? A fractured skull?"

Marianne covered her mouth with her hand as she chuckled. "No, no Jim. We thought a fractured forearm would do the trick. Nothing serious. I mean, I broke my arm during recess in the second grade when I fell on the concrete." Jim leaned closer towards Marianne. He thrust out his jaw as he spoke.

"Y'know what, no, you people are just too creepy to me. You've got too much power, and you don't seem to know what you're doing. You're playing God, that's why this is all so eerie. What if you're wrong *this* time too? Are you going to come back and bother me again after I let my daughter's arm get broken?"

Jim had slid towards the edge of his bench. Marianne raised both of her hands in the air to try to calm Jim. "Jim, now, stay calm, we're not perfect, but you can trust us." With his heavy hand, though, Jim smacked Marianne's blizzard off the table, sending its contents spilling over the floor. A teenage couple turned towards Jim and leered at the fracas. Jim rose, spun towards the door, and barged out with such force that the bell attached to the door rang loudly and repeatedly. Marianne lowered her head onto her hands and tears began to curve down her soft cheeks. She could hear the engine of Jim's pickup as he maneuvered it through the narrow parking lot and raced onto the highway.

CHAPTER 10

MARIANNE DID NOT sit until Mike had asked her to; her eyes were still moist and red from crying. Mike rested his chin on his fists as she recounted her failure.

"He's just deaf to any sort of appeal. He's fiercely protective of his daughter, and he doesn't like us very much."

Mike sighed. He spoke in a low voice and slowly articulated each syllable. "You try so hard to help people. You want to do the right thing, but nobody cares or ever gives you any recognition. Jim just does not recognize the debt he owes us."

Marianne shook her head. "I guess being a father can give you tunnel vision, especially if you've already found out what it's like to lose your child." Mike picked up a silver paperweight from his desk, and then tapped it against the desk's surface. A bubble rose up through the water cooler.

"That's no excuse, Marianne, no excuse whatsoever. Jim has to learn how to care for other people, to give other people their due— people like Angela. Maybe, y'know, we should just eliminate him."

Marianne tilted her head and curled her upper lip.

"Y'know, I mean, maybe we could give Jim a different personality by changing something in his past. I don't mean eliminate *him*— just a personality trait or two." The two fell silent. A couple leaves loosened from a tree wafted against the office window. After a minute, Mike rose to his feet.

"I'm going to call everyone. We're going to get everyone in here, and see what to do next, if anything. We all need to put our heads together." Mike lifted his hands up in the air and locked his fingers. Then, rapidly, he began to punch a number on the black phone on the desk beneath him. Marianne walked towards the water cooler to fill a small plastic cup.

Soon, in the meeting room, there was a growing sound of murmuring as more and more engineers entered. Some were shouting and gesticulating with their hands. Others sat silently, staring at the floor. When most of the chairs in the meeting room were occupied, Mike passed before the whiteboard again and lifted his hands in the air to get the attention of the group.

"Alright, everybody, let's quiet down, we're ready to begin." The sound of conversation dwindled shortly, and about twenty pairs of eyes watched Mike.

"Alright, we've got some bad news, folks, very bad news. Jim remains stubborn." Disgruntled muttering filled the room. "Angela's problems are getting worse. We've got some freakish weather going on in Australia that may have something to do with the restoration of Ruth. And, like I said, Jim is just stonewalling us. So, I want to open up a discussion on what exactly we should do next."

No one reacted for a minute, but finally a tall, thin man raised his hand. Before he spoke, he stood up and adjusted his tie.

"Let's try talking to Jim again. This time I'll go. Marianne tried a gentle approach. I'll try a hard approach. I'm going to try to scare Jim by listing all the evils we have to deal with as result of the botched recovery effort for his daughter. I'll lay it all out, and I think that he'll respond to that."

Mike nodded, then pointed to the next raised hand, which was that of a middle-sized man with willowy limbs.

"I agree with this speaker. We should just go after Jim, like a prosecutor. Don't soften the truth. We need to start playing hardball." Other engineers shouted their assent and one or two began to applaud the two speakers. Soon, the entire room had joined the clapping. Mike leaned against the whiteboard with his hands on his hips. When the applause died down, he stepped closer towards the long table.

"Keep talking with Jim?" he asked in a soft voice. A hush fell over the room. "This guy's already turned us down twice. Why should he listen to us the third time?" Mike looked at the two engineers who had spoken directly in the eye. The tall one scratched the back of his head, then answered.

"If we lay out our position in hard, logical language," the engineer said as he chopped the surface of the table with his hand, "Jim will be pliable. He's a reasonable man, a good man. I believe that I can get him to understand the full context of his situation." Mike then turned to the shorter engineer who also had expressed his opinion.

"I agree with the other speaker's approach, Mike, but I think I can do a better job of executing it. This is because I have experience in prisons because of a previous job. I've worked with some hardened criminals, real psychopaths, and I've had some success convincing a large portion of them to reform." Mike nodded, then retreated towards the blank whiteboard.

He tapped a finger against the metal ledge that held the markers. "You know what I think of all this?" Mike waved a hand towards the two outspoken men. "These two opinions? I think we're just pushing against a brick wall." The tall engineer's lips tightened and he shook his head. "Yeah, Don, that is what I think. Because Jim's not all there, or he's too biased—whatever the reason is, I just don't think we should waste our time with him." Mike paused. Marianne smiled as she adjusted a strand of hair.

"Yeah, Marianne, don't feel bad. It's not your fault, it's Jim's. So, everybody, wanna know what my idea is?" Mike clapped his hands together. The tall engineer, Don, clenched his jaw as he glowered at Mike. Mike waited dramatically for half a minute, then he lifted one index finger into the air.

"One word: Ruth." Some engineers in the assembly gasped. "Yes, you heard me, we will tell Ruth about her situation. We can try to convince *her* that she needs to suffer this small injury in order to rectify the problems we have created." Mike paced back and forth before the whiteboard, then stopped to face the group. Marianne lifted a slender forearm.

"Mike, I really disagree with that plan. Ruth's just a girl, it wouldn't be right to disclose to her all that we know. I mean, how could she handle the knowledge that she really ought to be dead and that her very existence has led to problems for people she knows as well as the world? I mean, what a blow to her self-esteem—the idea that she shouldn't be alive!"

Mike walked towards a window and opened it. A gust of wind ruffled the ties and hair of the engineers.

"I see your point, Marianne. But, sometimes, we need to weigh negative outcomes against one another. Okay, so Ruth has a hard time swallowing the idea that she really should be dead. But, let's say she looks at her situation reasonably—she's a bright kid, after all—and, after a brief period of adjustment, she sees things our way, we perform the operation, and then we can move on to bigger and better things." Mike faced Marianne, who was shaking her head.

"No, Mike, Ruth's not going to be able to deal with this so easily. She doesn't even know the realm of possibility exists. She's an adolescent, Mike! She doesn't know what she wants to do with her life, she's still learning about boys and money and getting a job. How is she going to be able to process this whole new dimension before she's even processed straightforward details about her own world?"

Mike smiled and shook his head. "Oh, but Marianne, you forget that it's precisely Ruth's immaturity that is going to allow her to be open to our advice. Young people are less sophisticated than adults, and therefore can adapt more readily to new ideas like the realm of possibility. Ruth will be drawn to our advice the same way she is drawn to a fantasy novel."

Marianne lowered her chin into her hand and looked at the floor pensively. "Well, Mike, if you're going to do this, you're going to have to find someone else to help you. You can count me out."

Mike licked his upper lip and brushed a strand of hair from his forehead. "Okay, we'll find some other people. Who here is ready to buy into my idea? Raise your hand!" Five hands shot up into the air. "Great! I want all five of you to come into my office. I will need just two engineers for this project, and I want to find out what each one of you is made of so I can make the right choices."

The group of five headed towards the door of the meeting room and passed through it into the hallway. The engineers still gathered at the table were motionless for a few seconds, then they got up and talked amongst themselves.

"I think things just took a turn for the worse," Marianne said to another woman.

CHAPTER 11

RUTH WAS WALKING through the puddles left by a midday storm. The weight of the books in her backpack bobbed up and down densely as she splashed along the sidewalk before the school. The sun had just broken through some clouds. Ruth was glancing at her reflection each time it passed over the puddles when she heard someone call her.

"Ruth, Ruth!" A secretary from the school had come through its tall entranceway and was shouting with a hoarse, weak voice. She lifted her bony hand above her white hair.

"Ruth, Mr. Snell wants to see you. Don't go yet." Ruth stopped and then reversed her direction. Mr. Snell was Ruth's English teacher. Ruth had a copy of "The Lord of the Flies" on her nightstand, since she was studying it at the time in Mr. Snell's class.

When Ruth entered the classroom to which the secretary had ushered her, she saw Mr. Snell sitting at the teacher's desk at the front of the classroom. Opposite him, she saw two men in dark blazers and ties sitting on some smaller desks for students. Ruth paused at the threshold of the door and stared at the men.

"These men are here to see you, Ruth. They seem awfully important, so I decided to get you before you had left school grounds." Mr. Snell's gray mustache gleamed in the harsh glare of the classroom lights. He extended his hand towards the well-dressed men, who both rose in unison and smiled at Ruth.

"Hi, Ruth, I'm Gary, and this is my partner, Jonathan." Gary was a young man with a shaggy black beard. Jonathan's bald head towered behind Gary; through his spectacles, Jonathan's narrow blue eyes peered down at Ruth. Ruth lifted her soft, thin hand towards each of the two men and gave a timid wave.

Gary turned towards Mr. Snell and said in a deep voice, "Alright, Mr. Snell, you can leave now. Thank you for your help." Mr. Snell slowly lifted his jacket from the chair and, after he had wrapped himself in it, shuffled out of the classroom. Just before he entered the hallway, though, he turned around and addressed Ruth.

"Don't worry, Ruth, they're from the government or something." Gary sat at the desk where Mr. Snell had been. Ruth watched Mr. Snell's curved back through the window in the door.

"Ruth, hey Ruth?" Gary reached out and tapped Ruth's shoulder. Ruth jumped back, then Jonathan steadied her with his long fingers. Ruth looked up and smiled at the tall, hawk-nosed man. She had been accustomed to being surrounded by loving adults. Jonathan pointed to a desk.

"Take a seat, Ruth, make yourself comfortable." Gary got up and placed a candy bar on top of the desk Ruth had chosen.

"This is for coming to this meeting. We know you would rather be home relaxing." Ruth slid the candy bar into a pocket of her backpack. Snickers was her favorite kind.

But Ruth remained standing and glanced back and forth at the two men's faces. They were strangers, and they had asked her to stay in a classroom at a time when she was used to relaxing and hanging out with friends. Ruth couldn't shake the nagging feeling that she was in trouble, but she couldn't imagine what she had done.

"I don't know what I did. I mean, if this is about Angela…"

But Gary chopped at the air to dismiss Ruth's fear as he returned to the teacher's desk. He rested his elbows on its surface and locked his fingers. "Ruth, we're not here to talk to you because you're in trouble. We actually want to talk to you because you're doing remarkably well." Gary pulled out a drawer of the desk and lifted some sheets of paper into the air. He leafed through them as he continued speaking.

"One hundred percent on your trigonometry test. An unheard of one hundred and two on the biology exam. Jonathan, can you believe this? A ninety six on the American history *final!*" Both men beamed at Ruth, whose face had reddened with embarrassment at the attention. She looked towards the floor.

"Well, y'know, I guess I just have a knack for school." A smile began to spread across Ruth's face as her initial discomfort lifted. She laughed when Jonathan put another Snickers bar on her desk. Jonathan pushed his glasses higher up along the bridge of his nose.

"And that's why we're here, Ruth," Jonathan interjected. "We… um, we're part of the administration of this school district. We know that you have a knack for school, and we're worried that you're getting too bored with the classes you're taking right now. Your teachers have to go slowly because of the other students. Don't you think you're getting somewhat impatient with the pace of your education?" Jonathan nodded his head as he asked the question. Ruth looked down again, this time at the surface of her desk.

"Um…yeah, I guess I could go a little faster." Ruth turned towards Gary, whose smile stretched out within his thick beard.

"That's our assessment, too, Ruth," Gary said while patting the desk once with his hand for emphasis. "So, the solution Jonathan and I have come up with is to have you take a more interesting and difficult course. We think it will definitely hold your attention. It's called 'The Physics of Reversal'. Both Jonathan and I, as school officials, are qualified to teach it, and we would be honored if you would be our pupil." Jonathan rubbed his hands together as Ruth lowered her eyes to her desk again. After a pulling at her fingers for a moment, Ruth sat up and faced the two men.

"Yeah, I guess we can do that. I mean, I'm really happy that you think I'm that smart." Both Jonathan and Gary began to clap excitedly and Ruth beamed as she peeled off the wrapper of her Snickers bar. "But," Ruth continued once the clapping subsided, "I don't know anything about that topic. Could you at least give me a summary of what it's all about?"

"Sure," Gary said while he pulled at the hair that sprouted from his chin. "In a nutshell, Ruth, y'know how in the physics class you're taking now you're talking about how things move over time?"

"Yeah," Ruth responded after a moment of hesitation. "You mean, like, velocity and force?"

"Exactly, exactly. Well, in the 'Physics of Reversal', we'll be talking about basically the same topics, except we'll be studying movement backwards in time. In other words, the changes an object undergoes in reversal physics involve going deeper and deeper into the past."

Ruth frowned as she mulled over the new concept. She was interested. "Yeah, I guess I can take it. Sounds interesting."

"Great decision, great decision," Gary said as he brushed some of his hair from his forehead. "Okay, Ruth, we're going to start lessons tomorrow, right after your regular classes end. We'll meet in this room—no clubs meet in here, right Jonathan?—alright, we'll meet in this room. The Physics of Reversal, Ruth! Boy, is your mind going to expand!"

The three sat there for a couple moments, then Gary stood up after sliding Ruth's exams back into the desk drawer. "Well, Ruth, we're done for the day. We both look forward to having you as our student!" Gary and Jonathan shook Ruth's hand, and Ruth retraced her path out of the classroom and the school and back onto the sidewalk. Before she had left, Gary had handed her a thick textbook that she had put into her backpack. By the time Ruth reached the front door of her home, her shoulders were burning. She dropped the backpack to the floor. It crashed on the hard tile and Ruth's mom bolted into the kitchen.

"What was that?"

CHAPTER 12

THE NEXT MORNING, Jim was taking deep swallows from a mug of coffee that steamed in his truck's cupholder. He was halfway to work, and Blackmun was about twenty miles behind him. He pounded his horn when a red Porsche merged suddenly into his lane.

"Watch it, buddy," he shouted as he stuck his head out the window. Ruth had told Jim the night before about the 'Physics of Reversal'. The conversation had ended with Ruth running up the stairs crying.

"But it sounds really interesting, Daddy!"

Jim's truck rushed along at sixty miles per hour down the two-lane road he took to work. "The Physics of Reversal," he muttered to himself. He knew who was behind the meeting with the two men Ruth had mentioned. Jim twisted the volume knob on the car radio so that when he passed a man walking his dog, the dog jumped to the side and nearly caused the man to fall.

Jim shut off the engine when he had parked with a violent push against the keys, then forced his door closed with a firm thrust. He looked towards a group of people drifting towards the entrance of the building. Mike was walking at the fringes of the crowd. Jim, ignoring the stares of the other workers, took a few long strides towards the young man, then called out in a hoarse voice, "Hey Mike, we've got to talk!"

Mike stopped and then made a comment to a couple men that had been walking alongside of him. He then trotted towards Jim. As he came closer, Jim saw that he was grinning.

"What's up, man?" Mike extended one of his hands towards Jim as he approached. Jim did not take it. Instead, he started walking towards his truck as he motioned Mike towards it.

"C'mon, we've got stuff to talk about." Jim opened the passenger door for Mike and then leapt behind the steering wheel. When Mike had climbed in beside him, Jim immediately leaned towards Mike's ear and began to hiss into it.

"What are you trying to do to my daughter, you little shit? Who are these goons you've set her up with? Look, I'll tear you to pieces. I can see your fingerprints all over this goddamn physics class!" Mike leaned back in the seat and ran his hand along its soft surface.

"This seat is comfortable. Is this truck fairly new?" Jim's eyes bulged even more from their sockets and he shifted closer to Mike's body.

"Look, kid, I ain't playing games." Jim pulled a large, folded pocketknife from his pocket. With a click, a blade of about four inches rotated out and shone in the horizontal light of the morning. Mike kept grinning, though.

"And I'm not playing games either, Jim." Jim lowered the knife when he heard Mike's calm, measured tone. Mike twisted in the seat so that he faced Jim.

"You can go ahead and kill me, Jim, if you want. It doesn't bother me in the least. You're forgetting my other role. If you kill me, some of my fellow engineers back in the realm of possibility can change things up a little bit and I'll be back. So, go ahead, do it."

Jim's hand shook as he held the knife. He slowly reclined in his chair, then, with visible reluctance, flipped the blade back into place. Jim slammed his palm against the steering wheel.

"You just can't win, Jim," Mike said, still smiling broadly. "I mean, c'mon Jim, why are you so hostile to me? I'm the good guy here, the one who restored your daughter. I'm the one who's trying to change this messed-up world. It's not my fault that restoring Ruth led to other problems. These problems, in fact," Mike said as his voice began to rise, "are more evidence that the way the world is set up is faulty. I mean, I'm not the one you should be angry with."

Jim looked down towards where his feet mingled with the gas pedal and the brake. His voice was soft. "Maybe I should just never have gotten involved with you. Maybe it would have been better if I had just accepted Ruth's death."

Mike shook his head. "You don't know what you're saying. I've had enough of this superstitious fatalism you're talking about. We have the power, Jim, and we need to use it. It's just an injury, Jim, things will be fine, you're being illogical!"

Jim pulled at the handle of his door and slid his leg out to the side of the truck. "I don't know, Mike, there's something fishy about all this. I guess there's nothing I can do, though, but hope for the best." Jim slammed the door and walked with a lowered head towards the Cisco building. Mike lifted his hands in the air and chuckled.

"Some people will just never get it, will they?"

Chapter 13

RUTH KEPT LOOKING at the clock throughout the day. After her last class, she was supposed to report to Mr. Snell's classroom again and meet with Gary and Jonathan. She was going to have her first session of the "Physics of Reversal". Ruth rushed past Angela on her way out of the classroom door once 2:30 came.

"Going to spend some more time with Tommy, huh?" Angela called out as Ruth breezed down the hall. Ruth focused on her locker, though, which was adjacent to a pair of glass doors that opened onto a grassy lot with a couple of picnic tables. After getting what she needed from her locker, she sat on a bench while the halls slowly emptied.

Gary and Jonathan were sitting in Mr. Snell's classroom talking when Ruth looked through the window of the door. Gary had gotten his dark beard trimmed. Ruth knocked on the door, and Jonathan took just two long strides towards it and held it open for her.

"Good afternoon, great to see you," Jonathan and Gary said in a friendly chorus. Ruth sat in a desk and within seconds had a notebook, pencil, and her glossy new textbook ready. She was eager to test herself against the difficult new subject matter. Gary and Jonathan exchanged some whispers in the front of the room and then Gary picked up a piece of chalk from the blackboard ledge.

"Alright, Ruth, it looks like you're ready, and we know that we are keeping you here at school longer than you are used to. So, why don't we just get started?" Ruth nodded and Gary turned to face the board and began to draw. Soon, some chalk dust began to float in the air. Ruth watched Gary as a stick figure took shape on the blackboard.

"Ruth, we're going to call this figure John. I know, I can't draw. But, anyway, John is a sixteen year old young man." Gary turned towards the blackboard again and drew two diagonal lines through John. "Something terrible happened to John, Ruth. He got killed in a car accident." Ruth scratched some notes. Gary continued when he saw that she was done.

"So, all of a sudden, John's family had a major problem on their hands. It's hard enough when someone dies after a life of eighty or ninety years. It's even harder when someone dies before they have even come into their own. John was still young, and no one got see what kind of talents he had and what kind of man he would become." Gary turned towards Jonathan, nodded and clasped his hands behind his back. Jonathan stepped forward before the desk.

"So, Ruth, this situation is simple and, unfortunately, pretty common. What do people generally do about these types of problems?" Ruth brought the eraser of her pencil to her lips.

"Well, I don't know," Ruth began after a moment's silence. "They don't do much, I guess. Maybe they have a funeral."

"That's right," said Jonathan, "there's nothing much people can do in these situations. Obviously, you cannot call a doctor—John is dead, so by definition he is beyond the help of medicine. So, we just cry a lot, maybe let ourselves be led on by a religious leader, and try to keep dragging ourselves through life."

Gary began to speak. "Alright Ruth, I'm going to change the example now, but not the topic. Are you ready?" Gary walked over to the shelf of books that ran below the windows. Ruth nodded at him after she had drawn a line under the notes she had already taken.

"Okay, Ruth, take a look at these textbooks over here. One is distributed to each student every year, so that they can learn about literature. I want you to think about these books in a new way, though. I want you to give me what I call a list of possible outcomes—in other words, what things could possibly happen to this particular textbook?" Gary bent down and pointed to one of the black textbooks with his finger. Ruth frowned at him.

"What do you mean? I mean, someone is going to read it."

Gary pressed his hands together and looked towards the back of the classroom. Then, facing Ruth, he said, "Now, don't overthink this. You're right, someone might read this book, but maybe I explained myself poorly. My question is actually very simple. Just tell me, what are the things that could possibly happen to this textbook over the course of time? Being read is one thing. What else might happen, though?"

Ruth rested her chin on her hands. "Well, it could be read, it… could be damaged by someone. It might just sit there because there are more books than students, it…someone might use a highlighter on it."

"Very good," Jonathan said while he stepped closer to Ruth's desk and adjusted his glasses. "Now, we really need you to focus to grasp this next point. Watch what I'm about to do."

Jonathan reached one long arm towards a textbook on the shelf, grasped its spine with his fingers, and then held it up in the air. "Okay, so now something has happened to the textbook. It has been taken from the shelf and it is now being held up in the air. Another possible state for it, before I lifted it from the shelf, was for it to just remain resting there, like you said. And here's where we get to the tricky question: what happened to this possible state? What happened to this potential future of just sitting on the shelf now that I've lifted the book up in the air?"

Ruth scribbled a couple more sentences in her notebook, then looked towards Jonathan and Gary. "Well, that state never really existed, right? It was just something that we imagined, but since it never happened, it never really existed."

Jonathan and Gary both chuckled. "That's what most people say," Gary said as he lifted an index finger in the air. "But, Ruth, the fact is that that possible state of resting on the shelf still exists." Jonathan continued to hold the literature book up in the air.

"That can't be, though. I don't see that possible state. I mean, where is it? The book's right there." Ruth pointed to the book, which Jonathan held up near his thin chest. Gary began to walk slowly along the front of the room.

"To help you understand this idea, Ruth, I'm going to ask you a series of questions. The first one is, can something come from nothing?"

Ruth held a finger to her chin. "Well, I guess not. I guess there has to be something already there for something to come about."

"Right, I can see we were right to select you for this class. It doesn't make sense for something to come from nothing, since something has to be built up with something else, and you can't build anything with nothing, it just doesn't make any sense. Okay, so that point is established. The next question for you, Ruth, is what was the state of being held up in the air *before* my partner Jonathan lifted the book up in the air?" Jonathan had tucked the book underneath his arm, but when Gary pointed towards him, he placed the book back on the shelf.

Ruth remained silent for awhile. Gary intervened. "It was a possibility, right, before it actually happened?"

Ruth looked through her notes. "Yeah, I guess you're right. Before Jonathan lifted the book in the air, that state was just something that was possible for the book to be in."

"Good. It's alright, Ruth, don't feel bad, this topic is hard. Okay, so now that Jonathan has lifted the textbook up into the air," Gary moved both of his hands up from his waist above his head, "it's no longer a possible state, but a real state. In other words, the state of being held up in the air now *exists*." Gary motioned to Jonathan, who placed the book atop the shelf and then loosened his tie.

"Okay, now we need to recall the principle that we first established," Jonathan said as he took a couple of steps towards the blackboard and began to write. Ruth copied each letter that arose beneath the slender piece of white chalk. When Jonathan had finished writing, he stepped back and extended his arms towards the sentence like a car salesman showing off one of his vehicles.

"Something cannot come from nothing. It follows, therefore, that, if the state of being held up in the air was real when I was holding it, it must have been real when it was a possible state. If possible states do not exist, then real states come from nothing, which is ridiculous. Therefore, possible states also exist." Ruth looked towards the bookshelf with a wide-eyed stare. She imagined all the possible states of the books as an array of hidden patterns floating in the air.

Gary spoke in a clear, ringing voice. "So, possible states do exist, contrary to popular opinion. Otherwise, none of them could ever become real states. And, that means that we *can* do something about things like a teenage boy's untimely death." Gary tapped the stick figure on the blackboard with his knuckle. "We have devised a method to access the possible states of a thing, Ruth, and activate them. This is an application of the physics of reversal: it's called reversal engineering."

Ruth began to page through her notes. She was concentrating so hard that lines had formed on her forehead. An hour had passed since she had entered the classroom. Gary pulled a bottle of water from a satchel on the desk and took a couple of sips from it.

"Alright, Ruth, we're going to wrap things up for today. We know that we've given you a lot to think about. But, before you leave, I just want to give you a preview of tomorrow's lesson. We're going to discuss the applications of reversal engineering. What exactly can we do with it? How can it help us? Alright, Ruth?"

Ruth was zipping up her backpack. She nodded at Gary and Jonathan, and her ponytail bounced up and down as she walked through the classroom door. Both Gary and Jonathan waved at her as she left. When she had disappeared, they drew close to one another and conversed in whispers.

CHAPTER 14

R UTH CAME IN through the door with a smile. Sarah looked up from a steaming pot of green beans.

"What are you making, Mom?" Ruth stepped closer to her mother, embraced her tightly, and then stood on her toes to kiss her cheek.

"My, what got into you today? Do you like that new class you got invited to? I'm so proud of you, sweetheart!" Sarah stroked the hair on one side of Ruth's head. Jim strode into the kitchen. His face was pale, and there was a faint redness in his eyes.

"Hi, Ruth, how was your day?" Jim muttered. He slouched as he moved to the cupboard to pull out a plate and a cup. Ruth sat down, and began to chat loudly and quickly.

"Well, I was just out by the stream on the other side of the block with Joanne. We saw some frogs and, also, a snake! It was just a small one, but there aren't that many of them in Blackmun, so it was exciting!" Sarah had placed a glass of water with a few ice cubes floating within it before Ruth. The feet of a chair scraped along the floor as Jim pulled it out and sat.

"And how was that new class, the physics class?" Jim rubbed one of his eyes. He leaned forward towards Ruth with his elbows resting on the table.

"Daddy, I love it! You wouldn't believe what I'm learning. Let's see if I can remember—it's really complicated. Mom, aren't you going to listen?" Sarah adjusted one of the knobs on the stove and dried her hands with a towel before moving to the table and sitting across from Jim.

"Well, today I learned about reversal engineering. It's incredible, Dad, you can change things that happen if you don't like them. Like if you lost a soccer game, you could just change the score. And you can do even bigger things—it's really cool!" Jim studied a small chip in the wooden surface of the table. He scratched at it with the nail of his index finger.

"That doesn't make sense Ruth—I mean, I thought once things happened, they just happened, and there was nothing that we could do to undo them." Jim still probed the chip in the table surface. Ruth grew calmer when she noticed Jim's blank stare.

"Well, that's what I used to think, too, but there is a way to change things, it's got something to do with—let's see—the idea that something cannot come from nothing, y'know, that doesn't make any sense." Jim rose to his feet and leaned against the counter next to the stove. He folded his arms across his chest.

Sarah frowned at Ruth as she put dishes on the table. "I guess they're exposing you to some new technology. I wouldn't know anything about that." Ruth rolled her eyes and lowered her forehead into her hands.

"You two are always so negative. I'm really interested in this topic! Aren't I supposed to like things I learn at school?"

Sarah positioned herself behind Ruth, rested her hands on her shoulders and kissed her soft hair. "Of course we're happy you like school, honey. Jim, we have to help Ruth stay motivated. She's got such a bright future. Tell us more about reversal engineering, Ruthie." Jim looked out the kitchen window as a large station wagon lumbered around the corner and then growled down the street.

"Well, it's like being a doctor, only better. You can fix a broken arm, but instead of putting in cast, you, like, make it not happen. It's kinda hard to put it into words." Lines formed on Ruth's forehead. Jim ran a hand through his hair.

"Yep, it's the Tower of Babel all over again." Jim had been paging through his Bible after the fracas with Mike. Sarah turned towards him and crinkled her nose.

"Since when have you become a Biblical scholar?" She lifted a hot bowl of broccoli with an oven mitt and set it near the center of the table. The thick aroma of the chicken then cooking pervaded the air.

"Oh, I was just reading through that story again this morning and I realized just now that it might apply to this new subject Ruth is dabbling in." Ruth slid her chair back and stood.

"Wait, so you're going to keep trying to discourage me. Okay, go ahead and tell me about this tower. I want to hear this argument." Ruth thrust out her lower jaw and her cheeks flushed.

"Well, okay. Y'know, honey, I'm just looking out for your welfare."

"You don't think I can find out what's good for me on my own? But, go ahead, try me." Jim pushed aside the plate before him and rotated his chair to face Ruth.

"Okay, well, in this story, people try to build this really tall tower because they wanted to have a great reputation. But, they had too much power for their own good. So God prevented them from working together by creating the different languages that divide people to this day. That's how I see this new engineering you've gotten exposed to. Sometimes, it's better if we lack control."

Ruth gripped the top of her chair and glowered at her father. "That makes no sense, none at all. How is power bad? Power is good, engineering is *good*, it can save lives!" Ruth stomped her foot and then lowered her head onto her mother's shoulder. Sobs shook her body. Jim could see the ridges of her spine pressing against her shirt. Sarah ran her hand up and down Ruth's back.

"Jim, why don't you just let the child find her own way, you don't have to be so controlling. There, there, honey, no one's going to stop you from pursuing your dreams."

After moving towards the front door, Jim stood looking through the screen at the steadily waning evening light outside. He scratched behind his ear, and felt helpless to change the way his life was developing. He looked to the side, and saw out of the corner of his eye Ruth's hot, red face as she hid herself in Sarah's body. Stepping towards them, Jim held his hand out towards his daughter's head, but held himself back as he crossed before the oven. He slid his hands into his pockets and then studied the designs on the tiles.

CHAPTER 15

THE NEXT AFTERNOON, Ruth walked slowly down the quiet school hallway with her head lowered. A couple janitors were pushing a cart piled with cleaning materials into a bathroom. Ruth pushed open the door to Mr. Snell's classroom and found Jonathan and Gary inside again. This time, she saw that they had turned two desks so that they could face one another and Jonathan, whose back was to Ruth, held his hands up in the air and spoke loudly.

"But that's bound to fail!" Gary motioned with his hand and Jonathan fell silent. The tall man spun around and stood up when he saw Ruth's slight figure.

"Oh, hey Ruth," Jonathan said as he finished unfolding his long body. Ruth craned her neck to direct her gaze up at his face.

"Um…sorry to bother you. Should I give you guys some extra time?" Gary hastily rotated the desks so they were in line with the others.

"Oh no, no," he said, slicing the air with his hand. "It's time to begin, there's no need to delay. We've got an exciting agenda today." Gary pointed toward an empty seat at the front of the room and Ruth walked towards it as she began to free her arms from her backpack straps.

"Good, because I'm *very* eager to begin today's lesson. My dad made sure of that." Ruth blew some air from the corner of her mouth and rolled her eyes.

Gary was walking towards the chalkboard, but stopped after Ruth had spoken. He turned around and looked at her with an open mouth in the center of his large, dark beard.

"What did your father say?"

Ruth crossed her arms across her chest as her face tightened. "He just told me all this...this crap about how reversal engineering is a way to get too much power. He was talking about this ancient story from the Bible about some silly tower."

Gary and Jonathan both exchanged glances. "Sometimes parents, Ruth, can get in the way of their child's progress," Gary said. "Y'know, Ruth, Jim's generation was never exposed to reversal engineering. Heck, they lacked some of the *medical* procedures we take for granted today. Sometimes people are just instinctively wary of new things. It's foolish, though, to think like this." Ruth played with her pencil, then looked up at Gary with a smile.

"Thanks, Gary. I want to continue with this," she said. Gary gave a small nod towards Jonathan, then turned back towards Ruth.

"We will certainly continue. Your father is not going to stop us." Jonathan shook his hand at Gary. Ruth's face fell. "I mean," Gary continued, "your father's a great guy, Ruth. I hear he's highly regarded at Cisco." Ruth frowned, but then she nodded and Gary began to write on the board. The word 'limitations' took shape on the smeared green surface at the front of the classroom.

"Okay, Ruth, yesterday we created some hype about reversal engineering. Today, we're going to take a realistic look at the problems with this kind of technology. Y'know, as responsible teachers, we're going to be perfectly honest with you." Ruth pressed her tongue against her upper lip as she wrote in her notebook.

"So, Ruth, you must have heard about nuclear energy, right?" Gary looked at Ruth with raised eyebrows. She nodded. "Okay, so when nuclear energy came out, it had some advantages over old types of fuel like coal and gas. First of all, one little pellet of uranium—that's what they use in nuclear energy—has as much power as 17,000 cubic feet of natural gas. Nuclear energy creates less pollution, and it requires less land than solar energy and wind energy. The point I'm trying to make, Ruth, is that nuclear energy is like reversal engineering: it's better than what we had before." Gary handed the chalk to Jonathan and retired to the side of the room. Jonathan opted to place the chalk on the blackboard ledge and began to pace back and forth with his hands in his pockets.

"Along with these advantages, though, disadvantages were discovered. Nuclear waste is very radioactive—this means it can cause cancer, birth defects, even death. The material used in nuclear reactors can also be used to produce bombs. The lesson here, Ruth, is that every technology has a dark side. No matter how hard we try, things can go wrong." A cat leapt onto the bricks extending from one of the classroom windows outside and with its green eyes surveyed the room. Gary noticed the cat and stepped towards it.

"Okay, now that this cat has sprung into view, we can use it as an example. You surely want to ask what the disadvantages of reversal engineering may be. Well, let's say that we had engineered this cat back to life—it had been, say, run over by a car and we shifted this reality back into a possible state and actualized another, better possible state." As Gary pointed at the cat, it leapt off the bricks and raced across the thick grass.

"Now, when we look at the various possible states into which the cat could have entered, we see that things are extremely complex. I mean, think about it, there are just so many things that could happen to a cat. It could get sick, it could catch a mouse, it could be purchased by another owner, etcetera, etcetera. And, on top of all this, all of these possible states are connected to the possible states of other things. So, for instance, if we were to actualize the state of the cat in which it captures a mouse, then the possible state of the mouse in which it dies at the hands of the cat would be actualized, and then the possible state of the homeowner whose house the mouse would have invaded had it not died is also affected. It just goes on and on. Now, listen carefully: it is very difficult—in fact, it is impossible—to identify all the consequences of choosing any possible state in the reversal engineering process. So, inevitably, when we do this, we find that, though we have solved one problem, we have created others down the line." Gary fell silent and the only sound in the room was from the water flowing in a pipe behind the wall. Ruth kept scribbling down notes. After a couple minutes of writing, she set aside her pencil and looked up at the two men with a puzzled frown.

"So, what we do, just give up on it all?" Ruth shrugged her shoulders.

Gary shook his head emphatically. "No, no, we go ahead and perform the operation, but it needs to be carefully monitored. For instance, let's say someone's dog got hurt and we wanted to engineer it back to health. So, we get it nice and healthy, but then we realize that this new state has negative consequences for some other situation. What we need to do, then, is to make an adjustment that will remedy the negative effects of the undoing of the injury to the dog."

Gary looked over at Jonathan and raised his hands slightly to indicate his frustration. He feared that he was not making sense to Ruth. Jonathan wiped his forehead and turned towards Ruth. "Well, okay, um…yes, there just needs to be an adjustment to circumvent these problems and things of that nature. So, for instance, we might need to injure the dog again. Of course, the dog would heal eventually. And, then, we could move on to a different problem."

Gary, who had sat down at the desk Mr. Snell often used, spoke again. "And, Ruth, we want you to know that there is a reversal engineering operation proceeding right now and we want you to be part of it. We want you to get some hands-on experience! Would you like that?"

Ruth nodded and rose from the desk. The presentation intrigued her, and was feeling a little defiant after her dad's attempts to discourage her. She stretched the muscles on her neck by shifting her head from side to side.

"Great, okay, the operation is going on right now, Ruth," Gary continued, "and it's very important, and we just need you to, like the dog I was talking about, sustain a small injury in order to make sure that this operation works out. Are you game?" Ruth flattened the hair on her temple with her hand and blinked a couple of times at Gary.

"Wait, I have to get injured? What kind of injury?" Gary looked towards Jonathan and parted his beard to scratch his face.

"Just a minor one," Gary responded. "Believe me, it will be worth it. You'll see." Gary began to walk around Mr. Snell's desk towards Ruth. He wanted to placate her. Ruth went back to her desk and sat again.

"Wait, why do *I* have to get injured? Since when was I a part of a reversal engineering operation?" Ruth's face was pale. She rested her chin on her hand and leaned forward in the desk.

"There's one going on right now, and you're definitely part of it." Gary spoke in a harsh tone all of a sudden. Jonathan looked pained as he fiddled with the cloth of his pants.

"What is the specific injury that you want me to get?"

Gary leaned against the blackboard and swung his fists back and forth in front of his hips. "It doesn't really matter. Don't worry, it's not going to kill you, you're not going to go back to that condition."

Ruth lifted her chin and frowned. "Back to that condition? What's that supposed to mean? This is all getting pretty strange. Are you talking about, like, before I was born?"

Gary held a hand to his forehead and muttered a curse softly but still audibly. "No, no, Ruth, just forget that I said that. You just need to sustain a minor injury so that this reversal engineering procedure can work. I think this is a great opportunity." Gary pointed down at the floor as he made his point. But, Ruth had placed her notebook into her backpack already and Gary heard a little metallic hum as she zipped it shut. She swung a strap of the backpack over her shoulder and began to labor along underneath its weight towards the classroom door.

"I can't keep doing this right now, guys, I just don't quite get it. I need to talk to my parents." When Ruth had stepped through the door and reached the end of the hallway, she let her backpack slam to the ground, sat on a bench, and cried with her knees held up to her face. It was humiliating for her to acknowledge that her father might have been right.

CHAPTER 16

"I TOLD YOU, honey, that kind of power is just too much for people. It's so great that it takes on a life of its own and people just can't control it."

Jim ran his hand up and down the bumps on Ruth's spine. She sat beside him on the couch, with her head resting on his shoulder.

"I don't know, dad, I'm still interested in it, but they just caught me off guard. I've never been asked to get injured in any other class. They seemed disorganized all of a sudden."

Jim nodded his head slowly as he rocked in a recliner in front of the TV. "Hey Ruth, why don't you just stop seeing these guys for at least a few weeks? Just to give yourself a nice break?"

Ruth took a deep breath. "Yeah, I guess you're right, Daddy. This sucks, though, I was getting pretty excited about this new subject."

Jim hooked his hand around Ruth's shoulder. "Young lady, don't talk like that! I'm going to put a profanity jar in here if you don't stop! Every time you curse, you have to put in a quarter!"

Jim started to make means faces at Ruth and she started to laugh hysterically. "Dad, cut that out!" She gave him a light slap on the shoulder.

Jim had to pay some bills, so he entered the study and pulled the door closed behind him. Ruth had the recliner to herself. She spun over towards the TV, on top of which an array of framed pictures leaned. There was one of her mom and dad's wedding day: Sarah was about twenty pounds lighter in the picture and her hair was long and curly. Ruth moved this photograph aside and pulled forward one of herself when she was three or four years old. She had been a plump child. In the picture, she stood in a pile of leaves with her arms in the air. Her smile revealed a couple missing baby teeth. Ruth brought the picture over to the recliner and held it in front of her. She thought back to a time five years before the picture was taken, when she had not yet existed. Gary's words kept running through her mind.

"It won't kill you, you're not going to go back to that condition."

Rascal rose from his bed, scratched at his side with a hind paw, and then ambled over to Ruth. She scratched the soft, pendulous skin underneath his chin. Behind Rascal's warm body, there was an entire set of possible states, one of which, lurking like a stalker on a dark city street, was the dog's death. Her own set of possibilities also contained a similar void. She could get sick, fall from a great height. Also, she might never have been born.

Ruth picked up a rubber bone, one of Rascal's toys. She tossed it up in the air. As it travelled up towards the ceiling, it blended in with the white paint there so that Ruth could no longer see it. When it landed with a thud on the carpet, Ruth noticed goosebumps on her forearm. Thinking about her own death had shaken her.

CHAPTER 17

GARY AND JONATHAN both waited before the door to Mike's office. Jonathan kept shifting his weight back and forth from one foot to the other. Gary pulled at the long strands of hair sprouting from his chin. The door swung open, and Mike's pale face emerged from behind it.

Mike's lips were compressed as he gestured with his hand towards the office interior.

"So, gentlemen, how did the project go? Did everything go as planned?" Mike lifted a stack of stapled papers from his desk and placed it in a drawer. The drawer scraped against the inside of the desk as he tried to shut it.

Gary cleared his throat. "Well, Mike, we think we made some inroads. We definitely created an opening."

Mike started back from the desk and looked at Gary. Lines began to form on his forehead. "What exactly does that mean? Does that mean that you haven't actually completed the job?"

Gary ran his hand down one of his sleeves. He cleared his throat again, and then poured himself some water from the water cooler. "Well, sir, I guess I'll just start from the beginning."

Mike extended his hands towards the two men. "Please, feel free."

"Well, okay, we had this plan to introduce Ruth to the idea that…she has to get injured. We led her to think she was taking a class on some new, advanced technology. We called the class 'The Physics of Reversal'. Ruth was really excited about it. We told her she had been invited to it because she was so bright. But, we found out later that Jim tried to dampen her enthusiasm."

Mike put his pen, which he had been tapping against his palm, on the desk and leaned back in his chair. "Maybe we'll have to teach Jim a lesson...Let him know who he's up against. But, go ahead. What are these inroads that you've made?"

Gary nodded to Jonathan, who began to speak with a finger held against his chin. "Okay, well, we taught Ruth about this new physics. She was really engaged, very excited, in spite of Jim's intrusion. We explained how the possibilities of something were not just ideas and did not go away once something had assumed a certain state, but that they are in fact real and we can access them and even manipulate them. She was drinking it up, Mike, really. So, then, a couple of days into this, we told her that she herself was part of a reversal engineering operation. We made it seem like we wanted her to get some hands-on experience. Y'know, get a taste of the real world. She was cooperative at first, but then we told her she had to get injured. She balked at this, and...then, I think it was you, Gary, right, who said something about Ruth being killed, and I'm afraid this comment is what has stalled progress at this point."

Mike was now standing. "Okay, so after this little mistake, what exactly is Ruth's attitude to you guys?"

Gary answered. "She was shaken up by the last meeting, and we have reports that she may not be attending for a couple of weeks, but it is still possible that we could eventually convince her to participate in this operation we are trying to get done."

Mike nodded. His lips were pale and thin. "So basically you're saying that the work's not finished?" He pressed his hands together.

"Well, er, I guess you..." Gary ran his hand under his nose and sniffed.

"Let me put it this way: has Ruth been injured in the manner prescribed by the research committee?"

Jonathan replied. "No, sir, she has not."

Mike sat down again. "Thank you, Jonathan. I'm a busy man, I like it when people are straightforward and direct." He chopped the air with one hand. "So, what's this about a verbal slipup, Gary? What exactly did you say that turned Ruth against you guys?"

Gary's face reddened. "Well, I guess things were moving pretty quickly at that point, and I was nervous, so I let out the fact—I mean, I sort of implied—that Ruth had once been dead. I don't think Ruth fully understood me, but it threw her off anyway and we lost some of her trust."

Mike glowered at Gary. He pulled open the drawer he had closed at the beginning of the meeting. He lifted a couple sheets of paper to the surface of his desk. With both of his hands and his teeth clenched, Mike tore the sheets in half.

"That, Gary, was your contract with us. You are now officially out of a job." Gary bent over and lowered his face into his hands. Jonathan began to rise from his chair.

"Hold on, Jonathan, there's something more I want to say," Mike said while reaching out towards Jonathan. Jonathan sat back in his chair. Mike disappeared beneath the desk again, and once again returned with a couple sheets of paper stapled together.

"This, Jonathan, is your contract." Mike ripped this in half as well. "You have also been officially fired."

"What?" Jonathan leaned forward towards the desk. "It wasn't my fault, it was this buffoon who blew it!"

Mike shook his head. "Nope, I'm not going to divvy up the blame that way. You were both responsible for the completion of a serious task, and that task was not completed. Therefore, you both lose your jobs. Very simple logic." Jonathan held a hand to his forehead. Gary's shoulders had begun to shake because he was crying uncontrollably. Mike turned to the side and said in a quiet voice, "It's just…intolerable, just intolerable, how you spend all your life trying to get what you want and it just keeps eluding you. Something always happens that either prevents you from keeping it or even from having it in the first place." Mike's face was red and he clenched both of his fists.

Jonathan moved up in his chair. He held his hands together before him, as if he were kneeling before the statue of a holy person. "Mike, I know you're upset, but…"

"No!" Mike screamed as he slid the papers on his desk to the side. They slid off and then fluttered away in various directions. "No, you guys are both done here. I'm going to take over this operation, I'm going to talk to Ruth, and she'll listen. We can't afford to waste any more time—I mean, more and more bad stuff keeps happening!"

Mike stepped towards the two men and placed a hand on each of their shoulders to escort them out of the office. Gary and Jonathan both walked towards the door slowly, with their heads lowered. "It's been nice working with you, gentlemen, but I think it's time for us to part ways now. No, no more negotiations, it's officially over." As soon as Gary and Jonathan had crossed the threshold of his office door, Mike pushed it shut. He leaned against the closed door and breathed deeply. A curled lock of hair had fallen onto his forehead.

After a half a minute, Mike lifted himself from the door and opened another, smaller door in his office that led into a dark corridor. At the end of it, there was a white, unsteady glow. Mike stepped within this glow, which came from two rows of televisions lined up on opposite sides of the hallway. Mike halted before one monitor and looked down at it intently.

It showed Ruth alone in her room, writing. She licked her lip as she hunched over a textbook. After a few minutes of writing, she looked towards the digital clock on her nightstand and sighed.

Mike adjusted his tie, then stood with both hands in his pockets, still gazing pensively at the television screen. He was so happy to see Ruth alive, and he wanted very badly to smooth out the problems in the reversal engineering procedure that had resuscitated her.

CHAPTER 18

RUTH CARRIED A long bag full of softball equipment on her back as she walked up the hill beside the field. She called out and waved to her teammates. There was red and orange paint on both of her cheeks.

Ruth stepped onto the warm concrete of the parking lot and twisted her way out of the long black bag. She wiped some dust from her uniform and then sat on the curb with her chin in her hands. Jim had said the previous evening that he would have to be about twenty minutes late.

A flock of Canadian geese waltzed across the lawn in the outfield. Ruth watched them: the furry young waddled in the center of the flock, while the long-necked adults patrolled its outskirts. The sight stirred Ruth's imagination and reminded her of the class she had taken with Gary and Jonathan. If the geese had settled on the outfield grass during the game, perhaps someone would have hit the ball in their direction by accident so that it slammed against the soft flank of one of the younger geese. The geese, on the other hand, could have landed at a nearby pond. There, Ruth imagined, someone's misbehaving dog might have broken loose from its leash and sent the geese scattering. There was more to the geese than what Ruth saw. On some deeper level of reality, a whole host of possibilities pushed for actualization.

Ruth dug in a pocket of the bag for her watch. She turned the face so she could see it. Ten minutes had gone by since she had sat on the curb. Someone was playing basketball alone in a court on the other side of the parking lot.

Ruth had begun to draw in the dirt with a twig when she heard a boyish voice ringing off the walls of the school.

"Got a ride?"

Ruth looked up and saw the thin figure of a young man about her age coming towards her. He was holding a basketball against his side and sweat had dampened his hair.

"Um, yeah, my dad'll come in a few minutes." But the boy kept drawing closer to where Ruth sat. His features became clearer and Ruth saw the hairless, soft face of a guy who had not reached his full height. His eyes twinkled in the horizontal evening light. Ruth shifted her bag, and the boy sat at the spot she had vacated.

"I hope I'm not too sweaty for you." He grabbed part of his shirt sleeve and toweled off his face with it. "Do you go here?"

"Yeah, yeah I do. I'm a senior." Ruth began to sweep more dust off her uniform, while her eyes remained focused on the stranger's features, which had an almost feminine delicacy.

The boy stretched out a thin hand, which Ruth found was light but fleshy, like a baby's. "My name's Mike. I don't think we've ever met." Ruth smiled as she shook his hand.

"I saw you guys lost," Mike continued. He leaned back on his hands. The basketball he had been carrying rolled slightly until it rested against the curb.

"Yeah, our season's lost, too. No playoffs this year. I blew it—got no hits."

Mike slapped Ruth lightly on the shoulder. "Hey, don't hang your head. It's just a game. What, is your father real hard on you or something?" Mike leaned closer towards Ruth, so that she could feel the warmth of his breath on her neck. There were only thin, white hairs above his upper lip.

"Well, no, my father's a pretty nice guy. The other night we got into a fight, but we get along most of the time." Mike looked down at a chunk of concrete at his feet with a grave expression. Then, he looked back at Ruth with a smile.

"Everybody fights now and then. That doesn't mean you have a bad relationship with your dad."

Mike pulled at a blade of grass beside him and glanced up at Ruth. "Oh no, my dad and I are on good terms. Sometimes…I don't know, maybe you don't want to hear this, but sometimes I wish he would let me grow up." Mike's easygoing demeanor made Ruth want to confide in him. Her shoulders relaxed, and she began to speak more rapidly. "I mean, it's not good for me to have someone always making decisions for me."

"Yep, I know exactly what you mean." Mike had torn the blade of grass into tiny shreds.

Ruth enjoyed being honest with Mike. "What's your dad like? Is he pretty cool?"

"Yeah, my dad's pretty cool, too. But, hey, I've got to go home and do some homework. I actually live right across the street, in that development over there." Mike pointed across the softball field towards an array of two-storey homes on the other side of the street.

"You live there? My family doesn't live that far away from there." Mike had gotten up and was pounding the basketball against the concrete again.

"Is that right? Well, maybe we should hang out some time."

Ruth looked down at the dark pavement of the parking lot and drew a strand of hair away from her face. Her cheeks flushed, but she eventually shrugged her shoulders and said, "Sure, that sounds good. Let me get you my number."

Ruth started searching through her softball bag, and found a notepad the team used to keep track of stats. She was usually open to meeting new people and she thought Mike was good-looking. She tore off the corner of a page where she had jotted down her phone number. Mike took it and slipped it into his pocket. The sun shone on the round curve of his cheek.

Mike waved, then hopped down the hill onto the field and trotted across it towards the street. Ruth waved at Mike's retreating figure, even though he couldn't see her. Mike's boyish appearance had charmed her, and she wanted to see him again. Soon, a few minutes after Mike had disappeared, Jim pulled up alongside the curb and she began to lift her bag into the bed of his pickup.

CHAPTER 19

RUTH BROKE THROUGH the chocolate shell around the ice cream. Mike sat across from her with a banana split before him. He had put in an earring before meeting her at the ice cream parlor. It glinted against his smooth skin.

Before she had left her home, Jim had accosted Ruth in the kitchen. Ruth had smeared light blue eyeshadow on her eyelids and her lips were glossy and red. She had spent half an hour in the bathroom running a comb through her hair, even though she had told her parents that Mike was just a friend.

"Hey, Ruth, I just want to know where you're going to be and who you're going to be with." Ruth's shoulders drooped as she sighed.

"Dad, I told you, I'm going to get some ice cream with this guy Mike. He's really nice!" Ruth started to walk towards the door. Jim, though, moved with her and touched her shoulder before she had twisted the knob.

"Ruth, as your father, I just want you to know—well, I was a young man too, and I know how their minds work. Honey, you should not by any means do anything that you're not comfortable with, do you understand?" Jim held his index finger up before Ruth's face.

Ruth replied slowly with an edge of frustration in her voice. "I get it Dad, but Mike's a cool guy. We're just going to get some ice cream."

"You've only spoken with him for a few minutes. It's easy for people to wear masks." But Jim removed his hand from Ruth's shoulder and watched as she slipped underneath his arm and walked to the end of the driveway while he still held the door.

"Bye now, Ruth, don't come back later than ten." Jim waved to his daughter, and then went back inside the kitchen to peer through the window at her while she waited for Mike to come. Soon, Jim could see the thin silhouette of Mike's body through the window of the compact car he drove. Ruth lowered herself into the passenger seat and Mike backed into the street and then sped off towards the setting sun.

Ruth had forgotten about her dad while she chatted with Mike in the ice cream parlor. Soft, old-fashioned rock'n'roll came from the jukebox at the other end of the shop. A family sat behind Ruth and Mike and another couple in their twenties ate in the booth across the aisle from them. Mike was talking about the problems he was having with calculus.

"I bet you could probably do well in that class. What are your grades like, A's and B's?"

"Well, I actually get straight A's. I'm a nerd." Ruth shrugged her shoulders and smiled.

"Holy smokes, I want you to do my homework!" Mike cut into the banana with a plastic fork. He glanced out the window while he chewed. "Hey, did I see you walking around the school after class had let out one day? I'm part of the chess club and I think I saw you walking in the building around 3:30, after the buses had left. Are you, like, part of some club for smart people?"

Ruth hastily wiped a smudge of chocolate from the corner of her mouth. "Yeah, that must have been one of the days I was in this special class. I got invited to this class called "Physics of Reversal". It was really interesting."

Mike's eyes widened in astonishment. "You got selected to study that stuff? Were you the only one in the class?" Ruth nodded. "Wow, I've read a little bit about that. I guess you can, like, change things that have already happened. Because you don't like them. Complex stuff!"

Both fell silent as they spooned ice cream into their mouths. One of the kids in the family behind Mike began running up and down the aisle between the tables.

Mike lifted a napkin to his lips and wiped off some ice cream that had been smeared there. He glanced at the surface of the table, cleared his throat, then said, "Hey, Ruth, can I ask you a big favor? I…I know I may not have what it takes, but I want to join you in this class. It's just so fascinating! When is the next time you're going to meet with the instructors?"

Ruth placed her cone on the table and smiled at Mike. "You're so enthusiastic!" she gushed. "I'd love to have you come, but…I guess I won't be going to the class for a little while. My dad doesn't want me to. Something happened. I'm really sorry."

Mike's eyebrows shot up so that lines formed on his forehead. "Would you mind telling me exactly what happened between you and your dad? I mean, what an opportunity!"

Mike's eyes twinkled, and his smile showed two dimples in his round, tan cheeks. Ruth began to talk quickly. She was happy that it was so easy to talk to Mike. "Well, things were going great, I was learning so much, and then Gary and Jonathan—those were the names of the instructors—said that they wanted me to be part of this experiment. They said that they would injure me. I didn't quite get this, y'know, but things were still cool. But then Gary made this weird comment—it was like, the injury won't kill you, that's not going to happen again. I couldn't make any sense of that. I mean, was he talking about before I was born? So, then, my dad talked to me about it, and he's got this whole Bible complex, and I guess I just chickened out."

Mike's face reddened when Ruth mentioned her father. His hand shook slightly as he placed his fork onto the napkin beside his banana split. "So, basically, your dad thinks he's smarter than the experts?" Mike's smile was gone and he looked intently into Ruth's eyes. Ruth noticed the depression at the base of his neck and the tiny links of a gold necklace that passed across the muscles of his shoulders.

"Well, yeah, I mean, I still want to go to the class, but maybe I'll wait a little while." The couple next to Ruth and Mike were holding hands across their table.

"Look, I'm no expert, Ruth, in this new science, but just think of the possibilities." Mike gesticulated excitedly with his hands. "My gosh, if we can change whatever we want, we could get rid of every problem—

all the awful things in the world—hunger, disease, war, everything! This new science would make everything else people are doing pointless. I mean, why would we need doctors anymore if we could just change the fact that someone had gotten sick in the first place?"

Ruth nodded, and licked up some more vanilla ice cream from her cone. Mike continued, "If you get involved with this experiment, you might be able to help make these new developments possible. Think of it: no more cancer, no more…whatever you desire, really, no more bad food! And the cost is that you sustain an injury! Ruth, y'know people get paid for participating in these experiments?"

Ruth swung a foot under the table, and hit Mike's shin lightly. "Like, how much?" she asked as she smoothed out her ponytail with her hand.

"Thousands of dollars, Ruth! I mean, this is a no-brainer! So, are you in? I can come with you."

Ruth turned her head and looked at the entrance to the ice cream parlor before looking back at Mike and answering. "Yeah, you can count me in. Maybe I can just not tell my dad." Ruth didn't want to alienate Mike in any way.

Mike stretched out his hand, clasped Ruth's shoulder and shook it a little. Both smiled. They chatted long after both had finished the treats they had bought at the parlor. The owner had begun to turn the lights off behind the counter when they finally slid out of their booth and walked through the door. Ruth had forgotten about the agreement she had made in the intoxication of talking with Mike.

Chapter 20

Jim sat slouched in his couch and stared blankly at the television while Ruth was out with Mike. There was nothing he could do to protect his daughter. Cursing, he switched off the television, got up, and began to pace back and forth across the family room rug. Rascal was lying there, and he kicked him out of the way.

"Go somewhere else, Rascal!"

Sarah came down the stairs, and Jim stopped pacing and began to pick up some loose paper that had fallen beside the television. He didn't want Sarah to see how perturbed he had become.

"You alright, Jim?" Sarah had put makeup on and she wore a pearl necklace. She was going to attend a dinner held in honor of a coworker, who was getting married.

"Yeah, I'm fine." Jim crumpled the papers into a wrinkled ball. Sarah nodded and left the room after she had adjusted her necklace before a mirror. Jim stood before the window. Outside it was very dim and gray. Jim looked down and bit the nail of his thumb. He peered into the kitchen where Sarah had gone, and saw that she was washing some lettuce. The water from the faucet thundered down into the sink, and Jim tiptoed up the stairs.

He walked down the upstairs hallway towards his bedroom. When he entered, he swung the door shut gently behind him. He walked towards the closet. Once there, he began to sort through all the clothes and boxes on the floor. After a minute of searching, he pulled out a slim notebook with a green cover.

Jim reached into the drawer of the nightstand, and plucked out a pen. On the cover of the diary, in the middle of a white diamond

surrounded by the green, Jim had written the words, "My Diary."
He leafed through the pages, reading snatches from some of them.
He closed the notebook and clasped it in his hands. He sat pensively
for a couple moments with his fingers held against his lips, and then
padded towards the closed door of the bedroom.

Once again, he walked down the hall. There was small table
there across from Ruth's room, about a foot shorter than Jim's waist.
A vase containing a couple pink roses rested on the table, and Jim
reached down and placed the notebook behind the brilliant petals of
these flowers. He squatted and looked at the cover of the notebook:
the title, "My Diary", could be seen through the thorny stems of the
roses. He stepped back and looked at the two items on the table
for another second—the vase and the notebook—and then passed
through the hall and on to the staircase.

On her way to bed that night, Ruth saw the green notebook
on the table. She walked right past it, though. She was tired, and
when she entered her room, she went towards the bed and pulled
away the covers. The next evening, though, after she had kissed her
father and mother goodnight, she paused before the table and then
glanced down the hallway towards the staircase. She could still see
the flickering, colorful array of lights coming from the television set
and so she guessed that no one would be coming up the stairs soon.
She picked up the notebook and looked down at the words "My
Diary" on the cover. Her eyebrows lifted. Closing the door softly
behind her, she went to her desk and switched on the lamp there.

She slid her nails in before the bookmark, and opened to the
page where it rested. Ruth pulled her chair forward and bent over
her father's handwriting.

*I know this is crazy, but I think this might be the solution. Most
people think that death is just something we just have to put up
with, but this guy Mike seems to have a way to circumvent it.
If Ruth had died as an old woman after a long and happy life, I
would have let her go. But there's something very wrong about a
parent outliving their child. It's too much for me to bear, and I'm
going to take up Mike on his offer.*

Ruth sat back in her chair. She pulled a loose strand of hair, hanging around her temple, behind her ear. She couldn't make sense of what she was reading. Had she been dead at one point? Then how could she be alive now? Was her father using some elaborate metaphor—maybe to express a serious illness that she did not remember? She bent forward again, and read more.

There's this place called the realm of possibility. Mike claims to have the ability to change the events that occur in the world. He's found out the event that was crucial to Ruth dying: if this event had not occurred, then Ruth would not have died. He wants me to enter the realm of possibility to try to prevent this key event from happening. I don't know about all this—maybe it's too good to be true—but I'm desperate and I'm willing to try anything.

Whenever Ruth read the name Mike, the face of the young man she had first seen playing basketball kept appearing in her imagination. Was there any relation between the Mike her father was talking about and the Mike she had just met? She thought it was highly unlikely, and she admitted to herself that she was becoming preoccupied with Mike. But, the idea that events in the world could be changed was very familiar. This was, of course, the purpose of reversal engineering. Ruth skipped ahead a couple of pages and continued to read.

I am so glad that Ruth is back. I don't care what it took to get her here. I don't want to deal with Mike anymore, so now I'm just going to enjoy my daughter. I'm grateful and everything, but there was something discomfiting about the guy. I felt a little afraid every time I was around him. It's like he knew too much. It's like with nuclear energy: sometimes our technology can take on a life of its own and becomes too much for us to handle. But, in spite of all this, I am just awestruck by the thought that the girl whose corpse I was crying over at the viewing is now fully alive and well.

Ruth slammed the notebook shut. She covered her mouth with her hands as she yelled. With her head buried on the desk, she sobbed and pounded her fist. The new information in her father's diary was incomprehensible and overwhelming.

CHAPTER 21

RUTH WAS QUIET as she ate breakfast that morning. Sarah, sensing her daughter's discomfort, added more Lucky Charms to her bowl and kissed her head.

"Is something bothering you, sweetheart?"

Ruth's face was pale, but she smiled up at her mother and Sarah nodded and went back to pouring dog food into Rascal's bowl. Ruth pushed through the front door as her stuffed backpack jostled the lamp at the side of the entrance. She said goodbye to her mother.

Ruth went through the school day mechanically. She took notes, chatted with friends, got an exam back, and ate lunch. When the final bell rung, she cut towards the receptionist's office through the crowd of guys dressed in athletic uniforms and people lugging large wind instruments. Ruth waited as a couple teachers asked questions about forms they held before the receptionist while she read them through her black-rimmed glasses.

"What do you need, honey?" The secretary had a mug on her desk, on which the words "World's Best Secretary" were printed with large black letters. Ruth stepped closer to the woman and began to articulate her concern.

"Um…I've been going to this class after school gets out, sort of like an extra-curricular activity. It's called 'The Physics of Reversal'. I want to know how to contact the teachers. Their names are Gary and Jonathan. I have some important questions for them."

The secretary frowned. "I've never heard of that class. I mean, of course, there's just plain physics for juniors and seniors. Mr. Jamison teaches the advanced placement section. Is that what you mean?"

Ruth shook her head. Another teacher came walking past the secretary. He patted her shoulder and began to tell her something as he smiled and gestured with his hands. Ruth became impatient as the conversation dragged on and she almost interrupted it. But the teacher finally left, and the secretary turned her black-rimmed glasses towards Ruth again.

"Yeah, I've never heard of that course, honey."

"Well, maybe you have the names of my teachers recorded somewhere. I don't know their last names, but their first names were Gary and Jonathan."

The secretary wheeled over to her computer, and opened up a file containing information on the school faculty. She scrolled through the names of the teachers with the mouse, then wrote down a couple names on a piece of scrap paper.

"Alright, we have two Gary's on the faculty, and just one Jonathan. So one of your teachers must have been Mr. Seltzen and the other was either Mr. Johnson or Mr. Dirkman. I didn't know Mr. Seltzen was into physics, though."

Ruth took a deep breath. "No, the Jonathan I met was not Mr. Seltzen. This guy was really tall, and he wore glasses."

The secretary rested her chin on her hands. "I just don't know what to say, dear. The list I pulled up on the computer there has names of everyone who teaches here—even people who come from other schools to do extracurricular programs." The woman shrugged her shoulders and sipped from a bottle of spring water she kept on her desk. Ruth frowned and started to turn away while lifting her hand to wave.

"Well, thanks anyway." The secretary nodded and grinned broadly.

"No problem, dear."

Ruth returned to the din in the hallway. Through the door opening into the gym, she could see the cheerleaders chatting amongst themselves with their pom-poms on the floor. The sound of a whistle pierced the musty air in the building and the cheerleaders stirred. Ruth rested against a wall for a few moments.

She then started walking rapidly towards the glass doors at the end of the hallway. Outside, she could see yellow schoolbuses lined up along the curb. Once she was outside, Ruth looked through the crowds of students waiting for the bus. She went towards the bus that went into Mike's neighborhood. But she could not find his delicate, smooth-skinned face among the raucous crowd gathered there.

After she had had a quick snack of graham crackers and juice upon returning home, Ruth brought the phone into her room and called up Mike. After a few rings, he answered.

"Hey, who's calling?" Mike spoke harshly and quickly.

"Oh, hi Mike, it's Ruth. Am I bothering you?"

The tone of Mike's voice suddenly became gentle. "Oh no, no. I did not mean to give that impression by any means. It's great that you called. What's up?"

Ruth paused, and then ran a hand across her clammy forehead. "Um, I just need someone to talk to right now. It's about this physics class I was in. I know you're familiar with it, and I thought maybe you would be the best...y'know, person to talk to."

"Oh, absolutely, Ruth," Mike responded with enthusiasm. "Do you want to talk right now, over the phone, or should we get together somewhere?"

Ruth glanced over at the green numbers of the digital clock by her bed. "Um, can we talk face to face? It's kind of a weird situation, I guess...And, I would like to see you."

"I'd love to Ruth. How's 7:00 o'clock tonight, on the picnic tables at Dawson Park?"

Ruth smiled. "Yeah, I'll be ready. Thanks a lot, Mike!" They said bye, and Ruth turned off the phone. She lifted her legs up so that her knees covered her chin and rocked back and forth on the chair for a minute. Then, slowly, she pulled out a pencil and a textbook from her book bag and tried to do some homework.

Ten minutes before seven, she heard a car horn honk in front of the home. She was wearing a bright red tanktop with spaghetti straps, and high-heeled sandals. Jim came out of the family room, where he had been reading the newspaper.

"Where are you going, sweetheart?" Ruth was already holding the handle of the front door.

"I'm going to spend some time with Mike, remember that guy I met?" Jim's face colored, but he remained standing at the entrance to the kitchen.

"Well, alright honey, just remember to call me right away if you feel uncomfortable. Do you have your cell phone?" Ruth paused at the door and sighed.

"Yes, I do Dad. And, my gosh, stop thinking like that, Mike's a nice guy. We're just going to talk."

Ruth pushed past the screen door and trotted down the driveway. Jim moved to the entryway and watched his daughter smile as she lowered herself into the passenger seat of Mike's car. He could see Mike's dim form waving at him through the window of his vehicle. After the car sped away, Jim closed the door so forcefully that the picture of Ruth hanging beside it rattled against the wall.

CHAPTER 22

A BREEZE BLEW THROUGH the leaves of the tall trees at Dawson park. The light of the setting sun cast a warm glow on Mike's skin. Mike's hands rested on the surface of the picnic table. Ruth kept moving one of hers towards them, but a few inches before touching Mike she would pull it back and place it on her lap again.

"So, I was leafing through my dad's diary, and I read through this part that was really bizarre. My dad was saying how I had been dead, and he was attending my funeral, but then he got me back, and he was really happy about this. He kept mentioning this guy named Mike, and this place called the realm of possibility. It reminded me a lot of this physics class I took. Can you make any sense of all this?"

Mike's lips tightened. He scratched at the picnic table with a twig. "Well, yeah, that does sound a lot like reversal engineering. I mean, the realm of possibility could be the place where the different possible outcomes for a particular object can be accessed, and only reversal engineering could bring someone back from the dead. Doctors haven't figured out death yet, of course."

In the distance, someone tossed a frisbee across the long green grass and their dog bounded through it to clasp the airborne disc in its jaws. The breeze moving through the trees caused some of Ruth's bangs to float up in the air. "So, is it possible that I was once dead, and my dad used reversal engineering to get me back? That's what the diary said, right?"

Mike looked down pensively at the table. Through its cracks, he could see an anthill rising up from a patch of bare dirt. He looked aside, saying nothing.

"I mean," Ruth continued, shifting her hands on the surface of the table, "is there some way I can tell if reversal engineering has been used on…me? Some mark—you've read some stuff, haven't you?"

Mike held two fingers to his chin. He attended once more to the anthill. "Well, Ruth, it seems possible that you got this procedure done. That's what your dad wrote, right?"

Ruth adjusted the straps of her shirt and compressed her lips. "It's just hard to think about…really, should I even be here? If I was dead…" Ruth pressed her hands together and then held them against her face. Mike looked up at her, then reached out and touched her shoulder. Goose bumps formed along Ruth's forearms.

"Y'know what might be happening? Your teachers—the guys who taught the physics class—maybe they wanted you to be part of that experiment because you *have* been part of a reversal engineering procedure. Ruth, you might actually have been dead at one point."

Mike rose up in his seat and looked down at Ruth with a glint in his eyes. Ruth frowned, and brought her arms against her chest as a strong, cool wind passed by them. "Well," she said, "I guess I should be happy, but it's kind of spooky." Ruth looked down at her palms. "Without this technology, I would be buried in the ground!"

Mike stood. The sun had nearly sunk beneath the horizon, and fireflies flickered through the dim air. Mike walked over to the side of the table where Ruth sat, and she allowed him to place his hand on one of her shoulders and massage it.

"I think you should talk to your teachers," he said. "We don't know much about what is going on." Ruth leaned over, so that her head rested against Mike's slender chest.

"If reversal engineering is really true," she asked, "does that mean we're never going to die?"

But Mike didn't answer Ruth. After a few minutes of holding one another, the couple walked towards the car around the grilles and picnic tables scattered throughout the park. Mike tapped Ruth's elbow right before they both entered the vehicle.

"So, are you going to talk to your teachers? I think it would be a good idea."

Ruth looked up at Mike. "Alright, I will." Her teeth shone in the light of one of the parking lot lamps.

CHAPTER 23

A LL THE ENGINEERS waited in the assembly room. An inchoate murmur rose up to the ceiling. Some people checked their watches and looked towards the open door. After one engineer had gotten up to look down the hallway beyond the door and returned to the assembly with his hands in the air, Mike finally passed into the room, striding rapidly. He clapped his hands together as he moved towards the whiteboard.

"Everybody, quiet, please, I've got some important news to convey." The room was silent save for the squeak of the marker Mike was using on the whiteboard.

"What some of you folks could not do, I was able to accomplish. I pretended that I was one of Ruth's classmates, took advantage of her adolescent hormones, and I got her to agree to undergo the operation she needs to undergo in order streamline the process that restored her life. I also managed to continue to work at Cisco so no one there would get suspicious." Mike had been able to find times to meet with Ruth that fit into his schedule with Cisco. When he worked as an engineer in the realm of possibility, he was outside of time altogether, since time can only characterize that which exists as an actuality, and so his engineering job did not interfere in the least with his role in the actual world.

Applause began to fill the room. One engineer, still applauding, stood up. One after another rose, until the entire group had joined in a boisterous standing ovation. After a few minutes soaking in the appreciation, Mike held his hands out, and said, "Thank you, thank you, you're too kind. Thank you, but please, I would like to speak now."

When the group was quiet again, Mike cleared his throat and said, "Yes, we have made progress in this stubborn situation. But, it's not over. Ruth is going to see Gary and Jonathan again. I'm going to have to hire them again temporarily. All they need to do is to explain to Ruth the situation she is in—that she has in fact been a participant in a reversal engineering procedure, and that it has some flaws, and that she needs to have a simple operation performed to get rid of these flaws. And if she's hesitant, we can use intimidation. We can suggest that we have the power to take away her dog, or harm her mother, and even her new boyfriend, Mike!" Mike laughed and rubbed his hands together. A female engineer raised her hand.

"So, wait, if we have to use intimidation to get Ruth to agree to this procedure, then she hasn't actually agreed to it? I thought you said that Ruth had agreed to undergo the operation."

Mike's face turned pale and he unbuttoned one of his sleeves and rolled it up his forearm. "Well, technically, all I've gotten her to agree to is to see Gary and Jonathan about the possibility that she has been a participant in a reversal engineering procedure. But, there, Gary and Jonathan are going to tell her the whole story, and she's a reasonable kid, she'll let us do our magic." Mike walked towards the whiteboard and picked up an eraser from the ledge there. He began to wipe off what he had written earlier.

"Alright, class dismissed. I just wanted to share the good news with you people, but you guys are—how does the Bible put it—stiff-necked. We'll get this done, though, in spite of everybody." Mike said the last sentence under his breath. He was tense, and the muscles on his jaws flexed as he held the eraser so tightly it was bent when he put it down again.

Chapter 24

I N HOMEROOM ONE day, a student placed a note on Ruth's desk. "This came from the principal, Ruth." Ruth had been resting her head on the desk. That morning, after she had gotten up and dressed, she crawled back under the covers. The bus passed by her house without stopping because she was not standing out there. Sarah came into her room, shook her awake, and took her to school in her car. Ruth's arms looked thinner, and Sarah told her to make sure she ate enough.

Ruth flipped over the note. In cursive written in blue ink, she read the words, "Please report to classroom 304 right after the last class of the day today." Her name was printed at the top of the card. Ruth flipped through her scheduling book, and jotted down some quick notes in the slot for that afternoon. Room 304 was Mr. Snell's room. She assumed there was some issue related to her schoolwork that Mr. Snell wanted to discuss with her—perhaps a test she needed to make up, or some grammatical mistakes in a paper she had written.

In chemistry class, towards the end of the day, Ruth's teacher surprised her as she stared out of the window. He had fallen silent when he saw her looking towards the building across the grassy lot outside, and slowly approached her when her eyes did not turn towards the blackboard. When he tapped her, Ruth gasped and looked up at the teacher's unsmiling face. All the students laughed.

Later, though, the final bell rung, and once again, students poured into the hallways out of the different classrooms like the tributaries of a river. Ruth threaded her way through the raucous hordes, some of whom twisted in the combinations on their lockers, while others chatted in large clusters. As Ruth made her way up the stairs to the third floor, the crowds thinned, and the building grew steadily more quiet. As she walked down the hallway towards Mr. Snell's room, she could hear the echoes of her footfalls coming back from the smudged walls.

She peeked through the glass window in Mr. Snell's door. Gary and Jonathan were there again. Gary sat in the chair at Mr. Snell's desk. He slouched and stared towards the back of the classroom. Jonathan rested on the edge of this desk and swung his long shin back and forth like a pendulum. His eyes were focused on the floor. Ruth was surprised to see the two men in Mr. Snell's classroom, but she was pleased, too, because she had some burning questions for them. Ruth came in and took a desk at the front of the room. After sitting through a long silence with the two depressed men, Ruth finally spoke.

"So, I wanted to ask you guys if it's possible to find out whether you've been through a reversal engineering procedure." Ruth leaned her chin on one of her palms. Gary ran his fingers through his beard.

"Well, we may as well cut to the chase, Ruth," Gary said as he used some of his shirt sleeve to polish his glasses. "You have been through a reversal engineering process."

Ruth blinked, and the muscles on her throat flexed as she swallowed. Gary continued. "We know because it's recorded where we work. We know that earlier in your life, you were hit by a car while playing with your dog. Your grief-stricken father came to us with a request: he wanted to undo the accident for which he felt responsible. So, after much careful research, we performed the procedure, and here you are today. The reason we brought you in is that, even though our research was very thorough, we were not able to anticipate the difficulties that would attend your restoration. In layman's terms, Ruth, you have to go through another procedure, in which you get injured, in order—we at least hope this will happen— to remove the problems that have cropped up because we brought you back."

Ruth rested her back on the hard metal surface of her chair and pressed her palms together in front of her face, the way kids do when they hold a blade of grass in their hands and blow on it to make a sound like a kazoo makes. After awhile, though, Ruth folded her hands on her lap and asked, "What are the problems that my life is causing?"

Jonathan started to pace back and forth on the floor in front of the desk with his hands in his pockets and his head lowered. He was so tall that when Ruth looked up at his face the light from the ceiling bulbs dazzled her.

"Well, there's the girl Angela. I know you know her. Her problems were caused by the fact that she did not receive the award for schoolwork that you got. She needed that award to feel good about herself, but the fact that you remained alive meant she couldn't get it."

Angela, with the red zits running along her cheeks making her appear almost diseased, had lain in a hospital bed in pajamas with an IV pumping nutrients into a vein in her wrist. Ruth looked down at her body. She felt all of a sudden like an illegal invader that had entered and occupied a territory that was the property of others. She held her hands so tightly as Jonathan continued speaking that they became inflamed.

"Along with Angela's problems, there was the bomb threat at a ballgame that we traced back to your restoration. There was a drought in Idaho that led to the demise of some endangered species there. There was also a psychotherapist in California who contracted a rare disease by eating at a restaurant she would not have gone to had you not been restored. More data is coming in, too."

Ruth's face reddened, and she lowered her head into her hands. Jonathan stared up at the walls. His face was expressionless as he recited the facts in a dull monotone. Gary kept stroking his beard. His eyes were downcast.

"So, that's why you need to get this injury, Ruth. Things have gone a bit haywire."

Ruth shook her head. "I guess…it's good that I'm still alive. But, I'm actually not supposed to be here, am I?"

Gary pushed his bangs out of his forehead. His eyes remained lowered to the dusty floor, even as he spoke to Ruth. Mike had told the two ex-engineers that they would receive compensation for this meeting with Ruth, but after this, their services would no longer be needed. Gary muttered, "Well, you can be here, it's just that you have to go through this second operation. But who knows if *that* will work?" Gary held up his hands, then dropped them limply onto his lap again.

Jonathan sipped from a can of coke that was sitting on Mr. Snell's desk. "Yeah, but Ruth, you better get this second operation done. I mean, the people in control of this technology have quite a bit of power, as you can imagine. They can change whatever they want."

Ruth rubbed the back of her neck. "You mean...they would, like, change what's happened in my life in order to harm me?"

Gary nodded with his eyebrows raised. "Oh yeah, you better believe it. You, as well as your loved ones." He slapped a hand on the surface of the desk. Ruth compressed her lips. Tears began to collect in the corners of her eyes.

"I guess reversal engineering is good," Ruth said as she wiped a tear away by running a finger beneath one eye. "I mean...I'm glad that I'm alive, and, yeah, I'll go through this. I'll get the operation. I don't want other people to suffer."

Ruth expelled air upward from her mouth so that some of her hair fluttered. Gary and Jonathan both looked at her for a few seconds, then Gary pushed his chair away from the desk, which generated a sharp scraping sound.

"Alright, then, I guess we're done." Jonathan strode out of the room quickly, and Gary followed right behind him. Just before he disappeared behind the doorframe, he snapped his fingers to get Ruth's attention.

"Um, yeah, someone will be in touch with you about the time and date of the operation." Gary held a hand in front of his mouth as he belched. Ruth stared at the chalk-smeared blackboard after the men had left. She brought her forearms close to her chest and lowered her chin onto them. Her slim shoulders shook as her tears pooled on the surface of the desk.

CHAPTER 25

LATE THAT NIGHT, Ruth picked up the wireless phone in the upstairs hallway and took it into her room. She could hear her father snoring behind the wall, but she brought the phone under her quilt and covered herself with it. She read the numbers on the keypad in the faint green light coming from the phone. Mike answered after a few rings. His voice was hoarse.

"Hello? Who's calling?" The ringing phone had disturbed Mike's sleep.

"Hi, Mike, it's Ruth. I hope I'm not calling too late." She heard Mike yawning at the other end, then coughing with his mouth away from the receiver. There was a crackling sound as he brought the phone back up to his ear.

"No, Ruth, it's not too late. We can talk. What's up?"

Ruth was lying on her side with her knees held up close to her chest. "Well, I talked to my physics teachers about some of the questions I had, like you told me."

Ruth smiled at the enthusiasm evident in Mike's voice as he answered. "Oh, great! Yeah, I thought it was important to get that cleared up. What did they say?"

"It was pretty hard to take. That's why I'm calling you." Ruth lowered her voice when she heard someone stirring in her parent's bedroom. She saw the light from the bathroom across the hall slice in underneath her door, then the faucet began to run.

"So, were you actually a part of a reversal engineering procedure?"

Ruth sighed. "I'm still in shock, but I actually was. I really should be dead. But my dad brought me back to life with this new technology." There was silence at the other end for a few seconds, then Mike spoke again.

"Well, that's awesome, Ruth! Isn't it great to be in the modern world? Y'know, back in the day, they used to use leeches and they had no anesthetic for surgeries. Yuck! Now we can undo even death itself!" Mike laughed, and Ruth couldn't help but giggle as she adjusted the sleeve of her t-shirt.

"Yeah, in a way it's good, but it's kind of weird, too. I sort of feel that I have no right to be here."

Ruth could hear a faint voice in the background on Mike's end of the line. Mike responded to it with the phone held away from his mouth, so Ruth could not make out what he was saying. When Mike finished with this other person, he said, "Hey, Ruth, I've got to go now, but I want to talk about this some more. Can we meet sometime soon?"

"Sure!" Ruth replied, but in her enthusiasm, her agreement was too loud. One of her parents knocked on their side of Ruth's bedroom wall.

"Okay, maybe I can just come and pick you up tomorrow evening around seven and we can play it by ear—y'know, maybe get a bite to eat, or just sit and talk somewhere."

"Okay! Sounds great!" Ruth lay on her back, looking up at the dark ceiling after turning off the phone.

When Jim saw Mike's car pulling into the driveway again, he lowered his eyes and kept slowly running a washcloth over a plate covered with crumbs and red sauce. He had a growing bald spot extending up from the corner of his forehead.

Ruth walked down the driveway eagerly. Mike pressed a button on his door handle to pop open the passenger door lock. Ruth sat in the car with a glossy leather purse on her lap. Exhaust fumes rose up from the car as Mike backed it out of the driveway and accelerated down the road.

Mike drove with one hand resting on the window ledge and the other gripping a corner of the steering wheel. The heavy, sweet scent of his cologne filled the interior of the car. Soft, slow jazz streamed from the car's speakers. Ruth kept glancing over at Mike expectantly.

"So, Ruth, I don't want to talk about this with you while I drive. Can I just park somewhere, and talk once we stop?" Mike looked over at Ruth, who nodded silently.

The car began to rock as Mike drove it over the rough surface of the parking lot behind the high school Ruth attended. People rarely used this parking lot; it was next to a field overgrown with weeds and there were many chips and dents in the concrete pavement. Loose gravel ricocheted against the bottom of Mike's car. Mike came to a stop at the edge of the parking lot. The setting sun cast an orange glow on the weeds and small shrubs of the field in front of them. Mike unbuckled his seat belt and stretched his hand behind him towards the backseat.

"Here, I brought some cookies. Want some?" Ruth took a couple of the soft, bite-size cookies. "We can just sit here," Mike said after he had chewed a cookie for a few seconds. "Here, look, you can put your seat back." Mike pulled a lever at the base of his seat, and it dropped back so that he could recline. Ruth imitated him.

"So you used to be dead," Mike said with his cheek resting against the seat so that he faced Ruth. "I'm glad you're still here." Ruth laughed softly. Mike wore a necklace that glinted against his skin in the light of the setting sun.

"I don't know, though," Ruth said, as she turned her head to look through the windshield. Mike's good looks were making her uncomfortable. "Gary and Jonathan said that there were problems with the procedure I went through. Do you know this girl, Angela Thomas?" Mike said he did. "Well, I guess I made her attempt suicide. If I weren't here, she would have won that stupid prize, and felt a lot better about herself. There's other stuff, too—a drought, a bomb threat. It's crazy."

Mike almost whispered as he said, "But you have every right to be alive. You shouldn't feel guilty about being alive!" Ruth glanced over at him, then back through the windshield, which was filmed with a thin layer of dust.

"I don't know, I just can't help it. It's like—okay, this may sound silly—it's like a softball game, and I've been taken out of the game for a pinch-hitter or something, but then I go back in. It's against the rules. If we win, it would be unfair!"

Mike's face tightened and he looked away through the driver's side window. His shoulders stretched as he breathed deeply. Then, he turned back to Ruth.

"Do Gary and Jonathan have any idea what should be done about these problems—Angela, the drought?"

Ruth rolled her head on the headrest of the seat to watch a squirrel pick through the weeds and loose gravel on the abandoned parking lot. "Well, yeah. They want to me to get this other procedure. I have to get injured."

Mike sat up and leant his hand on the emergency brake. "That doesn't sound that bad. Look, this all makes sense. The fact that you're alive has consequences, just like every other change. When the engineers, or whatever they are, let your dad bring you back to life, they probably couldn't see all that would happen as a result of this change. So, there are few a glitches, and you have to go back in and see them again, just like you would see a surgeon after a difficult operation. This is a new technology—it's not perfect."

"I guess that makes sense…But, what part of me are they going to injure? I do like sports. I start soccer in the fall."

Mike paused as he noticed the blue eyeshadow over Ruth's long lashes. The sight flattered him, since it seemed she had put it on for him. Then, he slid his hand in behind her neck and rested it atop her shoulder once he saw that she was not resisting.

"Look, Ruth," Mike said softly, "I want you to go through with this—it makes sense! It's like having a side effect from a medicine. You'll get the injury, but your body will heal, and all the problems you're feeling guilty about, like Angela and the drought or whatever, will go away." Mike squeezed Ruth's shoulder with greater pressure.

Ruth bit her lower lip thoughtfully, and slowly leaned her head towards Mike. Their faces were separated by mere inches. Mike whispered, "Do it…do it for me, Ruth. Do it for us."

Mike brought Ruth closer with his hand. She yielded and Mike kissed her on the lips as he embraced the back of her head. He thrust hungrily forward and pulled harder with his mouth, then he drew himself away and watched her flushed face. Ruth smiled, and then, in a quiet voice, said, "Alright, Mike, I'll do it."

Chapter 26

RUTH WAS SUPPOSED to meet two engineers after she had finished her lunch. In the cafeteria, right after she had taken the first bite out of her ham sandwich, she pulled out the note she had gotten that morning. She had to go to room 407. Ruth was quiet around her friends that day, and did not finish the vanilla pudding her mother had placed in her bag.

Once she was done, Ruth walked swiftly down the aisle, past the backs of hundreds of kids who were talking, laughing, and littering the surfaces of the tables and benches with crumbs and empty wrappers. Ruth pushed one of the doors to the cafeteria open, and found the hallway nearly empty at this time, with the exception of a few teachers. One man with a tie and polished dress shoes had a serious face and chopped at the air with one of his hands as he spoke to a woman with her head lowered. Ruth curved past this pair towards the stairwell.

The first faint traces of moisture had coated her forehead by the time she reached the fourth floor. She looked up at the numbers posted on the opaque glass of the classroom doors: 401, 402. When she got to 407, she knocked on the wooden surface and said, "Hey, I'm here."

There was some shuffling behind the door, then silence. Ruth knocked again, and she heard heavy footsteps moving across the room.

"Coming, just a moment," someone responded in a deep, male voice. The door swung open, and Ruth saw a man whose shoulders nearly extended across the width of the doorframe. He had a thick, bony jaw, and a bald head that gleamed in the pale glow from the ceiling lights. He pointed within the classroom, and Ruth obediently stepped across the threshold. The man closed the door behind her. Ruth could feel a rush of air as it rotated quickly on its hinges. A woman with a wrinkled face, thin lips, and stringy red hair sat in a corner of the classroom on a stool.

"Alright, Ruth," the man said in his deep, resonant, actor's voice, "we're here to take you to your operation. We're going to leave right away. Do you have any questions?" Ruth looked down at the floor while touching the pink clip that decorated her hair. When she did not speak for a few seconds, the old redhead and the stout man began to file out of the room. The woman motioned towards Ruth with a weathered hand just as she was passing out the door. Ruth took a step forward to follow them, paused, then went along with the two strangers.

They led her to a small, rusty car. The cloth on its seats was ripped in different places. Ruth buckled her seat belt, and, after the engine had squealed a few times and then died, the vehicle lurched forward and started to move through the school parking lot. Air began to whip through the interior of the vehicle as the deep-voiced man sped down the highway.

The man adjusted his rear-view mirror so that Ruth's reflection appeared in it. Ruth looked at the image of his brown eyes. "Alright, Ruth, what's about to happen may seem a little strange. But you just need to stay calm for me. We are going to enter the realm of possibility, and in order to do that, we have to get rid of our current actuality." The man pressed the gas pedal harder, and, with screeching tires, the small car accelerated even more.

The red-haired woman reached behind her and pressed her hand against Ruth's thigh. "Just stay still." Ruth looked past the front seats through the windshield. Just beyond a bend in the road ahead was a short brick building. It grew closer and closer. The man gripped the steering wheel firmly without turning it. Ruth could see the muscles on the back of his neck pressing against his collar.

"What are you doing—you're going to hit the wall! Stop!" Ruth stuck her foot on the back of the seat in front of her and lowered her head against her chest. The stout man had pushed the gas pedal all the way down to the floor, and his eyes were still focused on the brick wall the car was charging towards at breathtaking speed. In a massive explosion, the front of the car blasted against the brick wall.

A shower of glass and fragments of metal sprayed up into the air as the small car crunched up like an accordion. All three passengers fell heavily forward as the car's motion ceased. The engine, which had broken into the interior of the car, thrust up against the bodies of the man and the red-haired woman, and as the side of the car slammed into the wall as well, the metal exterior of the car bent in against Ruth's body. Darkness fell over the scene of disaster.

Ruth's eyes opened again upon a bright light. Her hand immediately shot up to her face to shield her eyes. She heard shouts coming from beyond the light.

"She's awake! This wasn't supposed to happen! Who was responsible for the anesthesia?"

Ruth squinted into the bright light. With her hand, she felt a hard surface inches above her mouth. She lowered her eyes, and saw that her mouth was covered by a transparent plastic mask. She ran her hand along it and then, beneath it, she felt a ridged tube.

She remembered that she had been driving with the two people—one of them was a red-haired woman, the other a man with broad shoulders. Then, a red brick building appeared on the horizon, and they kept nearing it at higher and higher speeds. The man had said something about dissolving her actuality, but he kept aiming the car towards the building, which Ruth, eventually, could see was a post office. The collision had occurred, with the harsh din of metal pounding on brick with all the force the car had gathered as it sped down the highway.

Now, in the dimness on the fringes of the bright light, Ruth could make out the stubble-covered cheek of a man who wore a light blue surgical mask. Ruth eyes wandered upwards, and she could see his eyes glowing in the reflected light of the bright beam that shone at her with fierce directness. Ruth tried to speak, but the plastic mask stifled her words.

"Dammit, someone get the anesthesiologist in here. This wasn't supposed to happen." The surgeon brought the blade he was about to use to slice into Ruth's side towards a counter in the darkness towards his right. As he drew it there, it caught some of the light shining at Ruth and her eyes widened when she saw it. She started to tug at the ridged tube connected to the mask, but she found that the mask was strapped tightly around the back of her head. She began to roll and struggle on the hard bed, screaming into the mask.

The surgeon lifted a dark, hairy finger to some people behind him. Two men came out of the shadows around the bright light with rubber straps in their hands. Ruth was clutching the side of her bed with one hand and grasping wildly at the empty air with the other. She kicked at the two men as they approached. But, with their large hands, they held her limbs against the bed, and soon Ruth could no longer move since the rubber straps were tightly secured.

The surgeon nodded at the two men, who faded back into the darkness. The swarthy surgeon then glanced behind him and pulled down his mask to shout.

"What's taking him so long? Put her back to sleep, I want to get this operation done." The surgeon's hands were trembling slightly. Soon, a pale man with a hunched back wheeled in a tall metal cylinder with a long black tube clipped to its side. He unhooked the tube, and Ruth felt a blast of air against her mouth as a bluish gas filled her mask. She closed her mouth for as long as she could, fiercely grinding her teeth together, but she finally breathed and almost at once her head fell back onto the bed and in a few seconds her eyelids dropped shut.

The surgeon studied Ruth's face. After Ruth had lain there nearly motionless for half a minute, he turned towards the pale man with the metal cylinder and waved him towards the darkness. Once again, he brought forth the long, shiny metal blade that had caused Ruth to try to struggle free from the bed. With his hands now sheathed in gloves, he parted the flap of Ruth's hospital gown so that the flesh of her lower abdomen was exposed. With the blade, he cut deeply across her stomach for about eight inches. After he had pulled the blade out, he lifted a plastic ruler from the metal shelf beside him and measured the incision.

"Eight and three quarters of an inch," he said into the darkness again, pulling down the top of his mask to do so. "Wilson, how long does this cut need to be again?"

A voice came from the shadows faintly. "Nine and one sixteenth of an inch. It has to be exact."

The surgeon grumbled, and covered the area around his mouth with his mask again. He wiped the blade clean with a cloth and then, with the ruler positioned along the cut, extended the cut the fraction of an inch necessary. He brought his head close to it and grimaced as he gently advanced the blade.

The surgeon put aside the knife once the cut was complete. With a fresh towel, he dried the sweat that had formed on his forehead.

"What next? Some sort of fracture?"

This time, a louder, nasal voice emerged from the shadows. "It has to be at the same spot as a large freckle on the top of her forearm."

The surgeon sighed as he held Ruth's forearm and rotated it slightly. There was indeed a large, squarish freckle atop Ruth's forearm, about an inch below Ruth's elbow. The surgeon brought a metal shelf, which rested on a flexible arm, closer to Ruth's body. He also lowered it, so that it was level with the bed on which Ruth lay. The surgeon then unfolded a slender metal extension from the metal shelf. He attached the base of a vise to this extension, and placed Ruth's forearm in the jaws of the vise. He started to twist the knob of the vise, so that its jaws closed around Ruth's arm. When the jaws were clasping Ruth's arm firmly, the surgeon held out his hand. Another hand stretched out towards the surgeon's and placed in it a hammer with a heavy leaden head.

The surgeon wielded the hammer. The hand that had given it to him disappeared into the darkness. Eyeing the freckle, the surgeon brought the hammer down once slowly, and then, in a curving flash, gave Ruth's forearm a violent blow. There was a crack of breaking bone, and some blood sprang out of the forearm where the surgeon had punctured the skin. The surgeon bent down and felt the area of the blow with his thumbs.

"Alright, folks, I hope this works." The surgeon removed his mask and gloves. He turned on a nearby faucet and began to roll a bar of soap around vigorously with his hands. People in bright green scrubs came into the light above Ruth's body. They all looked at the work the surgeon had done. A murmur rose up in the room as the workers chatted. When the surgeon returned from the faucet and joined the crowd that had gathered, they all began to clap and cheer. He grinned, but when the applause died down, he said, "We just have to cross our fingers and hope that I met the requirements exactly. Mike sent some very specific instructions about how we were supposed to go about this process."

An older man walked up to the surgeon and clasped both his shoulders in his hands. Both men smiled. Then, one by one, the group began to file out of the light and into the shadows, like actors departing a stage. Ruth lay on the table. Her right arm was limp, bloody, and twisted.

Part III
Chapter I

RUTH'S ROOM WAS bright when she awoke. Pushing her heavy lids open, she twisted a little in her bed to look at the clock: ten o'clock in the morning. She yawned, and with her left hand folded back her bed sheets. When she tried to hold herself up with her right arm, though, it buckled and pain spiraled up and down it like hot, spinning needles.

After catching her breath, Ruth looked at her forearm. It was sheathed in a cast. She then remembered that a doctor had told her, after she had been wheeled out of the operating room, not to put weight on her broken right forearm. The doctor had had a lean, muscular face.

Lifting herself up with her hips this time, Ruth rested her bare feet on the carpet beside her bed. A couple frizzy strands of her hair hung before her eyes. She lifted up the bottom of her shirt a little and saw a broad bandage attached to her lower abdomen. Blood had seeped from the incision and stained the bandage.

Ruth gasped and dropped the cloth of her shirt back down so that her stomach was covered. Someone had knocked on the door.

"Hey, Ruth, it's me, your dad. Can I come in? I brought you some breakfast." Ruth ran her hand up and down the smooth surface of the cast.

"Yeah, dad, you can come in." Ruth rested her head on the pillow again. Jim crossed the threshold carrying a full tray with two plates, a clear glass of orange of juice, and a steaming bowl.

Jim laid the tray on Ruth's desk and she saw that the bowl contained oatmeal. "Now, don't make crumbs. Your mother doesn't like to do this." Ruth nodded and sat up, clutching her knees against her chest. "It's a special occasion, though, sweetheart. How's the arm and that big wound?" Jim placed his palm on Ruth's forehead, as if she were sick with the flu.

"Still sore. I need a new bandage, this one is all bloody." Ruth lifted up the cloth of her white T-shirt again and showed her father the pale red oblong on the bandage.

"Alright, I'll get you a new bandage after I walk the dog. But, first, have your breakfast. You need to eat so your body can heal itself."

Jim handed Ruth a plate full of scrambled eggs mixed in with bits of ham. Ruth ate this, then stretched out her left hand for the glass of orange juice her father was offering to her. The food warmed her body.

"That dog is going to have to be put down. Just a vicious, vicious creature. Unacceptable." Ruth peered at her dad as she sipped some of the milk in which lumps of oatmeal floated. Some medical workers had told her on her way out of the realm of possibility that they would lead her parents to believe that a rabid dog had gone after her and taken a bite out of her stomach. The dog's attack had caused Ruth's right arm to smash against the pole of a swing set as she fell.

"I called the principal and told him that you would be late for school. I let you sleep in because of the accident, honey, but I want you to be at school before lunch. Your friends are going to want to hear how you're doing and you shouldn't fall behind in your classes."

Ruth arrived in time for the last ten minutes of her calculus class. Ruth scribbled down some notes, but the bell rang soon, and textbooks started to clap shut and sneakers began to scuffle along the floor. Ruth walked slowly down an aisle between the desks. She held her right arm close to her side as students streamed around her with different speeds and postures. At the door, she nearly fell against the whiteboard when she looked up and saw Angela's chubby face.

Angela was wearing a bright green turtleneck and a necklace with a thin gold chain. Her complexion had cleared. She touched Ruth's shoulder and smiled warmly.

"Did I scare you? You acted like you'd seen a ghost!" Angela bent over and held her hand against her mouth as she laughed. Ruth, with her shoulder resting against the whiteboard, watched Angela impassively. The girl rose up and patted Ruth's back as a few people began to crowd the area around the door that Ruth was blocking.

"C'mon, Ruth, you're holding everyone up. Are you alright?" Ruth followed behind as Angela crossed the threshold of the classroom into the dim, windowless hallway. Once there was space, Angela moved to Ruth's side. Ruth's face remained expressionless as she twisted a strand of hair with her finger.

"Have you recovered yet from that awful attack?" Angela was a couple of inches taller than Ruth because of the black platforms she was wearing. Angela reached towards her neck and adjusted her necklace while shaking out her flowing hair. The improvements in her appearance made her look pretty.

"Not quite. Not yet. How are you?" Ruth touched Angela's shoulder, as if she wanted to make sure that the girl was real. Angela smiled again.

"I'm great. I've got a new boyfriend!" Angela hugged her notebooks, which she was carrying in her arms, against her chest and twisted her hips so that her backpack shook a little. Ruth walked more slowly. Angela looked at one of the clocks protruding from the wall above the lockers.

"Hey, Ruth, I've got to run. It was great talking to you. Take care of yourself, though. Go to McDonald's or something. Chow down, you look thin!" When Angela waved, Ruth saw a gold bracelet that matched her necklace radiate twisting light. Ruth had stopped walking, and, her face grayish, she looked down at the scuffed hallway floor.

The people in the realm of possibility had told her that the operation had been successful, but Ruth was watching the news one day and saw a picture of an old woman she knew. She had seen Mabel walking around the neighborhood often with her frizzy white hair emerging from a broad sunhat with a flowery trim. Ruth sat up when she saw a picture of the old woman. She pressed her hand against her father's knee as the broadcaster described the situation.

"Yesterday morning, police, after looking through Mabel Darling's home, have classified her as missing. Her neighbor noticed that, for three nights in a row, her living room light was on.

The neighbor called the police, who are now saying that there will be a reward of fifty thousand dollars for anyone who can disclose information about Mrs. Darling's whereabouts. Mrs. Darling was an eighty-two year old widow who lived alone. She attended weekly bingo at the local senior center."

Ruth leaned back on the soft cushion of the couch and sank into it deeply. Her shoulders were lax, almost as if she had fainted. Jim looked over at her and placed his broad hand on her shoulder, covering it. Ruth's skin was clammy and cold.

"We know that old woman, don't we, Ruth?"

Mabel lived two blocks away from the Morrisses. A couple days a week, Ruth would see her from her bedroom window. When it was windy, Mabel pressed a gnarled hand atop her head so that her sunhat would not fly off into someone's yard. When Ruth was out when Mabel walked past, Mabel would stop, reach into her pocket, and pull out a mint or a piece of hard candy for Ruth.

"Of course I know her…That's awful, I wonder what happened to her." Ruth got up and moved among the living room windows. She peered through each one, as if she hoped to see Mabel wandering around the backyard. Colored, crisp leaves nestled in the corners of the windowsills. "Can we go look for her, Dad? There's a lot of weirdoes out there."

Jim held a deck of cards in between his hands. He split the pack, pressed the two halves of the deck together to shuffle the cards, and then split the pack again. "Sure, honey, we can go look for Mabel. Tomorrow, though, alright honey? Daddy's tired."

Ruth circled back and forth between the windows again. Then, she went back to the couch and sat with her hands on her thighs. She clutched a blanket from the corner of the couch and tossed it over her legs. She was wearing shorts, and there was a cool breeze that day. She looked in the corner where Rascal was resting on his bed. The dog expelled a puff of air from his distended nostrils and cocked an eyebrow as he looked at Ruth.

"I just feel…" Ruth breathed deeply as well while she looked down and frowned. Noticing Ruth's discomfort, Jim sat up from the couch, where he had been reclining with his hands clasped behind his head.

"What do you feel, honey? You can tell me." Ruth looked at the plaid shirt that covered her father's broad chest. She breathed in the heavy, dusty smell that always clung to his clothing because of his work at Cisco.

"I don't know...I guess it's hard to describe. I guess I just feel out of place." Ruth relaxed and let her body drift towards her father's. Jim wrapped his arm around Ruth's neck and they sat silently until the yard outside was dim.

"Alright, time to take Rascal outside," Jim said as the dog came up to sniff his feet.

CHAPTER 2

J IM'S HAIR WAS still wet from the shower he had taken that morning as he and Ruth walked down their block. They looked among the bushes beside which Mabel would often walk.

"Mabel only does two things, Dad. Go to the grocery store and then Thursday night bingo. There was no sign of a break-in at the home, so the kidnappers must have snatched her away somewhere out here." With her left arm, Ruth picked up an old sandwich wrapper lying on the sidewalk. She unfolded it and picked through the limp pickle and crusty ketchup.

"Ruth, put that down, that's filthy." Ruth dropped the wrapper and continued to survey the yards around her, as well as the bases of the trees and the dark interiors of bushes.

"You never know, Dad, maybe there's a piece of Mabel's long white hair in the wrapper. Maybe we could get a DNA sample from it—the kidnapper could have eaten from it." Ruth dashed across the street in front of a car. The driver slammed on the brakes and swerved onto the sidewalk. The man hit his horn hard and held it for four or five seconds. His window floated open, and he stuck his face out to talk to Jim.

"Hey, would you watch out for your daughter?" When Jim saw the rocking nose of the brown, old Cadillac plowing towards Ruth, he stopped moving, as though frozen. He stood silent and erect for a few seconds. Then, fluidity returned to his limbs and he rushed towards Ruth.

"No, Dad, I want to keep looking," Ruth said to her father, who was bending over her while holding her shoulder tightly. Jim was shaken up by the near accident, and wanted Ruth to go back home.

But, he stood up and held his hand against his chest while breathing deeply.

"How many times do I have to tell you to look both ways?"

Ruth, who had walked a few feet in front of her dad, turned her head to the side and shot back, "Yeah, it's like an obsession."

Jim watched as Ruth parted the thin, stiff branches of a bush and stuck her hand into its insides. She stretched her good arm and her muscles tightened as she grabbed hold of something. With her foot pressed against the base of the bush, she pulled out a misshapen sunhat.

"Check this out, Dad! I think it's the hat Mabel used to wear!"

Jim hurried over to Ruth. He held the brim of the baseball cap he had been wearing in his hand. Both he and Ruth inspected the coarse twine from which the sunhat was made and then Ruth ran the fingers emerging from her cast along the flowery band wrapped around the hat's top.

"It's got to be Mabel's. Dad, we've got to take this into the police station. There have to be fingerprints on it!"

The day had grown steadily brighter. A couple joggers had passed Ruth and Jim as they looked over the hat. "I guess we better," Jim said. "It does look like Mabel's."

Ruth and Jim went back to their driveway. Ruth, in her enthusiasm, trotted about twenty feet ahead of Jim. She kept stopping and waving towards Jim to encourage him to move faster. Jim grimaced and held a hand against one of his kneecaps as he ran.

"Ruth, I don't want you aggravating your injuries, you better slow down," Jim said in between long breaths.

Ruth kept up the rapid pace, though, until she stood beside her dad's pickup truck parked in the driveway. She waited outside of its passenger door. When her dad was near, she started pulling at the door handle.

"Unlock it, Dad. We're wasting time!"

The engine of the pickup started to churn and rumble. The chassis quaked. Jim began to maneuver the vehicle through the tree-lined, quiet streets of Blackmun, through which bands of sunlight were slicing.

Ruth saw that her dad was focused on the road, and she pulled up her shirt a little. A broad red stain had formed on the new bandage Jim had attached to her stomach this morning. Ruth clicked her tongue and frowned, but she dropped the flap of her shirt and brought the hat further up her lap. She looked out the window and saw that they were only a few blocks away from the police station.

Two receptionists sat before computers and telephones at the station's front desk. After waiting behind a very tall man who wore a suit and tie and held a briefcase in his right hand, Jim and Ruth approached the dark-haired woman who had beckoned them towards her.

"How can I help you folks?"

Jim stepped aside so that Ruth faced the receptionist.

"Hi, we've been gathering some evidence about Mabel Darling, the old woman who disappeared. Um, we're pretty sure that this is her sunhat. We found it in a bush." Ruth slid the sunhat forward on the counter. A stout man walked behind the receptionist and sorted through a stack of papers. When Ruth spoke, he put aside the papers and looked at her. The stout man adjusted his glasses as he ambled towards her.

"Hey folks, I'm Detective Arnold." The detective's fleshy hand engulfed those of both Jim and Ruth. "Folks, I really commend you for getting this evidence for the Mabel Darling case, but that case was solved late last night. We discovered that a couple of hoodlums were keeping her tied up in a deserted warehouse. They were hoping to get a sizable ransom. They're now behind bars."

The detective looked at Ruth and Jim with piercing, cold blue eyes. Ruth, with both her hands resting on the black counter before her, asked, "Is Mabel alright?"

"She's got some bruises where the ropes squeezed her body. The kidnappers wanted her well enough to plead with her family over the phone." The detective thrust his hands in his pockets and rolled some gum around with his tongue. "Psychologically, though, Mabel's pretty scarred. She keeps saying no one would bother an old lady back when she was young. She thinks society is going bad, which it probably is."

Ruth tightened her lips and held the edge of the black counter more firmly. "Can I see some pictures of the kidnappers?"

The detective frowned, checked his watch, then shrugged his shoulders. "Sure, I can show you. They're a couple of beasts, that's for sure."

The detective swung open the door of an office in a hallway behind the counter, and after a minute, came out with a couple of glossy photographs. He held both of them upright on the counter.

"Here they are." Jim glanced towards the entrance of the station and placed a hand on Ruth's shoulder, tugging it a little. Ruth moved closer to the counter, though, and stood up on tiptoe to see the grizzled faces of the two criminals. These two men had seized a thin, helpless old woman, driven her off in spite of her weak cries, and restrained her with ropes to get money. The corner of one man's mouth hung open beneath a broad, lined forehead and heavy-lidded eyes. The other man had a sunburn except for around his eyes, where he must have been wearing sunglasses. The white circles there looked clownish.

"Thanks," Ruth said with a somber look on her face. The detective nodded, and Jim arced his hand through the air.

"Thanks, detective. Nice work catching those scum." The detective was already walking away and had half-disappeared behind a door in the interior of the station by the time Jim waved. Once he had, Jim and Ruth turned back to the entrance and strolled into the parking lot. Ruth hung her head and dragged her sneakers along the concrete.

"What's wrong, kiddo?" Jim stuck his finger underneath Ruth's chin and lifted her face towards his. Ruth's eyes were moist and red.

"It's...just, it's just those men. Why did they have to pick on an old lady?" Jim ushered Ruth into the pickup by pressing his hand lightly between her shoulder blades.

"That's the way the world is, Ruth. Creeps have been around since Adam and Eve." Ruth wiped at the corner of her eye with her forearm and shook her head with such a subtle motion that her father did not notice.

CHAPTER 3

AFTER SCHOOL HAD ended, Ruth was walking past the basketball courts on her way to soccer practice. She was wearing high white socks and black shorts. With her left arm she carried a clipboard that held a stack of papers. The pounding of a basketball on concrete echoed against the school wall, and Ruth looked towards the courts. Mike was there shaking a guy's hand. The other fellow held a set of keys in his free hand that sparkled in the sunlight.

Ruth kept walking over the parking lot. She stepped over an oily puddle that had formed in a rainstorm that morning. No one was on the soccer field yet, except for a man rolling a cart along that painted white stripes on the grass.

Ruth looked back towards the parking lot, and she saw that Mike was alone. The guy who was shaking his hand had disappeared into his car. Mike trotted up to the hoop and spun the ball off the backboard. The ball caromed off of the backboard into the net. It silkily threaded its way back into Mike's hands. Ruth stopped walking and placed the clipboard on the gray, rough curb. She started to jog towards Mike. When Mike saw her coming, he stood still and faced her with his arm holding the ball against his side.

Some of Ruth's soccer teammates, who were just exiting the school, leered and then giggled as Mike kissed Ruth's cheek when they were close to one another. Ruth looked into Mike's eyes and smiled. Delight radiated from Mike's features. Ever since the kiss in Mike's car, Ruth and Mike had both agreed to be in a relationship. Mike had developed a genuine interest in her after spending time with her for a while.

"It's good to see you, Ruth." Mike stroked the part of Ruth's hair that hung below her shoulders. Ruth motioned towards a bench alongside the basketball court and Mike followed close behind her.

"What's going on?" Mike stretched his hand behind Ruth's back and hooked it around her shoulder. Ruth leaned into Mike's side. Her voice was low, almost a whisper.

"Oh, nothing much." Mike rubbed her shoulder. She was looking down at the pavement and stroking her chin.

"Are you recovering well from the operation?" Mike touched Ruth's cast lightly with his fingers.

"I'm still in pain. It'll be a few weeks before I can participate in practice again. Right now I'm just helping with keeping score and handing out water."

Mike looked off towards the squat brick school building and then back at Ruth. "That stinks, definitely." The chatter of Ruth's soccer teammates rose up from the field like the sound of a disturbed flock of birds.

After sitting there silently for a moment, Ruth spoke again while looking back towards the field. "I've got some other problems, too."

Mike brushed some dust off of Ruth's soccer uniform. "Like what?" Ruth noticed how Mike's hand was much more tender and frail than her father's imposing masculine hand.

"Did you hear what happened to Mabel Darling?"

"Yeah, I heard. Poor woman was kidnapped. They say she's at the hospital. But it's just because the doctors want to keep an eye on her because she's still shaken up from what happened."

Ruth breathed heavily, and then spoke with more volume and speed than before. "It's great that she's alright, but that kind of thing never used to happen around here. I just can't shake the feeling...that it's my fault. I shouldn't be here." Ruth's mouth curved downward and tears began to form at the corners of her eyes. Mike ran his hand up and down her spine, but there was some frustration in his voice.

"No, Ruth, things like that happen all the time. They've always happened. It's good that you're still alive. Creeps exist!" Ruth moved closer to him, so that she could feel his heart beating through his chest.

"No, nothing that creepy! I mean, Mabel was this sweet old lady! I've…just put things out of whack. The faces of those men—they were just heartless!"

Mike leaned closer to Ruth and listened to every word she said. He saw the fuzz on the slender curve of her neck and her musical girl's voice inspired compassion in him. Mike said, "No, don't think that way, you have every right to be alive. Look, you're in good hands. We—I mean, those people know what they're doing. That kidnapping is related to other things, not you. It's not your fault!" Ruth lifted her eyes up towards Mike and grasped his hand. His eyes were soft and vulnerable. A smile began to form on Ruth's lips.

"Yeah, I guess it's better being alive than in some cemetery." Ruth looked toward the field as the sound of a coach's whistle broke through the air. She pressed the bandage against the base of her stomach to secure it. "Look, Mike, I've got to run. It was great talking to you. Yeah, creeps are everywhere, I guess." Ruth walked away towards the slope that led down to the soccer field. Her eyes were still shiny from the tears as she raised her arm high in the air and waved. Mike waved back and, when Ruth had disappeared behind the hill, looked down at his clasped hands and sat on the curb pensively for a few minutes.

That night, Ruth lowered herself into bed gingerly: she held her right arm tight against her side as she rolled onto her left arm. She grimaced when she bent down to pull up the covers—a spear of pain shot up from the still bleeding wound on her abdomen.

She sighed, though, and wrapped herself in the covers. Warm air floated up from the ventilator on the floor beside her bed and her breathing soon became steady and deep. She stirred, though, when her father's voice, distorted by the wall, passed into her room.

"We just don't have the money for another one, Sarah. Look, Ruth is going to start thinking about college soon. You have to be patient."

Ruth heard her mother responding in an indistinct whisper. Cringing again, she inched herself to the edge of the bed, and walked stiffly over to the wall. She placed her ear against its rough surface. Her mother's voice became clear.

"Why can't you earn a promotion over at Cisco?" The bedsprings creaked as Jim shifted his position.

"Even that wouldn't do it, Sarah. Repairs need to be made to the house, Ruth is going to need a car pretty soon, too. You're going to just have to cool it!"

Sarah's voice rose in volume. Ruth pressed her ear against the wall. A bolt of pain electrified her right forearm when she knocked it against the edge of her dresser.

"I just want to hold another infant in my arms again, Jim. It's been so long since Ruth was little. I feel like I'm slowly becoming dispensable."

"I know, I know. Look, we're going to make this work, it's just going to take some time."

Her parents fell silent. As sweat slid down her cheek in a shiny band, Ruth pulled herself away from the wall and slid her feet along the carpet towards the bed. She lay on her stomach, with her face buried in her pillow.

Her pillow cover soon became warm and moist with drool. Ruth envisioned the baby brother she had always wanted. In her imagination, she clasped his hands as he tottered along the carpet with tentative, crazy steps. When he had made it across the living room, Ruth tousled his newly emerged hair. Later, when Ruth's brother was bigger, he and Jim would have a catch on a summer evening. Ruth and Sarah would watch on lawn chairs as the white ball arced across the backdrop of trees irradiated by the setting sun. On fall and winter evenings, Ruth imagined her brother studying with his tongue curled around his lip, writing out equations and essays.

Ruth rolled onto her back. Her nightgown was damp with sweat and the blast of air coming from the ventilator was uncomfortably hot. Ruth kept checking the time on the digital clock beside her bed: there were still hours until morning. She got up to use the bathroom. In the mirror, she saw that her hair was disheveled and there were faint red lines in the whites of her eyes.

CHAPTER 4

RUTH WAS VERY distracted during school the next day. She was quiet while eating her snack once she got home. She left three crackers and a slice of cheese on the kitchen table, and pulled herself up the stairs before her mom had returned from the laundry room. Sarah's singing in this barren room echoed tinnily off the machines and pipes there.

Ruth pulled her door shut all the way and walked over to her desk. She twisted the knob of her desk lamp with her left hand. She opened a notebook under the light and began to write in it. Ruth paused often, with the tip of the eraser on her lip, to think.

From the realm of possibility, Mike watched Ruth on a TV monitor. The image was black and white, as well as shaky. His face lightly flushed, Mike rested his hands against the edges of the monitor and held his face close to the screen. With his fingers, he brushed away some dust that had accumulated over Ruth's image. Mike titled his head as he watched the girl. There was a dreamy look in his eyes.

Mike noticed that Ruth was writing. He pressed one of the buttons on the side of the screen. The camera zoomed in, so that the image of Ruth steadily began to dominate the screen. Mike could eventually see, over her shoulder, the page on which she was writing. He tapped the button by the side of the monitor a couple more times so that he could read Ruth's words.

Mike frowned as the words formed.

Hello Mom and Dad. I know this hurts, but I want to you to know that you are better off without me. You may not understand, but you should not be upset about what I have done. It is the right choice, and you will be happier because of it.

Mike tore down the hallway. As he ran, he pulled off his blazer and loosened his tie.

"Scott, Scott, I need to be sent down, right away!" Out of a nook in the hallway, a man with a large gut and a cigar in one of his hands emerged. He pulled from his pocket a small rectangular box with two long wires hanging from it. There were metal clips dangling from the wires. Mike lifted his chin so that his neck was exposed. Scott attached the two metal clips to the skin on Mike's neck and then turned a dial on the box. All of Mike's body began to shake violently. His eyes rolled back into his head. He gasped repeatedly, and then, his legs having become rubbery, crashed upon the floor. Scott put some cloth from his blazer over his hand and checked Mike's scalp for blood.

Ruth was writing her name at the bottom of the page she was leaving for her parents. She stopped writing, though, when her cellphone rang. She lay the pencil down and lifted the phone to her ear.

"Hello?" Ruth said in a soft voice. She had paused before picking up the phone.

"H-hey, Ruth, it's Mike." Mike spoke quickly and slurred his words. Ruth could hear his shallow, frequent breaths as he waited for her to respond.

Ruth's eyes ran over the note she had been writing. She reclined in her chair, and brushed a thread of hair away from her forehead while sighing. "It's good to hear from you, Mike."

"Hey, Ruth, I just wanted to know if you had any free time. I mean, would you like to get some ice cream or something?"

Ruth wiped away some red fragments her eraser had left on the notebook open before her. "You mean, like, right now?" Ruth's eyebrows rose when she asked the question. Something metallic crashed to the floor of the kitchen. Ruth suspected Rascal was climbing onto the counter to get some food left there.

"Yeah, right now. I'd like to hang out with you."

Ruth fell into a pensive silence. After a few seconds, she flipped the notebook shut. "Yeah, I can come. I guess I can be ready by the time you get here."

Mike responded in an awkwardly loud voice that crackled through the phone. "Great. I'll be over there in a second."

Mike drove so fast that his tires skidded sideways a little when he turned into the Morrises' driveway. When he stepped out of the car, Jim noticed that Mike had buttoned his shirt wrong. He had drawn the second button from the top through the hole meant for the top button. Jim's face grew pale and serious as he watched Mike again through the kitchen window.

Mike smiled at Ruth when she got into the car. He placed his hand on her knee and rubbed it, while he managed the steering wheel with one hand.

"How've you been?" Mike asked. He removed his hand from Ruth's knee and then patted her shoulder.

Ruth pulled down one of her sleeves, which were decorated with colorful, shiny sequins. "Pretty well, I guess." Ruth's face was expressionless as she watched the rough concrete of the road pass under the vehicle.

"What do you want to do? Get some ice cream, pizza, watch a movie maybe?"

Ruth was silent for a while before saying in a shy, scarcely audible voice, "I don't know."

Mike decided to head for the deserted parking lot where he and Ruth had first kissed. Loose gravel rattled and clicked against the undercarriage of the car as Mike pulled into the lot. Time had corroded its lines into faint fragments.

When he had put the car in park and turned the engine off, Mike rotated his body to face Ruth.

"Ruth, has something been eating at you?"

Ruth's face reddened, and she gave a small nod. She brought her fist to her eye and rubbed it.

Mike leaned closer to Ruth. "What—is it about the operation? Aren't the injuries healing?" Mike frowned as he looked over at the cast on Ruth's right arm. Some friends had written notes in magic marker on the cast.

Ruth lowered her head and tears began to drip from her eyelashes. She turned towards Mike and embraced him. After a few moments, Ruth pulled herself from Mike and said, "I've been doing some bad things."

Mike nodded, and wiped a hand across one of his eyebrows. Ruth's face tightened with grief. "I…I was going to kill myself, just now."

Both stretched towards one another, and embraced each other more tightly than before. They rocked back and forth, and Mike kept whispering, "No, no," while stroking the back of Ruth's head.

Finally, they separated, though they still looked into each other's eyes. Mike swallowed heavily and bit his lower lip.

"Ruth, I think it's time for me to share something with you." Mike's grave tone made Ruth frown.

"What?" Ruth fingered some change in a cup just behind the emergency brake.

"This will hurt, but you'll be better off once you know."

Ruth's lips twisted. "Tell me."

The muscles on Mike's forearm tightened as he gripped the door handle. "Ruth, I'm not really a high school student. I actually do…I actually do what Gary and Jonathan do. I'm part of the realm of possibility."

Ruth stared blankly at Mike.

"Look, let me explain. I've only been leading you on like this because I care about you. I've been part of your life for a while now, Ruth, and I've been starting to feel like I want us to keep being close."

Ruth leaned forward in her seat and pressed her hand against a ventilator. "Wait, slow down. You've been leading me on?"

Mike shook his hand in the air, denying the accusation. "No, no, don't get me wrong, not in a malicious way. Look, let's take this one step at a time. I work in the realm of possibility. I'm a reversal engineer, not a high school student."

Ruth leaned back slowly until her shoulder blades rested on the hard car door. Her forearms were folded across her chest.

"So, as a reversal engineer," Mike went on after Ruth had maintained a tight-lipped silence for a few moments, "I knew what happened to you. I knew that, when you were eleven, you were struck by a car and killed. But, we helped your dad bring you back. Then, we found that restoring you led to other problems around you and in the world. Angela, the bomb at the stadium, the drought. What we concluded when we looked into the situation was that we had to injure you to prevent these bad consequences from happening. That was why I disguised myself as a high school student—I wanted to coax you into getting the operation you needed. I lied because I care."

A strand of Ruth's hair fell from her head and hung over her eye. She did not pull it back into place. She had shifted in the seat so that she looked straight through the windshield. Her expression was blank and her body was still.

"Ruth," Mike said while nudging her shoulder, "I didn't want you to have to be the cause of all kinds of evil in the world. I also don't want you to kill yourself. That's why I'm telling you this now. There's nothing wrong with the way things are calibrated now—I should know, it's my job. There's nothing to feel guilty about."

Mike lowered his hand gently onto the cushion of Ruth's seat after saying this. He watched Ruth, but she was totally still except for the rise and fall of her chest as she breathed. Mike faced the steering wheel and turned the keys. As the engine roared and its rumbling shook the interior of Mike's chest, he said, still looking out at the shoddy parking lot, "I want to put you at ease, Ruth. You're not the source of bad consequences anymore. All that was rectified after the surgery. You can live the rest of your life in peace."

CHAPTER 5

S ARAH OPENED RUTH's bedroom door the next morning, letting in a triangle of light from the hallway.

"Ruthie, time to wake up," Sarah said to the dark mound underneath the covers. When the mound remained still, Sarah walked across the bedroom and rocked Ruth from side to side with her hand.

"Ruth, Ruth," Sarah said, more firmly this time, "it's time to get up, I've already given you an extra ten minutes."

Ruth rolled onto her back. She blinked a couple of times while staring up at the ceiling. Then, directing her eyes towards her mother, she said in a tired voice, "I don't feel well, Mom. Can I stay home today?"

Sarah sat down on the bed and tested the warmth of Ruth's forehead with her hand.

"You don't have a fever, though, honey. Are you sure you want to miss class?"

With her left arm resting limply upon the bed, Ruth nodded before a yawn rose up in her throat and stretched open her mouth. "I feel really bad, Mom. I don't want to throw up on anyone."

Swirls of hair flattened upon the sheet radiated from Ruth's head. A faint smile flashed on Ruth's lips and disappeared. Sarah laughed and, in a whisper, said, "Alright, honey. I'm going to go to the kitchen to get you some ginger ale."

After an hour or so, the sounds of the sink running and closing doors subsided. Jim and Sarah had both left for work. A glass of ginger ale with ice cubes floating in it, as well as a bowl of red jello, rested on the nightstand beside Ruth's bed.

Ruth, wearing a long white nightgown, shuffled out of her room and down the stairs. When she got to the living room, Rascal padded up to her with his tongue lolling out and his tail wagging. Ruth walked over to the couch and sat down before wrapping her arms around Rascal's neck.

Ruth switched on the television. The shrill music and the bright colors of a cartoon came on, but Ruth watched it with glassy eyes. Often, her eyes wandered away from the television to another part of the room: the computer to the right of the couch, the stack of magazines on the coffee table. Rascal climbed up on the couch and stuck his nose into Ruth's lap. Ruth bent over and pressed her neck against the dog's furry side. She scratched Rascal underneath his chin, and then picked up a discolored tennis ball from the floor. Rascal's head perked up and he riveted his eyes on the ball. Ruth tossed it to the other side of the room and Rascal bounded after it.

Ruth rose up and left the living room without turning off the television. She walked with her eyes on the floor as she thought about what Mike had said. The scrawny guy whose boyish face had drawn her turned out to be a person with a mysterious profession trying to deceive her, allegedly out of concern for her welfare. Ruth glanced at Rascal gnawing on the tennis ball in the corner of the living room before disappearing up the staircase.

She sat in the chair before her desk and propped her feet up on its wooden surface. Her notebook was on her lap, and she flipped through its pages. Her eyes fell again upon the suicide note she had written. After a few moments of abstraction, her hand darted towards the top of the page and she tore out the note and crumpled it in one motion. She then hooked her arm behind her and sent the note flying into the trash can.

Ruth walked along the soft carpet of her bedroom towards the window. Rainwater dribbled down the pane. The sky was gray, and the branches of the trees jerked in the wind. Ruth bent over with her hands covering her face. She rested her forehead on the windowsill, and her back shuddered as she wept.

Mike watched Ruth on the TV monitor. When she began to cry, he leaned back against the wall with his hands in his pockets. Pulling his hair over the side with his hand, he looked down the hallway, which went on without a visible endpoint. He spoke to someone hidden in another hallway branching off from the one where Mike stood.

"I'm going to wait for the right time to talk to her again. I gave her a lot to deal with. I want to give her time to process it all." Mike rolled some gum over to the other side of his mouth.

The sound of footsteps came from the other hallway, and a throaty voice said, "Sounds like a good plan."

Mike rattled some change in his pocket. His eyes passed from the still sobbing Ruth to a poster above the television. The title above the poster read, "Outline of Comprehensive Upgrade". There was a complex diagram on the poster, with flashing lights connected by small lines and labels in tiny font at various points. Mike took a couple of steps towards and tapped it with his knuckle.

"The upgrade must continue, Charlie. I think Ruth is going to be fine, but there are a host of other problems demanding our attention. What a cruel way to plan out a planet."

Charlie emerged into the main hallway. He carried a wrench in one grease-stained palm. "I totally agree with you, boss. Things were so much worse before you got started."

Mike nodded. He had withdrawn his hands from his pockets and placed them on his hips. "Something else has been on my mind, too, Charlie. This Ruth—I think she might be a welcome addition to our team here. I…I really like her."

Charlie had pulled a rag from his pocket, and was wiping off the stripe of grease marring his palm. "I trust your judgment, boss. You call the shots here."

Mike looked down again at the image of Ruth on the television screen. She had sat down on her bed. Ruth was pulling back the covers and arranging the pillows so that she could go back to sleep. Mike tapped his finger on the television screen. "I just need to make her comfortable with the whole reversal engineering process. Take away her fear and guilt about still being alive, then she'll see how effective what we offer can be."

Mike fell silent and clasped his hands behind his back. Charlie watched his profile for a couple of seconds, and then moved back to the hallway where he had been making some repairs.

CHAPTER 6

RUTH STARTED GOING back to class, and lost herself in her schoolwork for the next couple of weeks. After these two weeks had passed, Ruth sought out Mike after the end of another day at school. She looked from side to side as she wandered through the hallways and then out near the athletic fields. She saw him by the basketball courts with his backpack on and wearing a baseball cap. He was chatting with another girl. Ruth walked more quickly so that she could catch up with him. When the girl peeled off and Mike was alone, Ruth cut into the crowd moving down the sidewalk to Mike's side.

"What are you still doing here? I know that you're not really a student." Ruth held some textbooks against her chest. She was wearing a white sweater with gold buttons along its sleeves.

"Oh, my, Ruth, c'mon, let's go over to this table and talk." Mike tried to guide Ruth with his hand, but she stepped out of his reach. Mike shook his head. They both lowered their backpacks to the ground when they got to the table. Ruth sat down quickly and looked at Mike with an intent glower.

"I need some answers. I've got plenty of time. What the hell is all this business about leading me on about?"

Mike picked at a splinter of wood jutting up from the table. His lips were pursed. "I just wanted to prevent from having a miserable life, Ruth, with all kinds of bad consequences associated with it. Your dad didn't want you to undergo the operation you needed. I thought that I would try to cajole *you*. I couldn't just tell you about all this outright—it'd freak you out. So I had to do some pretending."

Mike had risen from the bench while speaking. His voice rose, and he thrust out his hand to emphasize his points.

Frustration twisted Ruth's cheeks into swollen, red knots. "You were my boyfriend. You were cute, and it was normal, not some trick played by a mad scientist!" Ruth threw up her hands in disgust. Some students walking past the pair leered at the couple and snickered amongst themselves.

Mike pressed two fingers on Ruth's shoulder and steadied it as it heaved with each breath she took. "Ruth, lower your voice, c'mon. I'm not a mad scientist. The ideas that I'm introducing are new, but they're very practical. Look, you died at the age of twelve in a car accident. We took an interest in you and saved you. It wasn't a clean process, but we fixed the problems through the surgery. Now you have to move on with your life!"

Ruth remained silent. Her mouth was slack and she wiped some tears running down her cheek with her palm. Mike clasped her hand and leaned paternally towards Ruth. "Look, just hear me out. The whole reason I got into the reversal engineering business is that the world is just plain messed up. There's no rhyme or reason in the things that happen. It's like some sadistic moron is in charge of it. There's war, famine, poverty, racism, car accidents, kidnappings." Mike extended a finger for each item in this litany of ills. "And my colleagues and I decided that we didn't want to put up with it anymore. God is dead, Ruth. Now we're in charge, and we're making the world a little better each day." Mike's voice thinned to a whisper as he said this. He gripped Ruth's arm gently. Ruth lowered her eyes to the pocket knife carvings decorating the surface of the picnic table.

Mike peered earnestly at Ruth's face. "We're remaking the world, Ruth. You're just one piece of the puzzle. But, I also think that you're special. I wasn't just pretending to like you. I think you could support me, Ruth. It'd be nice to have you by my side." Mike rose from the picnic table and sat next to Ruth's slumped body. She was inert while he slid his arm behind her shoulders and wrapped her against his side. With his free hand, Mike cupped Ruth's delicate jawbone. Suddenly lunging towards her, he pressed his lips against hers and probed deeply into her mouth with his tongue.

Ruth tried to tear herself free from Mike's embrace, but he held her firmly. He kissed her thirstily, stifling her cries. Finally, he released her and leant back, breathing heavily. He wiped some shiny saliva from his lip. The buses lined up along the road before the school had long since departed.

Ruth planted her elbows on the picnic table and held her hands against her ears, as though to deafen herself. "Get the hell away from me, you creep." Mike twitched forward in surprise and reached out for Ruth's shoulder again. But, moving frantically, Ruth extricated her legs from the picnic table bench and began to lope away across the freshly mown school grounds. Mike turned on the bench to watch her departing figure.

Ruth avoided Mike for the next couple of weeks. When walking through the hallways in between classes, she walked along the row of lockers with her head bowed, swiftly passing in the midst of the obscure and confused stream of people. After school ended, she left with the same determined, single-minded gait, fixated only on getting home.

Ruth, though, ran over in her mind what Mike had said at the picnic table. A new inspiration began to fill her like an energizing elixir. Mike had disclosed to her the full scope of his project. Ruth paused one evening over the front page of the newspaper tossed slantwise on the kitchen table. Her eyes scanned the stories about the economy hemorrhaging jobs, the suicide-murder of the pregnant teenage girl, and the new disease being spread by a queer-looking foreign bug that had found fertile breeding grounds in parts of Missouri. She pictured Mike in front of a computer, typing in input for some algorithm that would magically reverse the daily losses of the world. The evil situations described in the newspaper got better because of Mike's efforts, as if the pieces of a broken vase scattered along the floor were to suddenly start dancing in the air and begin to reassemble themselves.

Her heart had broke a week ago for the slender, soft-spoken young man down the street who had hung himself from a pipe in his basement after confessing to his parents that he was gay. His father's rage had boiled to the point that he flipped tables and made dents in the wall by hurling knickknacks from the mantel. With reversal engineering, one could rewind these dark scenes and reposition the figures so that the outcome was different. It was like the kid who switches some of the pieces on a chessboard while his father is away in the bathroom. Solve the problem by going back to before it happened.

One night Ruth sat up on her bed and held her knees up against her chest so that a puddle of moonlight encompassed her entire body. Her skin was pearly in the pale glow of the moon. Reversal engineering made every problem temporary. She pictured herself in a white lab coat, ordering around technicians while she pointed at a flow chart. Here was a path by which she could leave her childhood home and her parents' restrictive guidance, and rise up to higher levels of prestige and power than she had thought were possible for her.

Her meditation complete, Ruth fluffed up the pillows and slipped under the bedcovers. She closed her eyes, but before she fell asleep, a firm resolution had formed in her mind.

Just as school ended the next day, Ruth was the first to exit her classroom. She strode quickly through the empty hallway before the hordes of kids burst forth through the doors. She headed for the basketball courts.

Mike was there again. He stood out of bounds holding a ball above his head and trying to thread it through the waving arms of the defender. Ruth trotted eagerly up to the chain-link fence around the court and pressed her face close to the metal wires. Shadows of diamonds checkered her face.

"Mike, hey Mike!" she cried and beckoned him towards her with her hand when he noticed her. Mike tapped the sweaty shoulder of one of the guys he was playing against and told him he had to talk with Ruth. He removed his white sweatband as he walked across the concrete surface of the court.

"Hey, hey, what's the occasion? Get a good grade or something?" Mike held his arms akimbo. Ruth grabbed his hand and led him towards the picnic bench where they had talked before.

After they had both sat, she began, "I've been thinking about what you said, Mike. About reversal engineering. And...and I decided I want to become one." Mike's face lit up and he leaned towards Ruth's side of the table.

"Ruth, that's great," he exclaimed and embraced her. Both beamed, as if they had just agreed to get engaged. Slowly, they released one another and Mike returned to his half of the table.

"What made you want to do this all of a sudden, Ruth?" Mike asked with a smile. The other basketball players had begun to play again, and the sound of the dribbling ball reverberated across the school parking lot.

Ruth was still beaming. "Well, first of all, there's a lot of problems in the world I want to fix, and reversal engineering is a powerful tool for doing that. And, secondly, if there are problems resulting from one engineering procedure, they could simply be corrected by another procedure. There's really nothing to lose."

Mike pounded his fist on the picnic table. "Exactly. Reversal engineering has the ability to refine its own processes. So, some bad consequence of a procedure can be corrected by another reversal engineering procedure. No problem. Oh, Ruth, there's so much good we're going to do." Mike pushed back some sweaty bangs that were clinging to his forehead. He looked up at the blue and deep sky rising behind Ruth. "The diseases we'll eradicate, the droughts we'll reverse! The possibilities of improvement are just endless. We'll take charge of the world ourselves, and erase all the unpleasant stuff." Mike held Ruth's fragile hand in his. "And we'll make sure you get educated by the best professors in the realm of possibility. You'll know so much about reversal engineering that, once you're done, you'll be second-in-command to me. Both of us'll be calling the shots!"

Three guys in baggy jeans stopped to stare at the rapturous couple. Mike and Ruth both pressed their palms together and laced together their fingers. One of the guys started hooting while pumping his fist, and the other two in the group soon joined the chant. Mike looked over towards them and detached his hands from Ruth's. His face was pale and the smile left it. He frowned at the guys with the ragged, long hair.

Chapter 7

THE CONDUCTOR WAVED his baton and the assembled tubas, trumpets, and clarinets began to play the stately melody of "Pomp and Circumstance". Ruth, along with a long line of other graduates wearing black gowns and caps with yellow tassels, walked proudly towards the stage. Mike handed out diplomas from a basket he was holding. Ruth remained standing beside him once she had gotten her diploma while the other graduates sat down in the rows of wooden chairs behind the podium. Ruth bent the flexible arm of the microphone extending from the podium downward, so that it was level with her mouth. She had grown three inches since she had entered the four year reversal engineering program in the realm of possibility.

The restless crowd became still as people saw that Ruth was waiting to address them. When the silence was nearly complete and thousands of rapt faces were turned towards her, Ruth began to read from some index cards with a stately rhythm and overdone articulation.

"In the beginning, there was total chaos, a realm of possibility that was absolute and unbroken by actuality. Nothing was; there was only that which could be. The Creator existed, but we cannot say that He was actual because He never transitioned from possibility to actuality. The Creator never did not exist, so He exists on a higher plane than anything else in the universe, as an actuality that is not associated with any possibility. For reasons we do not fully understand, since the Creator could not ever need or even desire anything since He was complete in Himself, the Creator decided to establish order out of the infinite unrealized possibilities that existed. He fashioned the basic realities of light, matter, and atoms. These he then arranged into the fantastic array of natural phenomena we all marvel at: wetlands irradiated by swathes of red light streaming from the setting sun, and savannahs where proud lions roam. To complete His creation, the Creator created people, those beings that share in the Creator's nature by being able to fashion from possibilities actualities that are both beautiful and functional. We can take the raw material of trees and turn them into homes, channel the mighty but random flow of rivers to generate electricity that counters the daily onset of darkness, and streamline inchoate ideas into organized, focused messages. We can turn the indefinite into the definite just like the Creator." When Ruth said this, she held her fist against her chest, showing her pride in the power of humanity.

Mike watched from a seat near the front of the stage with a pleased expression. Ruth paused to twist the cap off a bottle of spring water she had put on a shelf within the podium, sipped it, and then proceeded with the narrative.

"As human beings began to experience the world in which they were destined to live, they started to see how inhospitable and hostile to them it could sometimes be. Some of us questioned whether there was a Creator because of the flaws that were evident in the way the world had been designed. We saw how the ground beneath us, ordinarily so massively still, could shake violently so that our homes crashed down upon our heads and killed those whom we loved. The ocean would send out towering waves that assaulted the shore and inundated whole cities, devastating their infrastructures in a colossal, malicious blow. We noticed flaws in ourselves as well. Instead of being united in cooperative efforts to achieve prosperity and wellbeing, we would often become antagonistic, refusing to change our stances to accommodate others. We would often resort to killing, which always led to great grief afterwards. In short, the beauty in the world was overwhelmed by the more prevalent evils: natural disasters like floods, hurricanes, and tornadoes and then our own failings, which resulted in broken relationships and, on a large-scale, wars."

While Ruth listed the errors of the Creator, Mike held his forehead with his hand and closed his eyes, as if to block out an ugly sight before him. He shook his head, and then raised a wan face back up to Ruth when she began again.

"A group of people looked at the world's disasters and concluded that things could be better. Other people criticized this group, saying that they needed to accept these ills and that they did not know how to properly construct a world. This other camp argued that people had no right to judge that the world was defective, since we had only a limited amount of information at our disposal. We had no right, therefore, to make judgments about it. But, the other camp, from which this whole prestigious school was formed," Ruth spread her arms out over the assembly, "insisted that things needed to be set straight and they used their ingenuity to come up with ways to correct the situation. After painstaking research and inquiry, they first found ways to harness the power of nature to preserve human life. They formed medicines from the chemicals of the world and used the power of explosions to create automobiles that could make travel more convenient. This went on for awhile, with more inventions proliferating all the time to make life safer and more comfortable. But, then, closer to the current period, we discovered a more powerful way to keep the forces of evil at bay. In fact, with this method, we can completely eradicate evil from the entire globe! This method is called, as we all know very well, reversal engineering!"

The people in the assembly, all clad in gowns and caps, rose to their feet and broke into cascades of applause. The roaring ovation continued as Ruth walked over to where Mike was sitting, wrapped her hands around his and then bowed with him twice. Then, Ruth walked with an elegant, slow gait back to her place at the podium. The excited buzz of thousands of conversations slowly died down after Ruth had stood with her elbow resting on the podium for a couple of minutes. She continued.

"With the onset of reversal engineering, we can now access the layer of possibilities behind the actualities that form our world. Once there, we can pick and choose which ones we prefer. Instead of having to endure whatever the Creator sends to us, we can eliminate an actuality merely by bringing a contradictory possibility to realization. I was once dead from a car accident!" Ruth shouted the last sentence and spread out both of her arms to the side again. Once again, the crowd roared in affirmation and rose. They applauded Ruth's openness. Ruth spoke through the noise, and the assembly eventually fell silent. "I was once literally dead at the age of eleven because of a car accident. Without reversal engineering, my life would have been cut short before I ever had to chance to cultivate my talents, find love, and raise a family. My parents would have been heartbroken for the rest of their lives. Now, this situation, and millions of others like it, can be remedied!"

Ruth stepped away from the podium, and then to the side. Her high-heels added a couple of inches to her height, and she looked regal and beautiful up on the stage. As waves of applause rolled towards her from all sides, she bowed while holding her diploma in one fist. After a few bows, the ovation intensified as she waved to the crowd and left for the one open seat in the row of chairs behind her. In observance the strict conventions of the ceremony, Mike rose from his chair the moment that Ruth sat down.

He held his hand before the people in attendance in an attempt to silence the buzz of conversation and ongoing applause. It grew quiet finally, and Mike became aware of the full force of his nervousness. With Ruth's graduation, he was ready to take on new challenges. For the four years during which Ruth had been studying, he had dreamt of the brilliant conquests they would share in the near future, while at the same time growing more and more deeply in love with her. Now, this new chapter in his life was set to begin.

He moistened his dry lips with his tongue and started to speak. "My fellow engineers, future leaders of the new world, I want you to embrace a great plan I have been working on for four years now." Mike paused as murmurs of surprise and wonder swelled up from the crowd. "Humanity has suffered for too long under the clumsy governance of the Creator. We shouldn't have to put up with the flaws in His blueprint, and we're going to completely assert our independence from the Creator from this point forward. We've made some inroads so far, but after this gathering, I want to make a final, overwhelming push so that reversal engineers have complete control over every event in the world! And to do that...and do to that," Mike had to shout over the loud, spirited agreement of the engineers, "I'm going to delegate some of my duties as president of the realm of possibility to a special person. Ruth, why don't you get up again!" The sleeve of Mike's gown flapped in the air as he waved towards Ruth. Ruth rose, and stood with her eyes lowered to the stage floor, as if she felt unworthy of the honor that Mike was about to bestow upon her.

Mike pulled a small box covered in gray velvet from his pocket. He positioned himself in front of Ruth so that his back faced the crowd before the stage. He lowered himself to one knee, and, raising a beaming face to Ruth, who was already quivering with excitement, asked her if she would marry him.

Ruth was speechless, so she just nodded and Mike rushed up towards her and locked her in a fierce embrace. A couple professors seated on the stage pulled out handkerchiefs to wipe away tears. Mike and Ruth hugged in the afternoon sun for a long time and lost themselves in the joyful anticipation of their future together. After they separated, Mike held Ruth's hand up so that people close enough could see the large jewel on the engagement ring he had purchased. A couple young male engineers in the front row started to bark out comments at Mike as he stood by the side of his new, lovely fiancé.

"Way to go Mike!" one said before whistling with two fingers in his mouth.

"You damn stud!" the other said while giving Mike a thumbs up and winking at him.

Mike didn't pay attention to these cheers; instead, he kept his gaze fixed towards the rear of the audience and smiled broadly.

Part IV
Chapter 1

MIKE ADJUSTED HIS wet swimming trunks as the waiter placed a glass of wine with a cherry floating in it on the small balcony table. Ruth sat opposite him, wearing a long, elegant white dress and taking in the sight of the bright blue ocean beneath the balcony. Mike and Ruth were on their honeymoon.

Mike watched Ruth through the lenses of his sunglasses. Her skin had tanned after a few days in the tropical paradise where they were staying and she had slimmed down before the wedding and her figure was still svelte. She was so different, both physically and mentally, from the timid, indecisive girl she had been when he had first met her.

"Our future is so bright, sweetie," Mike said. He stretched out his hand and stroked Ruth's forearm. She rolled around an ice cube in her mouth. Mike unbuttoned the top button of his shirt and leaned back with his hands behind his head. "What glorious weather we're having!"

Ruth waved to the waiter and told him that he could leave for the time being. "And to think, honey, that, if it's bad, we can go ahead and change it!" Mike and Ruth clasped hands above the table and laughed.

"We have great power at our disposal, Ruth, great power for goodness and progress towards a better future." Mike picked up a bunch of grapes from a bowl on the table and began to pluck them and pop the glossy globes into his mouth. The couple sat in silence for a couple minutes. A gentle breeze caressed their hair and the waves kept rolling in to the shore in a steady, hypnotic rhythm.

"Well, it's quarter to five, I think we ought to start thinking about dinner." Mike rose up and placed the half-eaten cluster of grapes back in the fruit bowl. He stood and waited for Ruth, who was staring out at the ocean while the breeze dragged some of her hair towards the corner of her mouth.

"But, Mike, it's still the afternoon. We've talked about this already, it's very odd that you would want to get ready for dinner this early!" Ruth finally said after Mike had stood watching her with his hands in his pockets and his chin sticking out sternly. Mike sighed with exasperation.

"That's the way we did things growing up. My dad had to wake up early in the morning for his job at the post office, and so we ate rather early. That's the way life should be—early to bed, early to rise."

Ruth had deferred to Mike's unusual eating habits so far during their honeymoon, but earlier that morning she had resolved to put up a fight. She wanted a compromise, so she got up and thrust her index finger in the air as she spoke. Mike could see the faint blue line of a vein running down the pale skin beneath her forearm. He reflexively inspected her upper arm, to see if fat was collecting there.

"But, Mike, I don't like having to be so efficient! I mean, we're on vacation! Look, at least we can set up a schedule where we can have dinner at your time on some days and on other days there can be more flexibility." An old man sitting on the balcony just below Ruth and Mike put his book aside and peered up through the gaps in the wood above him.

"Okay, Ruth, let's not let this get out of control, we're on our honeymoon. How about today I grab something to eat for myself right now and you can wait until you feel ready? I'm really hungry. Then, tomorrow, I promise, I'll wait until you're ready to eat. Tomorrow is your day to run the show." Mike held out a hand in supplication and hoped Ruth would accept his plan.

The color slowly left Ruth's face and her shoulders drifted up and down as she took a couple deep breaths. "Okay," she said, mollified. "That sounds good, honey." She walked over to Mike, looking directly into his eyes, and began to kiss him hungrily on the lips. The old man below them had stood up and was squinting as he watched them so the sunlight wouldn't block his view.

After the long kiss, Mike closed his eyes and savored the lingering sensation of Ruth's lips. "No, dear, let's not forget the great future that lies ahead. We're not going to squabble, like so many other couples."

Ruth suddenly turned to the side and looked down the long stretch of golden sand extending all the way to a jetty in the distance. She pressed her hand against her mouth as her shoulders began to shudder with laughter.

Mike moved towards her and clasped her hips with his hands. "What's so funny, Ruth? Tell me what you're laughing about!" He began to tickle her sides and Ruth bent over in the fit of giddy laughter.

When she was able to speak, Ruth said haltingly, "It's…just occurred to me, Mike, that…if we do fight, we can always go back and make it so it literally never happened."

Mike slowly sat down, and looked pensively at the mound of apples, peaches, and grapes piled sumptuously in the fruit bowl at the center of the table. A small smile formed on his lips. He chuckled softly, and he said, "Yes, we are quite blessed, aren't we, dear?" With that, he got up and walked into the hotel room. He was going to make himself a ham and cheese sandwich. Later on, in the kitchen, Mike agreed to accompany Ruth to dinner at the hotel restaurant when she got around to going, but he said he would not have anything to eat.

Chapter 2

MIKE SAT ON the couch in the living room of the home he and Ruth had just purchased. The couch, as well as a coffee table in front of it, were the only pieces of furniture in the room at the moment. More pieces would be coming in a moving truck within the next couple of days. Mike had a pen resting behind his ear, and there was a notebook opened on the coffee table.

"Ruth, are you done in there? C'mon, we have to do some planning." Ruth was in the kitchen cleaning up the dishes used for dinner. It was five o'clock. Traffic was heavy on the highway outside the home as people poured back into the neighborhood from work.

"Just a minute, Mike." Dishes rattled as Ruth placed a stack of them back in the cupboard. The cupboard door slammed shut, and she walked into the living room with suds from the dishwater still on her forearm.

"Ruth, you missed those." Mike pointed at the suds, and Ruth returned to the kitchen to wipe them off with a towel.

With Ruth sitting beside him in a pink T-shirt and jeans, Mike plucked the pen from behind his ear and tapped Ruth's knee with it. "Alright, now is the time to start planning out what we want to accomplish with our reversal engineering expertise. You start. What problems would you like to tackle?"

Ruth rested her chin on her hand and looked out the window, where a man was walking down the sidewalk while holding his small daughter's hand. Ruth felt sad for a moment as she reflected on how far she had come since the days when her father Jim towered over her and held her tiny hand.

"Well, I think the first thing we should tackle is obvious. It's the most evil, sickening thing, really, and it would be the first thing that came to most people's minds if you asked them what they wanted to fix. I'm talking about the Holocaust. I mean, millions of beautiful people gassed or shot. Let's fix that."

Mike wrote in the notebook. He looked up, and stared vacantly at the blank wall. He chewed the tip of his pen while he thought.

"I like your ambition, Ruth, but I think we're in a situation right now where we can't take on a situation of that magnitude. To reverse that situation, we would have to conduct years and years of painstaking research. What are the implications of preventing just one of those people from dying? Maybe the prevention of one death could lead to another, even worse genocide. I mean, remember what happened when we restored you?"

Ruth felt faint and slightly nauseous as she thought about the Nazis piling dead bodies in mass graves. "Just out of curiosity, Mike—why would the Creator allow something like the Holocaust to happen? I don't buy any of that crap about how events like that are essential for some grand, ultimate goal. There was something I heard when I was little—history is like a giant tapestry, and each event is supposed to be part of this beautiful tapestry, no matter how horrific it is. What nonsense!"

Mike bit his lower lip in chagrin. "I completely agree. That's why we're doing what we're doing, that's why we have reversal engineering. Because we're impatient with the way things are, and we think things can be done a hell of a lot better than the way the Creator is doing them." Both Ruth and Mike fell silent as they grew absorbed in their own thoughts. Mike finally said, "Alright, let's get back on track. Great idea about the Holocaust, but it's got some feasibility issues. Got any other ideas about things we can change?"

Ruth pinched some of the flesh on her chin between her fingers. "Okay, this is on a smaller scale, but it was no less of an atrocity. Different in quantity, but basically the same in quality. The school shooting a few years ago in Oregon. Some kid was getting bad grades and kids were making fun of him, so he gets hold of a gun and kills a bunch of the students. The town in Oregon was so bucolic—y'know, a town where everybody knows everyone else— that they were totally unprepared for something like this, and all these precious young people end up dead. Like I would have been, were it not for reversal engineering. These kids were going to do great things, get married, have jobs, make the world better. Their families were absolutely crushed with grief. It's really sickening, just sickening. Can we tackle that?" Ruth pressed her fingers lightly against Mike's elbow as she asked the question. Shaken by the memory of the shooting Ruth had described, Mike placed his hand on Ruth's shoulder and began to massage it with a gentle, circular motion.

"That'd be more doable. You're right, it's like the situation we had with you. Kids who don't even get a chance to blossom. So much potential wasted. But..." Mike's voice trailed off, and he swallowed down some saliva that had collected in his throat.

Ruth leaned forward and slapped Mike's shoulder lightly. "But what? Do you have a better idea?"

Mike got up and Ruth saw how some of his hair had fallen onto his forehead and sweat had broken out on his cheeks. He leaned against the bare wall. Ruth consoled herself with the thought that they would have pictures to hang eventually. "There's just so many situations we could address. It's hard to choose. But there's one in particular I've been thinking of. It would be a good way to gain some experience and work out some kinks in our procedures. Back in the 80's, there was a plane that crashed during a blizzard over the Rockies. When emergency personnel came to the crash site via helicopters after the storm had died down, they were able to deduce that the people had not died right after the crash. Some had managed to survive the impact of the plane smashing against the mountainside, and so they passed away in very painful ways, like hypothermia or starvation. There were even some rumors of cannibalism. In any case, it was a horrific situation. Could you imagine dying of starvation? The horrific, maddening hunger you would feel?" Mike's face twisted in disgust. Ruth moved forward, so that she sat on the edge of the couch.

"I like that idea, Mike." She tilted her head as she brushed some of her long hair off of her shoulder. She flashed a broad smile at Mike. He looked handsome standing in the shadows. Mike, sensing her admiration of him, bent over her and kissed the base of her neck.

"That's what we'll address, then.," Mike said after a long kiss. "The plane crash in the Rockies."

CHAPTER 3

RUTH GRABBED HOLD of a handle jutting out from the side of the chopper as a surge of turbulence rocked the craft to the side. She had never been in a helicopter before, and Mike placed a gloved hand on her shoulder to reassure her. Through a small window, Ruth could see the peaks of the mountains, and below them, vast plantless and snow-covered fields. Ruth was encased in a thickly padded parka and she had a pair of goggles and a ski mask in her lap.

Mike tapped the leather jacket of the pilot sitting in front of him. The pilot nodded without taking his eyes off the vista of the mountain peaks thrusting themselves in the air. "We're about there, right?" Mike had to shout over the constant roar of the blades. The pilot nodded again, and gave a thumbs-up to both Mike and Ruth. Mike patted Ruth's knee and said to her soothingly, "Hang in there, the flight's nearly over." Ruth's face was pale and her arms were folded on top of her stomach. She had been complaining of nausea ever since the first hour in the helicopter had passed.

Ruth clutched the handle on the side of the helicopter tightly again when the flight of the craft slowed and it hovered above one mountain. There was a relatively flat spot beneath them where the helicopter could land. The pilot began to lower the craft down to this area, and Ruth nearly screamed when another draft running up from beneath them caused the helicopter to sway. Ruth could see the blade of the helicopter tilting precariously outside her window. But the pilot held the steering wheel firmly, and soon he had planted the vehicle solidly on this remote spot constantly buffeted by chilly gales and buried in snow.

"Put on your ski mask and goggles, Ruth," Mike said with his eyebrow cocked in warning. "You can get frostbite out here very quickly."

A team of engineers had already begun to work at the site of the plane crash. They had set up flares to demarcate the area where so many people had taken their final breath. They all stood watching the helicopter, the blades of which were spinning more and more slowly. The side door slid open, and Mike and Ruth stepped out, wearing large goggles, heavy light blue parkas and orange ski masks.

The other engineers stopped whatever they were doing and pushed through the heavy snowfall to gather around Ruth and Mike. The couple stood beside one another, erect and proud, conscious of their status as leaders of the realm of possibility. A gust of wind swirled past Mike. It sent circling flurries of snow around his head. He exchanged glances with Ruth and then, facing the crowd, spoke through the walk-talkie embedded within in ski mask.

"Greetings to all. I hope, and it seems like, the work here is progressing well." The other engineers and technicians switched on their walkie-talkies after reaching within their long, brightly colored jackets. When Mike's voice had finished crackling through their earpieces, they all nodded. One of them stepped forward and addressed Mike.

"This is definitely the crash site. The archivists who were tasked with finding the latitude and longitude of the site did their job, sir. We found sections of the wing buried under heavy rocks and snow and there's long indentation in the soil that we were able to uncover where the plane crashed."

Mike folded his arms across his chest and nodded. "Alright, good work so far. Continue to analyze the soil for chemical content, keep looking for body parts and fragments from the plane. We need as much information as possible about this crash. That way we can, hopefully, eliminate any bad consequences that may occur as a result of the reversal engineering procedure we're going to perform."

The engineer who had stepped before the crowd nodded and then returned to his group of subordinates. He rattled off orders to the cluster of hooded figures. Mike looked at Ruth and touched her shoulder. His hand was encased in a thick woolen glove.

"I'm going to talk to these people some more. I feel I need to jumpstart this mission. Just stand behind me and show your support." Mike feared that the dreary cold on the mountaintop, and the constant reminders of the tragedy that haunted it, would sap the morale of the engineering team. He clapped his hands, even though the heavy gloves and the whipping wind muffled any sound he made.

The crew noticed Mike was ready to talk again, and for the second time they milled and trudged through the snow to form an audience before him. Ruth dutifully stood behind Mike, clapping when he had completed a point and occasionally resting a hand on his shoulder while smiling.

"My fellow engineers, I fear that your spirits may flag in these harsh conditions. I therefore want to explain a few things to you. I want to tell the story behind the shards of wings that you're picking up, and the traces of the decayed human flesh that you're detecting in the soil here." All the engineers watched Mike through their goggles. They forgot everything except for the compelling voice ringing in their ears.

"There are two people in particular I want to tell you about. Both of them died here. One was named Miguel Montanez. He ran Mexican restaurant chain in Texas. He was travelling up here to visit his daughter, who was in a doctoral program in Colorado. Miguel never was able to get an education, but worked like crazy in the restaurant business and made enough money to send each of seven kids to college. His restaurants were known for serving the tastiest burritos in the entire state. These burritos were so renowned that one day the President, while on a reelection campaign, stopped by one of Montanez's restaurants to sample one. This was a good family man, a hard-working man who just wanted to visit his daughter. When the plane ran into the blizzard that was raging here on that fateful day in 1987, Miguel lost the bright future he was entitled to—a future of seeing the success of his children and watching his grandkids grow up. His children lost the support of their father. Some of them had to drop out of college, because all of a sudden money was tight, and take over the restaurant business themselves."

One of the engineers lowered his face into his hand. Mike could hear staticky sobbing coming from this man. He was pleased that his speech was eliciting such a strong response.

"Another individual was Michelle Fenton. She was an architect, and she was engaged to be married. The wedding would have occurred three weeks after the crash. Her fiancée was so devastated after hearing the news that, after six weeks of talking with psychotherapists and trying different antidepressants, he was found hanging by a rope from a pipe in his basement. Along with the collapsing frame of the plane, then, were whole futures, whole lives, that collapsed as well. That's why we're here, ladies and gentlemen. To wrest back what people like Michelle and Miguel deserve."

Mike looked toward Ruth inquiringly. He wanted her approval, and she gave a slight nod, accompanied by a smile. Satisfied, Mike lifted his legs through the deep snow towards the cluster of engineers and technicians that had been listening to him. He took in the scene around him. To his right, there was a tent that housed the equipment used to test the soil. Near one of the flares, there were two other large, broad tents where the workers slept, rested, and ate meals. After Mike had finished speaking, a female engineer plodded over to a tractor; once she started it, it began to shoot out snow from behind. It gradually revealed ridged, rocky soil. A young male technician, with a pale freckled face, was digging carefully through the exposed indentation in the mountainside where the plane had crashed.

Everyone was grim and intent as they worked on the cold mountainside. Canisters of oxygen were stacked in a plastic bin near the two large tents, and workers frequently had to walk over to the bin to pump oxygen into the masks they held over their faces. Mike and Ruth had separated and were inspecting different areas of the project. Mike walked over to the edge of the indentation. He visualized the crazy flight of the plane through the air and the violent crash as it exploded into a brilliant flower of flame and black smoke. Then, the survivors, prostrate on the snow, wearing only street clothes and surrounded by the dead bodies of other passengers and feeling their hopes die within them. The cold embraced and thoroughly penetrated them like a devouring ghost. Mike imagined their blackened fingers and bluish lips.

Mike looked up when he noticed the young technician in the trench carved out by the plane quicken the pace of his digging. The freckle-faced technician bent over and dug at the soil with his fingers. Mike drew closer to him, hoping to get a better view of what had caused the technician's excitement.

Mike saw a couple white ridges in the soil where the technician was pushing it away. The soil was hard and dense from the cold, and the young man crouched to pull at the dirt with greater force. He exposed more and more of the white ridges. They protruded in rows, and formed arcs above the hard soil. Mike drew nearer, realizing that it was unmistakable that he was seeing part of a human skeleton. The technician had climbed out of the indentation, shaken by the grim sight. He looked over at Mike, who nodded to acknowledge that he understood the technician's distress. Mike waded through the snow towards the edge of the indentation and pensively stared at the bones.

"You see how awful it is," Mike said through the microphone hooked up inside of his ski mask. The human remains stuck in the dirt mesmerized him. The technician frowned at Mike, wondering what he meant. "Y'know, I mean death. A rich, complex person becomes as simple as a stone, some sort of object. It's just too stupid to tolerate." Mike kicked some snow into the gash in the ground. After a few more seconds of reflection, Mike walked rapidly towards the encampment. He nearly pushed the young technician aside in his haste. He began to bark out orders to a group of engineers standing idly around the large tents.

CHAPTER 4

A COUPLE WEEKS later, after the team of engineers up on the mountain had gathered pages and pages of data, Mike sat in a spacious room in the building where he worked and scribbled down numbers on a huge sheet of paper that stretched across the entire table. The sheet was covered in fine print, as well as charts, graphs, and diagrams. Mike, Ruth, and their subordinates had tried to track down all the events that led up to the crash in the Rockies, and, on top of this imposing task, all the events that depended on this crash. Their calculations were recorded on the large sheet. Mike was writing on a small blank space on the sheet. He was putting the finishing touches on the project.

While he punched the buttons of a calculator, Ruth walked in carrying a steaming mug of tea. She placed the mug in front of Mike, then immediately stood upright and looked out the large window beyond the other end of the table, which revealed the rough gravel and faded yellow lines of a parking lot. She stood there silently. Mike exhaled audibly, and laid his hand upon the table surface.

"Ruth, I have to work. I've got an urgent matter to attend to!"

Ruth still glared out at the parking lot. "It's not that, Mike, I just don't agree with your conclusion. You can't solve the loss of innocent human life by taking away more innocent human life."

Mike pushed the calculator so that it slid down the sheet towards the middle of the table. The feet of his chair ground against the floor as he lifted himself upright. "Here, want me to go through the logic again! No, really, let me start at the other end of the table here and take you one by one through all the circumstances preceding the crash." Mike had walked towards the other end of the table, and was thrusting his index finger at various diagrams and passages of fine print.

Ruth's shoulders relaxed and then hung limply. She looked down at the floor with hurt eyes and held her hand against her forehead. "I don't know Mike, if that's the only way we can fix this crash, then maybe we shouldn't do it at all." She shrugged her shoulders. She looked tired and defeated.

Mike's face showed pain and shock. "Look, Ruth, we have to be persistent. Yes, it looks like at least ten people are going to have to die because of this rare strain of the flu we're going to have to invent. But thirty four people died in the plane crash. The lesser of the two evils here is the people dying of the flu."

Ruth sat down in the same chair that Mike had been using. "But, then, the cycle will repeat itself. The loss of those ten lives will have ramifications throughout history. Children will be without parents, and someone with two brothers will end up with none. Who knows how this will play out over time? You just can't win this game, Mike." While her elbow rested on the table, Ruth leaned her forehead against her hand. Mike turned ashen and he walked somberly over to the window.

With his back facing Ruth, he said in a flat monotone, "You've given up hope in reversal engineering, then."

Ruth sighed and started to massage her temple with one of her hands. "No, of course not, Mike, don't say things like that."

Mike spun around and Ruth could see the anger torturing his face into knots. "But, you have given up! That's what you just said! If we fix one thing, then something else will go wrong, isn't that what you just said? No, Ruth, dammit, no!" Mike was shouting furiously. "We can beat this, we're going to be in charge because we don't have to put up with the way life is!"

Ruth sunk in the chair and wrapped her fingers around her upper arm. Her posture was lax, and she could not bring herself to look at Mike.

Mike moved very close to Ruth, so that his face nearly touched hers. Ruth could feel the warmth of his breath on her cheek. "Now, look," he whispered, "are you with me or against me? Because engineering is more important to me than anything, even my marriage. Doing great things—that's what I'm interested in. If you don't want to join me, then we may as well end this." Mike motioned towards the space between him and Ruth, indicating their relationship. He had begun to breathe heavily.

"Well, what's your answer?" he asked with a cracking voice. Ruth appeared to be considering her response with great care. Finally, she spoke very softly and slowly.

"No, Mike, I don't want to lose you. I'm in. No matter what it takes." She reached out and laid her hand atop Mike's. The ridges of her wedding ring pressed against the loose skin on Mike's hand. But Mike withdrew his hand away with a swift movement.

"That's good. That's very good, but I don't want to hear any more doubts like I had to hear today. You're supposed to support me, not undermine me."

Ruth sighed and pulled down the sleeves of her red sweater. She managed to smile at Mike, and said, "Let's get to work, then, on that weird mutation of the flu virus."

Mike nodded at her without, however, returning her smile. The bottom of his blazer flapped up as he strode briskly out of the meeting room. When he had gone, Ruth slumped in her chair and stared morosely out the window.

CHAPTER 5

S HE WAITED UNTIL two in the morning to start the project. The only places still open were some of the bars and the occasional convenience store. When someone walked by, she huddled in the shadows away from the streetlights and treaded lightly on the concrete sidewalk so as to avoid notice. She was dressed in sweatpants and a T-shirt, and carried a grocery bag containing ice cream and a box of granola bars in her right hand. She was trying to pass as a mother who had to do some late-night shopping for her demanding children, and who didn't feel like she needed to dress up for an emergency trip to the grocery store in the middle of the night.

In one of the deep pockets of her sweat pants, though, the woman kept a test tube and some protective rubber gloves. She was a reversal engineer from the realm of possibility, and it was her duty to initiate the spread of the rare form of the flu that thrived in the innocent-looking clear liquid in the test tube. She had already broken into a restaurant and tainted some flour contained in large bins back in the kitchen. Her next plan was to wipe some of the infectious liquid within the test tube on some of the door handles of the bathrooms in a basketball stadium.

The engineer went about her work dispassionately and methodically. Every time she had finished distributing some of the flu virus on another well-frequented part of the city, she looked around and then started talking quietly on her cell phone. She was reporting what she had done to the headquarters in the realm of possibility. She was laying a biological trap for the people of the city of Sacramento. When the bustle of the workday started that morning, the invisible pathogen she had distributed would travel from person to person. The stronger people would weather its symptoms, but some of the weaker people would die. As she imagined this outcome of her nighttime labor, the engineer paused and sighed. She went on, though, confident that she was impinging upon a complex fabric of cause and effect that would save the lives of those who had died in the Rockies.

Six hours later, Randall Delgado pushed his aching limbs out of his bed slowly. He grimaced as he planted his wrinkled, fragile feet on the cold wooden floor. Delgado scratched the skin over the thin muscle of his calf and then, with another heave of effort, walked over to the bathroom sink. He lowered his face into the ceramic bowl encrusted with dried-up toothpaste and began to splash cold water against his skin and run it through the sparse hair he still had.

The fatal moment came when he drank from the cup that had rested on a corner of the sink. The engineer had walked silently into Delgado's unlocked apartment building early that morning and poured a droplet of the fluid in the test tube into this cup. She knew that only one person might use it, but the apartment building was large and crowded, and she figured that, throughout the day, amidst all the activity within the apartment, there would be many opportunities to spread germs. Randall Delgado drank from the cup, and at that moment, the virus began to probe his body, seeking cells in which to replicate.

For a while after the virus had infiltrated him, Randall Delgado's day proceeded innocuously. He was old, and had little to do. He walked down the apartment stairs to get his mail from the rows and rows of gray metal mailboxes in a small room that branched off from the main lobby. He took the stairs because he wanted the exercise, and by the time he reached the top of them again with a couple envelopes and an advertisement from a clothing store in his hand, he was breathing heavily and with a wheeze. When he got back to his apartment, he took a seat on the frayed cushion of his couch and watched the morning news. He wore sweat pants and a plain gray sweater with red stain from spaghetti sauce on one of the sleeves. Besides watching television and eating two more meals that day, Randall Delgado called both of his daughters and wrote down a few stanzas of a new poem he was writing. He had a small notebook full of verses that had occurred to him at various times during the day: in dreams, while out walking in the park, or while meditating over a microwave dinner.

The illness started to set in that evening, after he gotten into bed. He liked to fall asleep to jazz. Sometimes, the tenant living next to him would pound on the wall late at night because Randall had forgotten to turn off the radio. The easy, loosely cadenced melodies streamed from the speakers of Randall's radio again the evening he got sick, attended by the faint background hum of static. Randall settled into the soft depression in the bed his body had made over the years.

Soft, watery noises fluttered within his stomach. Randall placed his bony fingers atop the skin there and massaged it. As he rolled onto his side, he thought of the macaroni and cheese he had eaten for dinner that night. It had tasted good when he ate it, but now its memory was a source of nausea. The thought of the heavy, thick cheese and the somewhat crisp and undercooked noodles was something that he now wished he could forget. His stomach felt bloated and his mind was muddled and dizzy. He tried to soothe himself by rubbing his temples with his fingers, but the pressure in his gut was building. He forced himself to rise and go to the toilet. His legs were even weaker than they usually were, and he braced himself by pressing a hand against the bathroom doorframe. He sighed, and then held himself over the toilet with his mouth hanging open and his hands resting on his knees.

Sweat had begun to ooze from his forehead. He gagged, and the vomit rose up still closer to his throat. As he waited, he began to grow tired. He leaned against the sink and ended up squashing a blob of toothpaste with his hand. The vomit forced its way up his throat and formed a fountain arcing from his lips. Some of its cascaded into the toilet, but, because he had moved towards the sink, some splashed upon the floor. The muscles in Randall's throat and chest burned and ached as his stomach totally emptied out its contents. He waited for the light, purged feeling that he knew would come once the last heave had ended.

Finally, the outflow stopped and he rested his shoulder upon the edge of the sink, panting and tired from the strain. Flecks of vomit were caught in the stubble on his face. He grew more and more still as he slowly caught his breath. Finally, he just lowered himself onto the floor in an exhausted heap.

It took him almost a half an hour to recover enough strength to walk back to bed. Cleaning up in the bathroom was out of the question. As he hobbled along the floor, he was so tired that it was difficult to keep his eyes from drooping shut. He felt the warm slime of vomit with his bare foot, and he swiftly skidded along the tiles while his head streaked back and ended its flight by crashing onto the side of the tub.

With spittle and puke still dribbling from his mouth, Randall sent up a cry. His body was so tired, though, from the spasms of throwing up that no one in the apartment could possibly have heard it. As for the crash of his body on the floor, everyone was either asleep or, if they were awake, lazily assumed that, if a person had fallen, they would easily get back up again and continue with their lives.

Blood dripped into the bathtub from a crack that had opened in Randall's fragile skull. He closed his eyes tightly because of the pain. He coughed as some more vomit slid over his throat, turned his head to the side, and expectorated into the tub. He winced and grabbed his neck as a sharp pain shot up his side because of this twisting motion.

He had to relax for a few minutes, even though the side of the tub was hard and his neck began to throb sharply because of the angle at which it was bent. He considered just lying in the bathroom until someone came to check up on him once people noticed that he hadn't come out in a while and that he wasn't answering his phone. But he didn't want to be discovered lying with his old, bony limbs splayed over puddles of vomit. He took a few deep, slow breaths, and then grimaced as he tried to gain traction on the floor with one of his feet and push himself up the side of the tub.

He clawed with his thin fingers at the knobs for the water protruding from the wall and actually managed to bring himself upright. With one hand he gripped the rusty door handle of the bathroom and he rested his shoulder against some of the tile within the shower stall. A broad river of bright red blood, like a streak of paint, ran down his neck and stained his loose cotton T-shirt.

With a grunt, he rocked back and then pushed against the shower stall to propel himself forward. He began to walk clumsily but effectively towards his bedroom. While he was in the bathroom, though, the sun had gone down, and Randall's already weak eyes were not prepared for the solid blackness he found when he entered the bedroom. He stepped blindly out into the abyss his room had become and searched for a foothold. He lost his balance, and as he fell his skull cracked against the sharp corner of a nightstand where a lamp rested as well as some playing cards.

This blow was so violent that Randall lost consciousness. The corner of the nightstand had cut a wide crack in his fragile skull. Blood now started to pour from his head with frightening volume.

Three days later, after no one had seen Delgado and his family members were repeatedly unable to contact him by phone, the police got the key to Delgado's apartment from the landlord of the complex and entered. They found Delgado sprawled out on the floor with his head and neck resting in a glistening, broad pool of blood. The paramedics rushed towards his body and knelt beside him. One of them felt his wrist with his gloved hand, but it was clear just from looking at Delgado's pallid body and the gaping wound in his skull that the old man was dead.

CHAPTER 6

MIKE RETURNED TO the couch from the telephone resting on the stand in the corner of the living room.

"Well, we've got one death already. Old man falls and cracks his skull while coming back from vomiting in the bathroom. Dead because of a byproduct of the flu, not the flu itself."

Ruth shut off the television set. Her and Mike had been watching a sitcom, and Ruth took offense at the canned laughter and the crude humor after the news of the old man's death.

"Mike, that's awful! How can you be so easygoing about something like that?" Ruth leaned forward in her seat and clutched a cushion with her fist. Mike remained standing. He looked to the ground and ran a hand through his hair. He was exasperated with Ruth's frequent reservations.

"Remember the cause, though, Ruth, the cause. We're committed to the cause of the plane crash victims who died of cold and hunger up in the Rockies." Mike returned to the couch and put his feet up on a footrest. He turned the TV on again, and chuckled at the sitcom to show his contentment. Ruth morosely toyed with the tassels of a small pillow, then pressed the off button on the remote with undue force.

"No, we need to talk this out." Ruth had twisted herself so that she faced Mike squarely. Mike was startled by her vehemence and he reflexively pushed himself up against the couch's arm. "I didn't sign up for a dirty operation. I was idealistic, I wanted heroism, I wanted people to revere me after I was done. This project of yours... it's tainted!" It was a late summer evening, and there was a violent chorus of cicadas in the treetops in the backyard.

Mike remained calm during Ruth's outburst. He had considered these criticisms while alone. "Reversal engineering *is* heroic and pure. Your mistake is in thinking that we can have anything that's good without a cost. The meal we ate today—the delicious steak you made—involved butchering a cow. Any great endeavor, a work of art, a scientific discovery, has to include hard work and suffering. The cost is always going to be there, and just because there's a cost to reversal engineering doesn't mean that it's not heroic."

Ruth sat on the edge of couch. Her neck muscles were tense and her face was serious. "Those things are different. Hard work is not the same as an old man cracking his skull and lying dead in his apartment for three days. I want a clean conscience again."

Frustrated that his analogies had not convinced her, Mike gesticulated animatedly as he responded to Ruth. "Look, why can't you stick with me for a while! I know it's a little messy, but we're still trying to refine these procedures. Show me some respect, Ruth! Sometimes things take time!"

Ruth shifted in the couch again so that she faced the TV. She leaned back and relaxed her upper body on the soft cushions. After a silent pause of a few moments, during which Mike raptly awaited her answer, Ruth got up with her arms crossed across her chest and walked towards the window. In the gray light outside, a group of shadowy figures moved along the sidewalk. Ruth stood there and contemplated the twilight scene.

"What are you thinking?" Mike said softly. Ruth's silence, and her pensive pose before the window, had made him abruptly mellow.

Ruth turned around towards Mike and rested her hands on the windowsill. "I was thinking...I was thinking that there's just not going to be an end to this refinement process you keep talking about. Let's say we decide to correct the Sacramento flu deaths after we have solved the Rockies problem. Well, in order to correct these deaths, then we'll have to harm other people. Then, in order to correct these later problems, we'll have to do damage to another group of people. When is it going to stop? Evil is built into life. No matter how hard you try, it's going to happen."

Mike reclined on the couch and slid his hands into the pockets of his jeans. He stared vacantly at the carpet, deep in thought. Ruth had given voice to an anxiety that, he admitted to himself, he had harbored for a long time. Mike began to murmur in such hushed tones that it seemed as though her were talking to himself. "It's the Creator. There's so much here already that He's created. The flaws go back to the very origins. To remedy them, we have to go way, way back. To the basic structure of the universe really. To the origins. Because that's the ultimate cause of all evil. The very moment of creation."

Ruth took a step towards him and cocked her head in surprise. "You see, we just can't win. You see what I mean, Mike!" Ruth, in her passion, bent forward towards Mike. She thrust out one of her hands to emphasize her point.

Mike looked up from the carpet and stared stonily and directly into Ruth's eyes. "Yeah, I see what you mean. But, I'm not going to give up." With that, Mike pushed himself to his feet and marched out of the room. Ruth watched him with a crestfallen look, and then covered her face with one of her fragile hands and wept.

CHAPTER 7

RUTH KEPT WORKING to correct the plane crash in the Rockies. She couldn't dismiss even the dim hope that, amidst all the possible and actual turns of fate, there was some way to recalibrate the whole complex fabric of reality so that everyone was happy. One day she was sitting in front of a computer and scrolling through a large line graph with thousands of blue, red, and green jagged lines twisting across the screen. She perked up and called over to Mike, who was pacing up and down the hallway behind her with his hands in his pockets.

"Hey Mike, come and check this out!" She waved towards Mike and pointed towards one of the lines on the screen. Mike's red tie swung as he strode quickly down the corridor. "Look, the old man's death is actually connected to a cancer victim in Ireland. According to my calculations, this man is not going to get cancer now that Delgado is dead." Mike squinted at the screen as he tried to follow Ruth's reasoning. But, before she had finished explaining her discovery to him, he turned aside and stared at the desk. He was so deeply preoccupied that he had lost track of what his wife was saying.

"Mike, hey Mike, aren't you listening?" Ruth slapped Mike's arm lightly. Mike kept staring at the table, though. After Ruth had hit him a couple times, though, he exhaled and clasped her neck with his hand.

"I'm sorry, dear. That's great, a great observation!" He forced himself to smile, but the enthusiasm in his voice was weak. He stood upright and sighed again. He had dark stains under his eyes and his hair was a little disheveled.

Mike had been absorbed in his thoughts for a couple of weeks now, and he had been spending much of his time alone in his office. He drifted off down the corridor. Ruth could hear him muttering to himself. She tried to keep studying the line graph, but finally she decided to confront Mike.

"Mike, c'mon, we need to talk." She pressed her hand against his chest.

"What? Now? No, I'm fine." Mike frowned at her and went on pacing. He glowered at the floor. It was clear he was brooding over some difficult problem.

But Ruth held her ground. She moved closer to him and, looking him earnestly in the eyes, she said, "No, we have to."

Mike looked up at her and, seeing how serious she was, he drew his hands out of his pockets and nodded. "Alright, let's go into this office here so we can have some privacy."

There was an empty, unused office down the hallway. Boxes full of papers were stacked in the corner, and the couple's entrance stirred up a cloud of dust. Mike pushed open one of the windows and began to wave around a manila folder he had picked up from the office desk.

"Gotta get this dust cleared out. I can't remember a time when this office was being used."

Ruth wheeled a chair over from a closet and positioned it in front of the desk. Mike sat on a chair with his elbows resting on the desk's bare surface. His golden wedding ring looked tarnished in the dim, musty air of the office.

"So, what's up?"

Ruth sighed and crossed her arms in front of her chest. She looked professional in a white button-down blouse and black jacket that extended just below her hips. "Well, let's see, last night you weren't home for dinner again. We've been together for a meal exactly twice in the past two weeks. You've spent whole nights working and when I ask you what you're working on, you're very evasive and uncommunicative. You've obviously got something on your mind, and I have a right to know. I'm your wife." Ruth thrust her chin out as she adjusted her jacket.

Mike shifted nervously in his seat. He looked levelly, though, at his wife, and said, "No, nothing's seriously wrong. Just the ordinary stressors of a major project. I am in charge here, you know."

Mike's answer did not placate Ruth. She watched as he fidgeted with a paperclip lying on the dusty surface of the desk. "I don't believe you. You've never worked this much. I'm your wife, you can't hide things from me. I know something is going on, I just don't know exactly what." Ruth removed her jacket and hung it over the back of her chair. She was ready to wait for a while.

Mike stared down at the desk, then glanced up towards Ruth as if he was about to speak; but suddenly he looked down again. Mike breathed in and then exhaled with a weary sigh. "Alright, you're right. I'm onto something. But, Ruth, this is a good thing. You shouldn't be angry with me."

"Well, what is it?" Ruth asked after a long, pregnant pause. "Am I going to have to bring a hot lamp in here or something?"

"No, no, I'll talk. Look, I've done some long, hard thinking. And…and I've reached the conclusion that your insights about reversal engineering have some validity. We'll just keep running into a wall if we focus on small-scale situations. Y'know, we correct one problem only to have another problem crop up as a result of the correction, and then we correct the correction only to have another problem crop up. The problem is not with a particular situation, Ruth, but with the entire universe. When the Creator made the universe, He set it up for failure. And, y'know, I've been trying, y'see, to find a way—this may sound a little crazy—to bring reversal engineering to bear on the very origins of the universe. If we remake the whole thing, then we can pull up evil by its roots, instead of just trimming its leaves."

Ruth leaned forward as Mike spoke and braced herself upon the armrests of her chair. She was alert and interested now. "That's exactly what I was thinking, Mike. A more fundamental correction, fixing the very foundations. But, can we do that? It seems so ambitious."

Mike nodded excitedly. "I think we can. Look, there was a point when the entire vast universe was compressed into this very, very tiny speck of matter with a very high density and pressure. And I think now that all the problems we now face began here, in the configuration of this tiny speck of matter. Perhaps if we could just tweak the composition of this iota of matter, there would be no more evil. The structural defect that makes the universe hospitable to evil would be removed, and life's problems would have been solved."

Mike looked at Ruth and waited for a response. She was toeing the carpet, though, with her foot as she tried to take in what Mike had said. The silence made Mike uncomfortable, and so he kept talking. "I think that the universe was poorly engineered. The problem we face is evil, in all its manifold forms. We have to research why this problem has come about. I think it goes way, way back, to very origins of the universe. We have to find a better alternative to this flawed design. I just hope there is one."

"I hate to be the cynic again, but are you hinting that evil may be something inherent in existence itself, and not just some form of existence? I mean, does the fact that something exists means that there will be evil?"

Mike swept his hand over the desk to indicate his dismissal of Ruth's fear. "You need to have a positive attitude. I need you to have a positive attitude."

Ruth smiled with genuine joy and relief. "I'm just so glad, Mike, you're doing this. I'm glad you're not as hardhearted as I thought you were." Both got up from their chairs. Mike circled around the desk, and Ruth leapt up towards him and wrapped her arms around his neck. After burying her face against his chest, she tilted her head back and kissed Mike on the lips. The couple then embraced again and forgot themselves as they held one another firmly for a long time.

CHAPTER 8

MIKE LOOKED THROUGH his safety goggles at the image on a computer that represented the bit of superheated matter suspended within the glass chamber. A hydrogen sensor fed data to the computer, which the computer used to generate an image. The hydrogen sensor used palladium to detect the hydrogen, since palladium selectively absorbed the hydrogen gas and formed the more easily observed palladium hydride. Mike removed a handkerchief from his pocket and wiped the beads of sweat that had formed on his forehead. He was alone in a large, cool room illuminated only by a pale blue light.

The infinitesimal bit of matter hanging in the glass chamber was a replica of what the universe had been like during the first few minutes of its existence. Mike had reproduced it with painstaking precision. He surveyed the image on the computer from different angles, bending over to get a closer look. He recoiled when a crash pounded near the doorway and then reverberated hollowly throughout the room.

"Don't come in, I'm busy!" Mike shouted nervously. He took a couple strides towards the door and craned his neck to peer within the shadows. He saw that a filing cabinet had fallen over, but the door to the lab remained closed. Mike went back to the glowing image of the tiny bit of matter.

He knelt down and twisted some knobs at the base of the glass cylinder that rose all the way to the ceiling. The bit of matter twisted and then tilted in synchrony with the turning knobs. Mike scrutinized it again. The bit of matter consisted in hydrogen and helium molecules that Mike had fit to a pattern. This configuration would determine the way in which the universe would develop over time. Mike studied the configuration of the helium molecules by looking at another computer screen, which showed the wavelength of the light emitted by the matter within the glass cylinder and the location of the source of each emission with a bar graph. This computer screen was hooked up to a spectroradiometer, which measured the wavelength of the light emitted by the matter in the tall glass cylinder. Mike knew that helium emitted light at a specific wavelength.

Mike went back to a panel of buttons in a corner of the room. The power that surged through the panel gave off a faint hum. Mike hit one button, and the images on the computer screens multiplied. The glow of the new images was dimmer and there were also distinct differences in their shape. One bar graph was elongated, whereas one representation of the distribution of hydrogen was very dense and compact. One other such representation was T-shaped. These images were different possible configurations of the primal set of subatomic particles. They would unfold into different and, so Mike hoped, more viable universes.

Mike squinted towards the door of the lab again. The hallway visible through the narrow rectangular window in the door was still dark. Mike then clutched a lever protruding from the wall beside him. His chest rose as he inhaled deeply. Then, with sudden force, he pulled the lever downwards and one of the images on the computer attached to the hydrogen sensor flashed with a brilliant green light.

The green light radiated from the cluster of matter on the screen and danced around the room like a strobe light. The beams swung around slowly at first, so Mike's eyes did not become uncomfortable. Then, as he stood, still holding the lever with the round knob at the end, the streams of bright green light rotated more rapidly and grew more intense. The amplifying light became so bright that it soon brought Mike to floor, where he buried his head behind his knees in the hopes of finding some relief in the darkness there. Still, though, the crescendo of luminosity continued, until it seemed as though the beams flashing past had become solid. Instead of green light beams, it was as though a green propeller were swirling around and imperiling Mike's body. Each passing stripe of green light battered him, and soon he was lying on the floor and weeping with the agony of the repeated blows. In spite of the weakness of his body, he tried to scream for help.

While watching the door, hoping that somehow someone would walk in and stop the nightmare of whirling light, Mike saw that his shoes and ankles were growing fainter and fainter. Color drained from them, so that they became pale, and soon there was nothing but a shadowy outline. Then, even this disappeared, and it was as though a surgeon had amputated Mike's legs at the ankles.

Mike stopped screaming and pulled his legs towards his body. He was so frantic that his breath came in short, constricted wheezes. The process that had begun with his feet was working its way up his body. The full flesh of his arm was dwindling down to nothing more than a cylinder as transparent as the glass tower in the center of the room. Horror tortured Mike's mind as the erasing agent, whatever it was, made its way inexorably up to his head. After a few minutes of this attrition, the place where Mike had huddled in the laboratory was unoccupied, an eerie gap where he still should have been.

Early the next morning, Ruth sleepily rolled over in bed and reached towards the side opposite her. She ran her hand along the edge of the mattress, searching for Mike's body. When she realized he was not there, she lifted herself up and peered around the room, which was lit only by dull light.

"Mike, you in there?" Ruth projected her voice towards the bathroom. There was no light outlining the bathroom's white door. Ruth had read a book on the couch in the living room until eleven o'clock the previous night so she could be there to greet Mike when he returned. By 11:30, she had reasoned that she had done all she could and that he would have to come back in without her attention.

She was sure that she would see him in the morning, though. She slid her feet into her warm slippers and padded in a t-shirt and red pajama pants through the upstairs rooms. The home was silent and still. It was so quiet that she could hear the grinding, creaking machinery of a construction crew operating on a sidewalk a block away from her home. Having explored the upstairs as well as the downstairs rooms, Ruth sat in a chair before a large mirror in her bedroom and rested her chin on her hand. She looked directly at her reflection. Her face was still shapely and smooth-skinned, but there was a growing anger inside of her. It had to do with Mike's frequent absences, and her disappointment with reversal engineering.

She picked up the phone by the nightstand and dialed Mike's cell phone number. She tapped her fingers on the wooden nightstand while waiting for him to answer, but she turned the phone off with frustration when the rhythmic ringing of Mike's phone transitioned to the recorded message of the voicemail. She shrugged her shoulders and placed the phone back on the nightstand. With a serious face, she went over to the closet and pulled out a pair of gray pants and a red blouse. She was headed to work.

Once she had said hi to a few coworkers she passed on her way in, she sat down at her desk and began to work on the chart she had left incomplete the previous evening. She was part of a team working on an experiment on airplane engines. They were documenting the acceleration capacity of seven different models, to see if one of them was capable of pulling away from the winds of a powerful storm. The hope was that reversal engineers could replace the original machine of the plane that had crashed with the new, more powerful machine and in that way they could save lives. Ruth sorted through some folders in her filing cabinet. She wanted to find some old data that interested her.

After a few minutes of work, though, she found that she could not concentrate. She reclined in her chair and unscrewed the cap of a bottle of spring water, then pulled her cell phone from her pocket and checked to see if there were any text messages or voicemails. But, the stillness of the screen indicated that there were none. Ruth rose from her desk and stepped out into the hallway. She wanted to see Mike, to find out how he was doing. He was, after all, her husband.

Some of her coworkers looked up at her as she walked past, since she was supposed to be present when the results of another experiment were announced that morning. Ruth headed, though, straight towards the lab where Mike often worked. It was in the basement of the building, in a quiet room next to the area where the archives were kept and outdated lab equipment was stowed.

Her heart fluttered when she saw that the interior of the basement lab was dark. She clutched the metal handle of the door and tugged at it. The door was heavy and she ground her teeth while she pulled it back just far enough so that she could squeeze inside the lab. She groped the wall beside the door for the light switches. They flickered on, and then flooded the room in a bright light that hurt her eyes like the glare of the late afternoon sun, which confronts people directly.

The room was empty. There was a glass pillar in the center that caught Ruth's attention. Mounted outside of it was an image of cluster of red circles which looked like the skin of a raspberry. Ruth walked towards it. She pulled her gray jacket tighter around her body, since the underground laboratory was chilly. The click of her high heels rattled off of the walls. This imitation of the sound of her walking made Ruth think someone was following her.

She had seen Mike fine-tuning the interior of the glass cylinder with the knobs located at its base. One was labeled pressure, another temperature. The harsh ceiling lights lit every inch of the laboratory, but Ruth peered around anyway. Her mind was beginning to race now. She kept inventing ways to explain Mike's absence that were more and more disturbing. She was not sure what the significance of the image attached to the glass cylinder was.

Something pounded far down the hallway, and Ruth stood erect and attuned her ears to the sound. It was isolated, though. The smooth, quiet hum of the ventilators winding their way behind the basement walls soon replaced the single pound.

Ruth thought Mike might be combing the storage area in the basement for some spare part that he felt was useful. She returned to the hallway and walked into the interior of dusty, rarely used storage area. In the dim light, she could see the hulking blocks of old incubators and monitors. A narrow aisle wound through this forest of defunct equipment.

There was a rusty metal panel attached to the wall from which two light switches protruded. Ruth flicked both of them on, but she was alarmed when one of the lights suspended from the ceiling sizzled and then, after a blinding flash, sent down a rain of glowing sparks. That light went dark, but there was enough left for Ruth see Mike, if he was in fact there.

As she wound her way deeper within the storage room, Ruth heard a faint murmuring and crackling. She stood still and held her head erect. She moved in the direction in which she thought the sound was coming, and it grew clearer, until she realized that it was a song playing on a radio. The tempo of the song slowed as she neared the radio, and the singer intoned a final, drawn-out note. Then, a male voice began talking. At that moment, Ruth rounded a stack of plastic vats that nearly reached the ceiling and seemed ready to topple. Behind them, she saw the thin, long back of a man she had rarely seen but often heard about: Carl, an engineer who kept to himself and who was known for coming up with bold ideas that were frequently the object of ridicule but which sometimes led to great success.

Ruth waited behind Carl. He was tinkering with something hidden by his body. There was a desk lamp set up on the table in front of him, and he had positioned its arm so that it shed a harsh, revealing light on whatever device it was with which he was fiddling. The male voice on the radio had stopped talking, and another song had begun with rhythmic, forceful guitar chords. Ruth moved towards Carl, and laid her hand gently on his shoulder. She had tried not to startle him, but his large spectacles nearly flew off when he spun around to see who or what had touched him.

Carl began to wipe his glasses clean with his shirt while sighing with exasperation once he realized it was Ruth who had emerged from the empty storage area and been the cause of the sudden light sensation on his shoulder.

"My, you startled me," Carl said in his British accent, which was often the object of jokes and caricatures among his coworkers.

"Sorry, Carl. But, I'm looking for Mike. Have you seen him lately?" Ruth was in no mood for chitchat. Lines of worry had formed on her tense forehead.

"Oh, Mike? Why, yes, I have seen Mike. A couple of days ago, in fact, he came over here while I was working and started to talk about some project about which he was very excited. He said he was working on it in the lab down the hall, and he didn't want anyone to know about it. It was all very abstruse, and I didn't get much out of what he was saying. He kept reiterating, though, the phrases 'primal stuff' and 'original matter.'" Carl randomly patted the gleaming peak of his bald head and then turned back to the intricate amalgam of gears and cables on which he had been working.

"Primal stuff?" Ruth asked with a thoughtful air. She recalled the discussion she had had with Mike about the deep roots of evil, and how this scourge originated at the very beginning, which meant that reversal engineering, in order to be truly effective, had to address this initial flaw rather than problems that occurred later and that were secondary. She whirled without thanking Carl and wound her way back through the dim mounds of old laboratory devices. She entered the broad room with the glass cylinder where

Mike, it seemed, had been trying to engineer a different beginning for the universe.

She began to walk around the perimeter of the room, peering intently at the floor and the panels of knobs and dials protruding from the walls. She came to a closet door, and pressed a button that caused it to open with a pneumatic hiss. Some light from the lab invaded the dark, narrow space, and Ruth saw that all that it contained were more intricate instrument controls, with tiny numbers etched onto their surfaces and red indicators pointing to the symbols of some obscure scientific code.

What astonished Ruth was that there was not even any trace of Mike in the lab, let alone Mike himself. If he had been working here, she expected to find a discarded lab coat lying crumpled up on a shelf or a notebook open to a page on which Mike had been writing. But the shelves and counters of the lab were bare or bore neat arrangements of equipment, as if a janitor had just cleaned it. There were no open bottles of chemicals or even a pile of antiseptic gloves in the waste disposal bin. The lab was mysteriously and eerily neat and orderly, even though the janitors would not have interfered with it had Mike used it as recently as Carl said he had.

Ruth paused and went over the various possible ways one could account for Mike's absence. Where else could Mike be? He had not announced any plans to travel. Usually he would type in his travel plans in the electronic calendar that hung by a magnet from their refrigerator. A red light would flash on it whenever the date for Mike's departure neared. Ruth felt a tremor shake up through her knees. She pulled aside a chair that sat underneath one of the instrument panels in the lab and lowered herself upon it with a relieved sigh.

As she gripped her temples in her hands, she resolved that all she could do was wait. After all, Mike was not helpless. He would contact her at some point, since he knew that eventually she would need reassuring. She tried to convince herself that he was just very busy and her panic was silly. But, the silence in the lab was so deep that it felt to her like some ghostly, watchful presence. Abruptly, she pushed herself away from the instrument panel and then made her way to the stairway leading up to the first floor.

She muddled through the day's work, and then exceeded the speed limit on her way home. When she swung open the front door, giving the glow of the evening sunlight access to the clean white spaces of the interior of her home, she twisted her head and craned her neck to see around all the protuberances of walls and furniture. She even walked towards the narrow door of a closet where she kept cleaning supplies, and sorted through the interior, which was crammed with detergent and mops leaning against the walls. Mike could never fit into such a narrow space, but she shoved away a stack of old washcloths anyway.

Ruth retired early to escape the tightening grip of her anxiety. A couple of times that night she dreamt that Mike was walking through their bedroom door while unloosening his tie. When she shot up in the bed, her emotions fierce, it took her just a couple of minutes for her eyes to adjust to the darkness enough to see that Mike was not there and she was surrounded by the same inert silence she had found in the basement laboratory.

After a night of fitful sleep, she woke at the first penetration of sunlight through her bedroom curtains. She rolled out of bed and began to search the house in her bathrobe, since she thought that Mike might have arrived that night while she slept. She kept calling Mike's name, and getting no response, and the lack of his presence became so frustrating that she began to scream his name. She no longer tried to reassure herself with comforting excuses. She let her panic rise up within her, and the conviction that something terrible had happened to Mike finally took hold.

Once at work, she charged towards the office of an older engineer, John Stacy, to whom she often turned for counsel, particularly when her relationship with Mike was strained. He immediately took notice of her agitation and shut the door behind her once she had stepped inside of his office.

"What's wrong, Ruth? Here, take off your jacket and have some water." John's gravelly voice soothed Ruth, and she was able, after a pause of a few moments and some sips of water, to explain her dilemma.

"When was the last time you saw him?" John was rocking slightly in his chair. There were fringes of gray, slack hair on his temples, but the top of his head was entirely bare.

"Um, it must have been...let's see, two days ago, in the morning. He woke me up when he was washing his face in the bathroom. Y'know, the sound of water coming from the faucet. It was 3:30

am, and when he saw that I was up, he whispered to me that he was working on an important project and he wanted to get started as soon as possible. I thought nothing of it at the time, and went back to sleep."

John had a sip of water himself. "And, Carl—he told you that Mike approached him in the basement?"

Ruth told her how Carl remembered fragments of the conversation he had had with Mike.

"When Carl's working on something, it's very hard for him to think about anything else. It'd be nice to have more information than he fragments he recounted to you...but, they're a start." John leaned forward and rested his chin on one of his large fists. A decorative pendulum swinging on the desk was the only movement in the room for a while as both he and Ruth sat thinking.

John tapped the pendulum gently with his index finger. Ruth spoke up, hoping to fuel his meditations. "Mike and I had been sharing doubts with one another about reversal engineering before his disappearance. What was troubling us was the idea that the flaws in the universe that led to our problems run deeper than any particular situation. We theorized that error crept into the Creator's design from the very beginning, and that's why we kept having to do bad things to compensate for the negative results of the adjustments we made with reversal engineering."

John's bushy eyebrows rose. "So you and Mike actually doubted whether there was any point to reversal engineering? Our fearless leaders?"

Ruth shook her head. "Not exactly. We just discussed whether it would make sense to adjust our target. We were bouncing around the idea that we should try to reverse engineer the very origins of the universe—y'know, recalibrate the original mixture at the big bang and ensure that things ended up developing smoothly. In fact, I think that's what Mike was working on before he disappeared— that's why he was telling Carl about the primal stuff and all that."

With his finger now extended onto the upper part of his chin, John nodded and then looked up at nothing in particular into the dim corner of the office ceiling. A few minutes passed, then John leaned forward towards Ruth and looked into her eyes earnestly.

"My goodness, I don't think we'll be seeing Mike again, Ruth. He's still alive, but not as a real person. He's lost forever in the infinite realm of possibility, where we can never find him."

Ruth did not understand what John was saying, but his serious demeanor and eerie words made her feel as though her insides were collapsing upon themselves. "What are you saying?"

John got up and poured some water from his water bottle into a paper cup, which he handed to Ruth. He pressed his fingers against her shoulder in an effort to soothe her. Tears had sprung into Ruth's eyes. John's words had shocked her—they were so abruptly cutting and hopeless.

"What are you saying, what gives you the authority..." Crying broke through and distorted her speech. John waited for the bout to pass, then spoke.

"Ruth, let me explain. I really think that Mike's gone. You see, there's a flaw in the project he was working on before he died, a major flaw. Think about it: you try to change the origins of the universe. The problem is that you yourself are part of this universe. You change the universe of which you are a part, and then you yourself are no longer present. Then, the act of reversal engineering never occurred, since you, who did it, never existed, and the universe remains the same. That's why we're still here, and Mike is gone."

Ruth's lip trembled and she dabbed at the corner of her eyes. Having finished, John looked down at Ruth and spread his hands apart in a gesture of helplessness.

CHAPTER 9

THE NEXT FEW days, Ruth kept trying to reach Mike by cell phone. Always, though, after a few rings she would get the cold, mechanical recording of his voicemail, where she had already left a number of messages. She spent some time trimming the tall bushes that lined the rear of their backyard. The sound of Mike's voice would seem to emerge out of the intermittent sounds of nature around her—a twig cracking when a squirrel leapt off of it, a groove in the siding of her home funneling some wind and causing a faint whistle—only to turn around and see the same mute and still facade of her house. The rooms within the home seemed larger now that no one was around to share them with her. The living room, where she and Mike had often watched television together, seemed as cavernous as some auditorium.

At night she sat on the porch and looked up at the rough patterns the stars formed. She had often come out there to relish the endless expanses of sky above her. When she quarreled with Mike, it was as if the walls of the bedroom had drawn inward, and she exited into the dark outdoors as from a prison. After Mike's disappearance, though, anxiety started to churn within her while outside and she fled within the home instead. She had found there was something incorrigible about the universe itself, and the feeling of freedom she had enjoyed while outside no longer came.

In her imagination she pictured Mike existing on some different wavelength of reality, trapped there because of his own action. He was pounding on the wall of his prison, and he was so distant from her that she could not hear his screams. She could only see the outline of his shadowy figure. As she moved through each day, performing tasks at work and running errands, there was not a crowd large enough to fill the void created by Mike's absence. The emptiness stunned her each time she walked into the home, or flicked on the television set after lowering herself into the couch. At night she dreamt about her youth in Blackmun, Missouri, where she would hurl a tennis ball up in the air so that Rascal would chase it. The beauty of these scenes, flooded with the mellow light of evening, filled her with sadness and often she had to spend fifteen minutes or so crying to relieve the deep nostalgia these images had stirred up within her.

Made in the USA
Middletown, DE
18 October 2015